# The Donut Trap

Dear Reader,

Thank you for reading *The Donut Trap*. In addition
to the romance, this story features a donut shop
owned by a Chinese Cambodian American family
and explores the dynamic between first-generation
immigrant/refugee parents and second-generation
children.

There may be potentially triggering content, including brief references to the Khmer Rouge, fat-
phobic language, and drug/alcohol use. Please take
care while reading.

This story was written with love and humor and
I sincerely hope that comes across the pages.

Love,
*Julie*

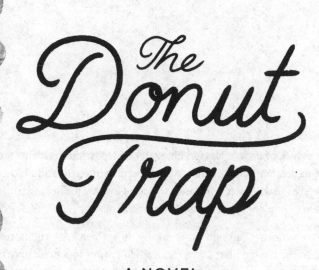

# The Donut Trap

## A NOVEL

# JULIE TIEU

**AVON**

*An Imprint of* HarperCollins*Publishers*

FIRST EDITION

*Designed by Diahann Sturge*

*Title page, chapter opener and running foot art © Olya_Beli_Art / Shutterstock, Inc.*
*Emojis on pages 120 and 252 © FOS_ICON / Shutterstock, Inc.*
*Emoji on page 157 © Cosmic_Design / Shutterstock, Inc.*

Library of Congress Cataloging-in-Publication Data has been applied for.

ISBN 978-0-06-306980-0

21 22 23 24 25   BRR   10 9 8 7 6 5 4 3 2 1

*To 爸, 妈, Phuong, and Sue,*
*for being trailblazers*

# The Donut Trap

## Chapter 1

*A*ll of my customers have told me at one point or another that Sunshine Donuts is their happy place. Who can blame them? There are colorful sprinkled donuts. The smell of coffee mixed with the cloying saccharine aroma of glaze is intoxicating. Friendly customer service is the utmost priority. It is a great place to visit. To live and breathe it every day—that's a different story.

I slammed a stack of pink card stock on the stainless-steel front counter. Folding donut boxes every day was the bane of my existence. In order for the box to close properly, every edge had to be precisely creased at a 90-degree angle. There was no shortcut to creating these boxes. Just mindless, tedious manual labor.

After I tucked in the lid on the last box, I rubbed off the bits of pink card stock that clung to the palms of my sweaty hands. Normally, folding a day's worth of pink boxes dried my hands. Except today, the air conditioning wasn't working and the hot air coming from the commercial refrigerators made it unbearably muggy. It was so hot that I forgot to say *mm-hmmm* to give my mom the impression that I was listening to her as I tuned out her nagging.

"So, what do you think, Jas?" my mom asked, looking at me over her glasses with eyes that begged me to agree. Gray hairs have invaded the center part of her hair. She was going to ask me to help her dye her hair soon. My mom rolled up the sleeves on her lavender oxford shirt and dusted a patch of powdered sugar off her jeans. She looked just like the moms in the laundry detergent commercials, except she didn't pat herself on the back when a chore was completed. She would simply find another thing to do.

"What?" I lowered my head to my shoulder and dabbed my forehead with my T-shirt sleeve. I was sweating like a pig. If the A/C didn't get fixed soon, customers were going to start complaining about their coffee tasting salty.

My mom grumbled, annoyed that she had to repeat herself. "Auntie Helen's nephew's visa is expiring soon." She stopped to muster some enthusiasm before continuing her pitch. "Since you're not dating anyone, why don't you marry him so he can stay? You can find your own boyfriend later." She said it as if it was a no-brainer, win-win situation.

My jaw dropped. Auntie Helen was not my aunt by any definition, but rather my mom's best friend, who called every afternoon to dish on the daily gossip. I was grateful that I didn't inadvertently agree to marry a stranger.

"Ma! No! That's crazy!" I shouted. What the hell? Did being single at twenty-two make me a spinster already? The warbled sound of the door chime stopped me from yelling further.

"Good afternoon, Mrs. Tran!" said Carlos Solis, who owned the liquor store next door. Our donut shop and the liquor store have operated side by side for the last twenty years in an otherwise empty strip mall. The vacant stores at the opposite ends of the lot and the overall outdated beige stucco exterior did not help attract business for us outside of our regular clientele.

My mother, Lily, quickly plastered a smile on her face.

"Carlos! Glaze donut today?" she asked extra sweetly. She always knew how to ramp up her personality when it benefited her. That's why everyone liked her. It was one of the many characteristics that I did not inherit from her.

"You know me so well, Mrs. Tran. How's business?" he asked, fanning himself with an orphaned section of the newspaper that was left on our counter. With his salt-and-pepper beard and low-hanging gut, Carlos was beginning to resemble a Mexican Santa Claus.

I quickly scanned the shop. All ten seats in the eat-in area were empty. A heat wave in July does not make for peak donut eating season.

"Business is fine. I'm sure you'll be busy on the Fourth of July," my mom deflected. My mom never liked commenting about the shop to anyone outside of the family, whether it was good or bad. She wanted us to be like that unadorned donut she held in her tongs. Plain, not like a sprinkled donut that drew everyone's attention. What was so special about sprinkles, anyway? They were just artificially colored rice-grain-shaped crunchy pieces of chalk.

"Yes, very busy. We always run out of ice," he said in all earnestness. My mom and Carlos continued to exchange boring pleasantries as she handed over his donut. Carlos pinched his fingers around an inch of napkins before turning around. The second he exited the shop, my mom's smile relaxed into a scowl.

"Always takes so many napkins," she muttered. My mom knew the cost of everything in that store and saw every extra item that customers took as a loss in her profit margin. I imagined my mom's brain just saw dollar signs wherever she went, kind of like this:

Extra napkins? Cost: fifteen cents. Profit margin: down to 10 percent.

Raising Jasmine? Cost: gazillions of dollars. Return on investment: 0 percent.

"So, what do you think? Do you want to marry Auntie Helen's nephew?" my mom asked eagerly with her hands clasped tightly. It never failed to impress me how quickly my mom could switch gears. She had a smile on her face, wanting to keep the conversation positive, but her white knuckles displayed her desperation for the answer to her prayers.

"Ma," I said gently, "I already said no. It's so gross. And immigration doesn't work that way."

"*Gross* shì shénme?" my mom asked, scrunching her nose.

I explained to her what *gross* meant in Mandarin, cobbling

basic synonyms together. Her eyebrows furrowed as she nodded, filing away this new word.

Even though Auntie Helen is not technically my aunt, it still felt like this nephew of hers was my cousin. Who wants to marry their own cousin? Also, what if a real boyfriend came along? Dating while being married to your cousin could really kill the romance. My mom had previously attempted to play matchmaker with me and her friends' sons, but this was her Hail Mary pass.

"Ma, all through high school, you kept telling me, 'No boys! Focus on studying!' And then, in college, all you asked me about is why I haven't found a boyfriend yet. It's not that easy," I said, even though I explained this to her every other day.

And this supposed boyfriend couldn't be any random guy. If it were up to my mother, this perfect boyfriend for me would be Asian, have decent (read: high earning) career prospects, and be pretty much perfect in every other way. As if those were a dime a dozen.

"I told you to take Chinese classes. I bet you there were plenty of boys in Chinese class," my mom accused.

"I wasn't going to take a Chinese class just to meet boys," I hissed.

I *totally* took Chinese classes at UCLA to meet guys.

I never told my mom about it because it was a major fail. The class was held in an auditorium, so it was hard to check out guys if I saw only the back of their heads. Even during conversation practice, I could tell none of the guys were interested in me.

Was it too lame to hope that I would find love while we were learning how to give directions to the museum? Three terms of Chinese classes, and all I took away was a wonky Beijinger accent that came out only when a hostess or a 99 Ranch employee greeted me in Mandarin. My parents never questioned where it came from, but found it incredibly pretentious, preferring the Southeast Asian–inflected Mandarin that nobody outside of my family understood.

"And how am I supposed to find a boyfriend if I'm always here at the shop?" I countered. The shop opened at 4:30 A.M. and closed at 10:00 P.M. every day. There wasn't any time to date. What were the chances that the boyfriend of my parents' dreams would walk into the shop? While Hacienda Heights had a fairly equal mix of Asian, white, and Latino residents, very few of our customers were Asian. There were too many Asian bakeries in the city to compete with. If we ever encountered a new customer, they were usually disappointed that the shop didn't have a croissant/donut love child or donuts shaped like a unicorn that pooped Froot Loops.

"If you find a nice boy, you can leave early." My mom's encouraging me to get out more caught me by surprise. "But . . ."—my mom paused and looked up and down at my outfit—"make sure you try to look nice, though."

I looked down to see what she was looking at—a faded Black Keys T-shirt, leggings, and a pair of black low-top Vans that unfortunately had a glob of chocolate icing on them. I thought it was perfectly suitable for working at your actual mom and pop's donut shop.

"What's wrong with how I look?" I immediately regretted asking the question.

"Con," she said, sighing. My parents never spoke to me in Vietnamese, preferring that I learn Mandarin. They felt it was the practical thing to do. However, they reserved that term of endearment when they wanted to appeal to me. "Just put on some makeup," she said as she flitted her hand across my face. Then, she pinched the tender skin under my arm. "And stop eating croissants every morning. It has a lot of butter!"

"Ow!" I jerked my arm away from my mom. I happened to be very comfortable being a size medium, even though it seemed like extra-large by her standards. "Well, you think it's good enough for Auntie Helen's nephew, whoever he is," I grumbled under my breath.

Ignoring my comment, my mom picked up her phone to break the news to Auntie Helen. I started to stack the pink donut boxes in the corner as my mother talked about me in front of my face. At least my mom had the courtesy—if we could call it that—to talk about me in different languages so that I wouldn't completely understand. I picked up on the Mandarin parts.

"*. . . if only she took Chinese class . . . She needs to cut her hair. It's getting too long . . .*"

My parents always switched between the languages they knew—Mandarin, Khmer, and Vietnamese—creating an odd pidgin language. This meant that—instead of becoming proficient in Mandarin like they hoped—I learned the most random words and phrases in all these languages and was fluent in none.

Most of the time, I didn't think too much about it. I knew enough to get by, except there were moments when I wished I could say more than the simple version of how I really felt. To explain the why and not just the what. I suppose language fluency didn't really matter these days when it was the same old conversation every day with my mom. My dad usually stayed out of it, not because he disagreed. He was just as tired of this topic as I was. After I finished stacking the pink boxes by our coffee machine, I began to wipe down the counters, trying to tune out my mom's conversation.

"No more boyfriend talk," my dad interjected as he emerged, limping from the back of the store. Years of baking took their toll on his body. He thought the air conditioning had tripped a fuse and it would be an easy fix, but no such luck. "But when are you going to find a job, Jasmine? You graduated last year."

*Great.* If it wasn't the boyfriend talk, it was the getting-a-job talk, as if those were the only two measures of success for my life.

"I'm still figuring things out, Ba. It's not that easy."

"What do you mean? You went to UCLA. How hard is it supposed to be? Pat has a job and he's still in school! You should have majored in computers."

"It's just an internship!"

"Same thing!"

It wasn't the same thing, but I was too annoyed to bother explaining the difference.

My shoulders slumped as I plopped down on a stool behind the front counter. My parents were so proud when they found out that my little brother, Patrick, landed a summer internship at "Gugo." They were eager to show him off to customers when he came home after the Fourth of July.

"Yeah, yeah. Okay, Ba."

My dad didn't press further. I've repeatedly tried to explain to my parents that I wasn't interested or smart enough to do computer science or be premed. I remembered the day my parents saw the C I got for trig during high school. Whenever report cards arrived, I knew my dad would leave me a Post-it with a happy face on it when he saw my straight A's. I always liked the way he drew his happy faces, with two little dots for nostrils. Because of that stupid trig class, it was the first time I received a sad face Post-it. How do you say *sine* and *cosine* in Mandarin to someone who didn't have more than a middle school education?

I stood up and walked to the bathroom in the back of the shop. The heat intensified the stench of the industrial cleaning solution stored in the bathroom. As I washed my hands, I caught my reflection in the mirror. My round face was pink and sweaty. The outgrown highlights in my hair had lost their luster. I never wore makeup to the donut shop, but if I had, it would have melted right off today. My mom was right. I looked like crap.

I glanced at my phone. It was only 2:30 P.M. *Shit.* Seven and a half hours to go before closing time. This was my life, seven days a week, including most holidays. As crappy as it was, I couldn't complain when my parents had been doing this for over twenty years.

Like many refugees new to the United States, several of my aunts and uncles had already established their own donut shops. It wasn't as if my family planned to create a donut empire. Hometown acquaintances who arrived before them figured out that a donut shop was a viable business model to make some sort of living without an advanced education or proficiency in English. All they needed was some capital. Without any credit, my parents were able to turn to my aunts and uncles for money to start Sunshine Donuts. They crowdfunded before it became a thing.

Eager to pay off the loans and to start earning their own income, my parents worked nearly around the clock. They never spent money on things that they considered to be frivolous. They rarely bought new clothes for themselves. They would never consider taking a vacation because it would mean closing the shop and losing business. While my classmates were whining about going to Kumon after school, I couldn't convince my parents to spend money on tutoring or extracurricular activities. "Just work harder," they would say. Money would always be tight, according to my parents.

To minimize overhead costs, they never hired anyone to help them run the shop. Why hire someone when they had their own children, who were fluent in English, to deal with suppliers?

By the time I was ten, I had already negotiated down the price of apple filling with our vendor. It was a delicate task, with my mom complaining to me in Mandarin while I was interpreting on the phone.

I swiped my phone screen. Without thinking, my fingers hovered over the Instagram app, but I stopped myself from tapping it. Like the mirror in *Beauty and the Beast,* my phone was my only gateway to the outside world. Did I really want to see how everyone from college was living their best life, floating in a pool on an inflated flamingo in Palm Springs or eating questionable things on a stick in some faraway place like Bangkok or the OC Fair?

Meanwhile I'd been stuck here, serving donuts and coffee, with chocolate icing on my shoes. I grabbed a paper towel and wiped it off, leaving a brown smear. It looked like shit. Literally.

Fuck this. I locked my phone and stuffed it in my back pocket.

AFTER CLOSING THE shop, my mom and I had a late dinner. We ate quietly at the dining table with only the clink of our chopsticks scraping our porcelain rice bowls breaking the silence. There wasn't much to say when we spent nearly every minute together. My dad just left for the shop to bake donuts for the next day. My mom and dad worked opposite shifts, overlapping a few hours when the shop opened. My parents knew I would never be able to get my ass up at four A.M., so they let me start my shift at six. I didn't know how my parents kept up this routine all these years. I had worked at the shop full time for only the past year and it had already drained my spirit. I rested my chopsticks on top of my bowl of rice.

"Full already? There's still a lot of food." My mom gestured at the food with her chopsticks. "You love eating thịt kho."

"Aren't you afraid the pork belly is going to make me fat?" I asked sarcastically. Thịt kho was actually my favorite of all the dishes my mom made. It was worth waiting for the pork belly to braise. I eyed a hard-boiled egg, but I knew my mom would give me crap for eating another one.

"A little bit is okay! There's not that much fat left," my mom said, trying to sound convincing. I raised my eyebrow as I examined the thick, gelatinous stripes of fat still very much left in the pork belly. I popped a piece in my mouth before shoveling in some rice. The fat coated my mouth. My chopsticks reached for some much-needed sweet and vinegary pickled vegetables when my mom blurted out, "Baba and I are worried about you."

My chopsticks hung in midair, holding on to a flower-shaped carrot slice.

I glanced at my mom. "About what, Ma?" I asked warily, my mouth still full of rice. As I swallowed, it became clear that my mom made my favorite meal so that I would be more receptive to this conversation. I should have seen this coming. It was just like the time she made spring rolls when she tried to talk to me about the birds and the bees.

My mom let out a heavy sigh and put down her bowl on the

table. "You have been very unhappy. After last year, we thought things would get better."

"Things are better, Ma," I said, quietly, unsure where all of this was coming from. I looked down at the table. "I've been at the shop almost every day since moving back. I'm always at home after work. There's nothing to worry about."

"You come home and watch TV alone every night. It's not normal." She shook her head in disapproval. "You should be going out more. I saw that Linh is in Las Vegas with her boyfriend."

Linh was my best friend and former college roommate. My mom loved Linh the moment they met during my dorm move-in day freshman year because she felt like she was looking at a much younger version of herself.

I gaped at her. "How do you know about that?"

"I saw on Facebook," my mom said casually, like it was no big deal.

"You're Facebook friends with Linh?! Since when?" We kept our Facebook accounts only because our parents started to use it to communicate with our extended family. Free access to our cousins' lives was like catnip to my parents.

My mom waved her hand, dismissing my question.

"What's the big deal . . ." I started to say, when it came to me. Why was my mom so eager to get me paired up? "Is this because of the wedding tomorrow?"

The bride was the daughter of an acquaintance they knew

from their hometown in Cambodia. There had been festivities all week in preparation for the big day, but my parents decided to attend the morning ceremony, come back in the afternoon to help me, and then attend the reception in the evening. I assured them that I could handle working at the shop alone, but they didn't like the idea of leaving me alone all day.

My mom willfully ignored my accusation. "Finish eating before the food gets cold."

"You're afraid of what your friends are going to say when they ask about me." I could already hear their shady questions. They weren't much different from my own parents' questions, except for a minor adjustment.

Jasmine *still* doesn't have a job?

Jasmine *still* has no boyfriend?

"Your aunties can say whatever they want. I want you to be happy."

Sure, that's what this was about. *My* happiness. If that was the case, I wouldn't be back at square one, living with my parents and helping out at the shop, as if college never happened.

"Fine. Whatever," I said, hoping it would placate my mom.

She didn't respond. Instead, she watched me as I stabbed my chopsticks through a hard-boiled egg. I expected her to tell me that it was rude or bad luck to stab my food like that, but she remained silent.

"Fine," I finally relented. I mustered some sincerity. "I will try to go out more." It was the best I could offer short of a guarantee. I kept my face down as I dropped the egg in my bowl and basted it with the fat-laden dark soy braise.

When she didn't respond again, I looked up to find that she had resumed eating. She got what she wanted. Therefore the conversation was over.

## Chapter 2

*I* was settling into bed with my laptop when my phone rang. Just who I wanted to see: Linh, right on time for our standing FaceTime call. Linh and I quickly became best friends when we met during our freshman year of college. She was the ultimate boss babe with the blunt personality to match. It was hard not to be in awe of her sometimes. She worked hard, she played hard, and she was the only person I knew who could do a smoky eye without watching a YouTube tutorial. After college, Linh moved back home with her parents in Garden Grove. So we tried to FaceTime weekly to really catch up in between our daily texts, which mainly consisted of our trying to outdo each other with gifs and memes.

A familiar shriek came through my phone. "*Jaaaas!* Uh-oh. What's wrong?" Linh pointed across the screen at the sheet mask that clung to my face.

"Nothing," I said dejectedly.

"Don't be so emo. It must be bad if you're having a treat-yo-self night. Lemme guess. You're watching Chris Hemsworth videos on YouTube and eating a bag of Flamin' Hot Cheetos." Linh looked expectantly across the screen.

I pursed my lips, reached under my comforter, and held up my unopened bag of Cheetos. "No Chris Hemsworth tonight, though. My date tonight is with the King of the North," I said, adding a quick wink.

"You're still catching up on *Game of Thrones*? You're way behind."

"Whatever," I said. "That Talisa is a lucky bitch."

"You obviously haven't watched the Red Wedding," Linh deadpanned. "Come on. What's going on?"

"You know. Same old, same old. My mom asked me to marry my cousin. She thinks I'm going to die alone. That's all." I peeled off the mask and rubbed in the remaining layer of slick, clear serum on my face. I slipped on my huge thick-framed reading glasses that my optometrist insisted that I wear because of all the screen time I inflicted on my eyes.

"What the *fuuuuuuuuuuuuu*—"

"I know! She's so desperate for me to date."

"I mean . . . it's not the worst idea, Jas."

"Anyway, how's Vegas? You look like you're about to head out," I said, spotting her revealing neckline and eyes shadowed to perfection. Linh had invited me to go with her to Vegas this weekend, where her boyfriend, Owen, had been working for the past week. As a management consultant, Owen often traveled to meet with his clients. His project had just wrapped up and Linh had recently left her legal assistant job, so she met up with him to celebrate.

"I wish. Look at this." She switched to the outer camera on her phone, to show me Owen's lifeless body, his face turned to the side, where a trash can was placed strategically underneath for anticipated projectile vomit.

"Linh," I asked gently, "did you murder Owen?"

She switched her camera back to selfie mode. "He got carried away day drinking. He couldn't handle sitting through dinner, so we came back to our room. His roommate had to help me bring him up." She lay next to him and rubbed his back while he grumbled in misery.

"Owen has a roommate now?"

"Yeah, one of his coworkers. I wish you had come, Jas! Some of his coworkers are pretty cute," she lilted, trying to tempt me back into dating. "What do you think about Mark for Jas?" She elbowed Owen. "They would make a cute couple." Owen replied with incoherent but thoughtful word-like sounds.

"No thanks," I replied. "Remember last time when you tried to set me up with your coworker? The guy took out his retainer in front of me and left it on the table. His drool was everywhere." I stuck my tongue out in disgust.

"Hey! In my defense, I didn't know he wore a retainer. I never saw him eat. Plus, didn't he give you flowers? That was sweet."

"He brought one single rose," I corrected. "You know what my mom would have said about that?" In my best critical-mom voice, I imitated her oft-said quote: "Are you supposed to fall in love with a man just because he gave you flowers?" Personally, I loved receiving flowers. Not that I received any from my nonexistent admirers.

"Your mom is hilarious. Tell her I said hi," Linh said. Linh loved my mom, and the feeling was mutual. Linh was the daughter my mom didn't have—ambitious, successful, and had a boyfriend. "Jas. You need to date again. Or at least get laid! When was the last time you got laid? Don't tell me it was—"

"Let's not bring him up," I rushed to insert. "That person is dead to me."

"Okay, then just tell me what you're looking for. What makes guys attractive for you? So I know who I need to set you up with."

"I don't know," I said. I wasn't in the mood to discuss my dismal love life. "What makes someone attractive?" I wondered out loud. "I mean, many people are good-looking, but it doesn't necessarily mean you're attracted to them. I guess, he has to be confident, but not cocky. He has to have a kind smile, and when he looks at you, there's that glint of curiosity."

Linh snorted. "This is exactly why you fall in love with every Starbucks barista you meet. Honey, the only thing he's curious about is your coffee order."

I narrowed my eyes at Linh. "Forget it then, Linh. Don't ask if you don't like my answer." I sighed, dreamily. "Remember Bryce from Northern Lights Café? God, he had those hazelly eyes."

"Earth to Jas! I'm trying to help you get back out there, okay?

But first . . ."—Linh pointed her finger across the top of my screen—"you need to take care of those eyebrows. And just make sure you don't get friend-zoned before you profess your love, like what happened with Justin. Or was that Andrew? I forget. You were chasing so many guys in college."

I slid further into my bed. During my sophomore year of college, after batting zero in Chinese class, I tried to spend more time with some guy friends to see if they would turn into a friends-to-lovers situation. Both Andrew Kim and Justin Huynh would have ticked off all the boxes on my parents' list of desirable qualities: Asian, smart, likely to have well-paying professional careers, and nice.

Andrew lived two doors down from my dorm room. Even though he practically lived in the same gray hoodie and worn jeans, he still gave the impression that he showered regularly, with his hair always gelled and cleanly parted at the side. We were both taking Anatomy during the fall quarter and he invited me to join his study group, which consisted of his premed friends from the Korean Christian Fellowship club. We spent almost every Tuesday and Thursday night studying together. His friends always brought pizza and wings because they had the expensive meal plan. The only time Andrew suggested that we meet outside our study group was when he asked me to attend their next fellowship meeting. He didn't get my joke when I asked if Frodo would be there. I did not end up developing any feelings for him, but I did pass Anatomy with a B−.

Justin, on the other hand—I was completely gaga over him. I

had googly eyes for him the moment we met. He was tall, lean, and GBD—golden brown and delicious. My mom would have hated his unruly hair, which he covered with a beanie, and his faded black Chuck Taylors, which were split on the sides. Justin was part of the Film Commission, which put on free film screenings on campus. Every time I went to pick up tickets at Ackerman Union, it was always Justin handing them out. When I picked up tickets for a little-known art-house indie, Justin introduced himself, impressed by my taste in movies. After that, I volunteered to help him set up the screenings in order to spend more time with him.

We watched movies alone together from the projector room. He added commentary like a film critic and I, being nosy, asked him personal questions. With each screening, I learned that we had more and more in common. Both of our parents came to the United States as refugees. Justin and I connected over growing up in a traditional household and having to explain to our parents that they don't teach us how to translate insurance documents in the third grade. It was nice to find someone else who shared a similar upbringing because I didn't have to explain or justify my experience. I also came to appreciate his dry sense of humor. Ninety-nine percent of the time, he didn't intend to be funny, which made it a thousand times funnier.

At the screening for a movie that Linh would describe as "artsy-fartsy with too many quiet moments," Justin was commenting on the cinematography while we watched from the projector room when I blurted out, "I think I'm in love with you,

Justin." In my head, I planned to tell him at a more opportune time and he would declare his feelings for me. When he didn't respond right away, I cut the awkward silence by rambling.

"I'm sorry. It's just that we've been seeing each other a lot, and every time I see you, I look forward to your hugs. Because you're, like, super good-looking and my face perfectly fits at your shoulder. And your texts make me laugh and you always use the winking emoji, so I wasn't sure how much I should read into that, but then you invite me to spend time with you alone here and then sometimes we go eat after, so I figured it was time to just put my feelings out there because maybe . . . you felt . . . the same?" By the end of the spiel, my voice went so high, I was pretty sure it was at a frequency that only dogs could hear. Justin responded with a slight look of panic on his face and bumbled about how he was flattered, but sorry if he misled me. I never went to another film screening afterward.

I frowned. Thinking of Andrew and Justin put me in a worse mood. If Linh was going to give me a hard time about dating, I wasn't about to tell her about the conversation I'd had with my mom.

"You know what? As much as I like to relive my dating fails, I have better things to do."

"Oh, please! Watching *Game of Thrones*? Thirsty Thursday was yesterday," Linh said, referring to my typical Thursday night plans of watching a movie or show with a hot leading actor. A while back, I developed a schedule of sorts to break up the monotony of working at the shop every day. Monday was

Movie Monday. Tuesday was New Music Tuesday. Wednesday was Reading Wednesday. Friday was Food Show Friday. Without this schedule, the days would all meld together. This way, I had something to look forward to.

"Look. I know you haven't been on Insta lately, but you should check out my Vegas pics. Maybe you might see someone you like," Linh said, waggling her eyebrows. "They were all cool, I swear. No retainers as far as I could tell."

I rolled my eyes. "I'll let you know. Do you know who your roommates are yet?"

Linh took a gap year to prep for the LSATs and worked as a legal assistant to boost her chances of going to law school. Unfortunately, she didn't get into any of the schools she applied to in California, and she was leaving for New York University soon.

"Not yet. I hope they're cool, though."

"As long as your new roommates know that I'm the best roommate you've ever had, we'll be cool."

When we ended our call, I quickly resumed my original evening plans. I opened my bag of Flamin' Hot Cheetos and inhaled the spicy, acidic aroma. I pressed play on my laptop and started a *Game of Thrones* episode before my fingers became encrusted with red Cheeto dust.

After a couple of episodes, I yawned and almost rubbed red Cheeto dust into my eyes. I closed my laptop and got up to wash my hands. My room was pitch-black. As my feet landed on the carpet, I followed the flat, worn-out path that led out the door. When I returned to my room, I took the same path back but managed to stub my right little toe on the bedpost. *Fuck!* I winced in pain and hopped forward on my left foot, landing on a fluffy, previously undisturbed part of the carpet.

Limping to the bed, I checked my phone. It was almost midnight. I saw an unopened text from Linh. My eyes widened the second I saw the photo that Linh sent with the message "Just in case you're interested."

In the photo were Linh, Owen, and presumably three of his coworkers standing in front of the pool at the Marquee Dayclub. Linh looked amazing as usual in her white bikini. Owen either drank too much or didn't put enough sun block on because he could blend in with a flock of flamingos. What caught my attention was the guy who stood behind Owen.

*It can't be him.*

I slid my fingers across the screen to zoom in. All I could see was his face, since Owen's damn body stood in the way. Even with his face partially hidden behind his sunglasses, his wide, slightly crooked smile was a dead giveaway. It was Window Guy.

During my junior year at UCLA, I realized I did not have any employable skills. The only thing on my résumé was "Child labor/dutiful daughter at Sunshine Donuts." I mean, playing Tetris to fit a dozen donuts into a 9-by-9-by-4-inch pink box was an underappreciated skill, but that wasn't going to help me find a job after college. So, I found a job selling tickets for athletic events at the Pauley Pavilion Box Office.

One day, after taking my midterms and long hours of selling basketball tickets, I was ready to clock out. I took off my name tag and began to clean up my station.

"Hey. Do you have any tickets left for the Stanford game?"

The smooth baritone voice coming from behind the plexiglass window made my ears perk up. When I looked up from the computer and turned toward the window, my eyes landed on a navy UCLA T-shirt that fit neatly on top of a set of broad shoulders. As my eyes crawled up, my mind took stock of the face staring back at me. Defined jaw with the slightest five-o'clock shadow. Inviting dark brown eyes. A full wave of shiny black superhero hair. *Damn.* Stunned, I stared at him without saying a word.

"Um," he said as he glanced behind him, "is there something on my face or something?" He chuckled softly as he self-consciously rubbed his face near the corner of his mouth. This drew my attention to his lips, which stretched into a wide, confused smile. It turned out that there was something on his face—one tiny dimple on his right cheek.

I snapped myself out of a trance. "I'm sorry. Um, let me check." *Be cool, Jas!* I focused my heart-shaped eyes on the screen and tried to work off my nerves as I typed on the keyboard.

"There are three seats left on row M. How many tickets were you looking for?" I asked, aiming for normal eye contact.

"Perfect. I only need two tickets." Window Guy slid his student ID and credit card in the tray under the window. That's when I learned that his name was Alex Lai, fellow junior. When I typed in his ID number, his contact information and a log of all his past ticket purchases populated on the screen. I slid Alex's credit card through the machine, waiting for it to process.

"Give me a second, Alex. It takes a while to go through."

"Have you worked here long? I've never seen you here before," he said, leaning forward toward the window, his hands flat on the metal counter. Our faces were inches apart, separated by the blue-tinted plexiglass that hopefully mellowed out my now-blushing face.

"I just started this quarter. It's pretty cool. Sometimes I get tickets to events on campus," I said breezily, briefly making eye contact with him before brushing imaginary dust off my station.

"Oh? Do you ever get tickets to the football or basketball games?"

"No." I chuckled. Everyone I knew asked me about that, hoping to get free tickets from me. "There are never any leftover tickets for football or basketball. I actually haven't gone to any games ever." I heard the beep, signaling that the credit card transaction was approved. I tore off the receipt and slid it under the window along with Alex's tickets, ID, and credit card.

"That's too bad," Alex said as he quickly signed the receipt. "You should at least go to one game before you graduate. I hear there's one seat left on row M." Alex slid the receipt back in the small indentation under the window. I was too busy watching Alex's hair flip over as he looked up when I reached for the receipt and my fingers found themselves on top of his. My fingers curled up like a roly-poly bug in an instant from the contact.

Mortified, I looked up and we briefly locked eyes. Alex's mouth pulled into a lopsided smile as he tapped his tickets on the counter. "Thanks. Have a good one." His eyes stayed on me as he backed up a few steps before he turned around and walked away. Once he faced the opposite direction, I let out a deep breath. Damn. He looked just as good walking away.

When I relayed the story of Window Guy to Linh later that night, Linh slapped my arm.

"Ow! What was that for?" I asked as I rubbed my arm, even though it didn't hurt.

"Jas! He was flirting with you," Linh declared, like it was plain as day.

"No," I said, shaking my head. "It was just small talk. Why would he flirt with me? I was acting like a dork."

"First of all, why wouldn't he flirt with your hot ass? Did you do your hair today? You look so cute," Linh said as she glanced up and down at my outfit. I wasn't so sure if my uniform, a baby-blue UCLA polo, qualified as cute. "Second of all, what's his name?" She grabbed her phone. "Let's look him up on Instagram!"

"Don't bother. I already tried and I couldn't find him."

"Ugh, fine." Linh stopped typing. "But I'm telling you. Window Guy was flirting with you and you missed your chance."

"You think so?" I started to replay the conversation in my head. "Do you think I should . . ."

"Should what?"

"I could look up his phone number tomorrow at work. Is that too creepy?" I asked.

"Super creepy," Linh replied. "Shoulda asked him when you had the chance." Linh caught me still contemplating this poorly hatched plan of violating Alex's privacy. "Jas. Don't do it. It's a bad idea."

*Is it? No one will know.*

I went back and forth on it the entire next day. When it was almost closing time, I decided to go for it and broke all kinds of confidentiality rules and my morals and saved Alex's number into my phone. Not wanting Linh to judge me when I called, I decided to call him on the walk back to my apartment. As I lifted the phone up to my ear, I started to panic. What was I supposed to say?

"Hi, I'm Jasmine. I sold you basketball tickets yesterday and then stole your personal information like a creeper." How would Alex ever resist me after that?

After several rings, the call went to voicemail. But not Alex's voicemail. It sounded like a landline voicemail message. *People still had landlines?* Apparently, I had called Alex's home phone number. That moment of confusion allowed some common sense to seep into my brain and I promptly hung up. I was so relieved that I didn't end up humiliating myself. I pledged never ever to invade people's privacy again in my quest for love.

That is, until today.

Seeing Alex's face again sent all kinds of awkward girlie feelings into my body.

*Damn it! Why was Owen standing in front of Alex's shirtless body?!*

I swiped my phone and stared at the Instagram icon for a minute. I hadn't looked at social media in months. It was a huge time suck and it was always disappointing when nobody liked the things I posted. It was a fucked-up way to get a sense of validation, so I stopped feeding into it. My Facebook and Instagram accounts were still active, but I made a lot of things private and turned off most of my notifications. I knew if I just stopped posting, I would fall off the radar or simply not exist. Most of my "friends" wanted to keep in touch only if it was convenient. Besides Linh, very few friends from high school or college reached out to me.

*Who cares about them? More Alex pictures!*

God. The thirst was real.

Curiosity got the best of me. I opened my Instagram app and ignored the forty-seven notifications as I searched for Linh's account. Linh posted several Vegas photos. Owen and her playing penny slot machines, drinking free cranberry vodkas. Owen, struggling to hold his fork and knife at some fancy steakhouse. Finally I came across the same group photo at the Marquee Dayclub. I tapped on the photo to see if Linh had tagged any of them. Several handles appeared. There he was: alex_laiiiii. Five *i*'s in that screen name. I double-counted.

I tapped on his name and a seemingly endless grid of photos appeared.

*Who doesn't set their account to private?*

The irony of that thought wasn't lost on me as I started with his profile picture. It was a silhouette of him on a dirt path, looking off to the side, surrounded by overgrown grass and a view of the beach ahead of him. Was he the outdoorsy type? I looked to see who he followed. We both followed Linh and Owen but otherwise didn't have any mutual connections. His Following list consisted mostly of other actual friends, unlike me, who followed all the Avengers and Dr. Pimple Popper.

It was too dangerous for me to have a repository of Alex's pictures at my fingertips. I hadn't made my way through them all yet, but my eyes already popped out of my eye sockets. Alex holding a golden retriever puppy? *Adorable!* Alex shirtless in the pool? *Drool!* Alex proudly holding up his homemade cornbread for last year's Friendsgiving? *Too cute!*

In the mix were pictures of his travels and almost every meal he's ever eaten. The Vegas skyline at night. A steaming bowl of ramen with the perfect soft-boiled egg and glistening slices of pork belly. Giant sequoias at Yosemite. A steak with crisscross grill marks on top between wineglasses on a table with white linens. The Bund.

I scrolled so far down that I came across his graduation photos from last year. He stood proud, his blue sash draped on his shoulders, with presumably his grandma by his side. The shy smile on his face as his grandma squeezed his arm was so sweet, my teeth hurt looking at it. All the pictures after that couldn't compare. Basketball games at Pauley Pavilion and a dark photo of what looked like the back of an EDM concert, with hands up and neon lights shooting across the stage. Ugh. I couldn't listen to EDM anymore without wanting to hurl.

I rubbed my eyes and glanced at the time. *Whew!* Only fifteen minutes had passed. Anything longer than twenty minutes would have made me a stalker. At least that was what I was telling myself. But then those forty-seven notifications called my name.

Before I knew it, two hours had passed. I went through nearly all my friends' profiles. Eight of my friends had gone to the beach in the last week. Their smiling selfies with their windswept hair that only the salty air could produce were in stark contrast to my random obscure pictures of everyday things at the shop, which I stopped posting a few months after I started working there again. There were only so many pictures of pink boxes and apple fritters I could take and fake excited captions I could write. I mean, I was thankful to be employed—it was better than nothing—and I'm sure some people would love to be surrounded by donuts every day, but not me. I've had enough of it for a lifetime.

My eyelids started to feel heavy. I wanted to get one last look at Alex's profile before calling it quits. As I finished typing his name, my body shut down, unable to resist sleep any longer. My eyes closed and my hands relaxed. The second my phone slipped from my hand, I gasped awake. My drowsiness kept me from reacting quickly enough. Like a slow-motion sequence, I clumsily tried to catch my phone before it hit me squarely on my glasses.

"Fuck!" I whisper-screamed.

The loud cracking sound of my phone and glasses colliding made me fear for the worst. Fortunately, both items were unscathed. I checked the time before I tossed it on my desk. I was supposed to get to the shop by six A.M.

*Four hours of sleep?*

*Tomorrow is going to be a long day.*

## Chapter 3

"Kuài diǎn! How come you're late?" my mom quickly scolded me under her breath. She was pissed, but she would never make a scene in front of customers. I hurried past the line of customers and threw my purse on top of a fifty-pound bag of flour in the back of the shop. After snoozing my alarm one too many times, I frantically jumped out of bed at five-fifty. I had only enough time to change into my usual outfit—a T-shirt and jeans—and brush my teeth before running out the door. I grabbed a Styrofoam cup and poured out a medium coffee. I really wanted it for myself. Lord knows I needed it, but instead I handed the coffee to Sam, a Sunshine Donuts regular.

"Jasmine! You read my mind." Sam chuckled as he reached for the half-and-half. Well, it wasn't rocket science. He had only ever ordered a medium coffee the entire time I had known him. "Sorry, kid, but it's all I got on me today," he said as he produced a clear sandwich bag full of pennies from his dingy sand-colored Members Only jacket.

*Oh, come on! Who carries a hundred pennies around?* I gave up on my fake strained smile. Sam was pushing eighty and he was sweet, but he totally didn't give a fuck that he was holding up the line.

Resigned, I said, "Take your time, Sam. I'll be right back when you're done counting." I turned away and ended up helping four customers by the time Sam completed his task.

"Here you go, sweetie. Thanks for the coffee!" Sam said as he walked out of the shop. I didn't bother counting. I swept them all into my hand, opened the cash register, and dumped them with the rest of the pennies.

I refocused on getting through the morning rush. While my dad finished putting the final touches on the last batch of maple bars in the back, my mom and I moved deftly around each other to fulfill the orders, our movements like a choreographed dance. As I reached up to grab a croissant, my mom dipped under my arm to toss in a few free donut holes before boxing up a neatly arranged dozen donuts. We knew all of our regular customers' orders by heart, to the point where the customers didn't even have to ask. When they stepped up to the counter, their orders were already waiting for them. The shop ran like a well-oiled machine, unlike one of our blenders, which gave out while my mom made a strawberry-banana smoothie.

By 8:30 A.M., the flow of customers settled down to a manageable pace. My parents started to head out to the wedding.

"Okay, Jas. We'll be back. Lunch zài bīngguì. After the wedding, I'll go pick up a new blender too," my mom said, already halfway out the door with my dad. As they stepped into their car, I turned toward the fridge to see what my mom brought for lunch.

*Bzzz. Bzzz. Bzzz.*

I heard my phone vibrate. It was probably Linh, bugging me again about the photo. I dug through my messy purse and found my phone. Apparently, I missed several text messages from Linh.

*7:40 A.M.*

**LINH:** JAS!
**LINH:** Why is Owen's roommate asking me about you?
**LINH:** Do you know him????

Owen's roommate?

*8:02 A.M.*

**LINH:** You liked what you saw huh?
**LINH:** Why aren't you responding?
**LINH:** TEXT ME BACK WHEN YOU SEE THIS!

*8:07 A.M.*

**LINH:** Sorry. I had to do it.

Do what?? Then, I noticed that I had other unread messages. From an unknown number.

*8:28 A.M.*

Hi Jasmine. This is Alex.
Linh gave me your number.

What the fuuuuuuuuuuuuuuuuuck?! Alex is Owen's new roommate?! I needed to sit down. My mind was spiraling.

**JAS**: LINH! WTF is going on?
**LINH**: You tell me! He said you followed him on Instagram.
**LINH**: Do you know him?

*Shit shit shit!* With trembling hands, I swiped my phone and there it was.

I officially followed Alex on Instagram like some random creep. I tried to recall the sequence of events last night. I must have accidentally tapped it before the phone smacked my face. I called Linh.

"You're welcome," Linh said, clearly pleased, like she couldn't have orchestrated it better herself.

"No, thank you. What the hell am I supposed to do?" I whined. Panicking, I started pacing behind the display case.

"Hold up. You have to tell me how you know Alex and why he's asking me about you."

I let out a guttural sound. "He's Window Guy, and I may or may not have stalked his social media last night."

"Who's Window Guy? Did he fix your window or something?"

"No! Remember when I worked at Pauley Pavilion? The guy whose phone number I stole because maybe he was flirting with me?"

"Oh. OH!" Linh started cracking up. "You either have the best luck or the worst luck."

"Linh, can you not?" Her cackle started to hurt my ears. "How am I supposed to impress him now when he knows I stalked him online?"

"So, you *do* want to impress him," Linh said excitedly.

"No! That's not what I meant. Ugh. This is a bad idea."

"Just let me introduce you guys. We can double-date!" Linh gasped. "YAAS! Let's double-date!" she squealed. "How's Sund—"

"No! No double date. Look, a customer just came in—"

"Bullsh—" Linh's voice cut off.

My face reflected back on the black screen. My phone died. Oops. Sorry, Linh. I went to the back of the store to plug it in and waited a minute before turning it on. Unread texts from Linh were waiting for me.

LINH: Did you hang up on me?
LINH: You're gonna pay for that.
LINH: Just give this a chance.

**Linh:** If he wasn't interested, he wouldn't have asked me
about you.

**Jas:** Sorry. My phone died. I swear!

**Linh:** It's already been done.

**Jas:** What did you do?

**Linh:** I showed him this.

I felt the blood drain from my face. It was a screenshot of
Linh's text conversation with Alex. She sent him a hazy picture
that she and I took in the bathroom mirror from a club we went
to senior year. Linh insisted that our dresses be short and tight.
Linh had on a rust-red bodycon dress with a cutout under her
boobs. I didn't own anything that short or tight, so I borrowed
one of Linh's dresses that was normally knee-length on her.
With our height difference, the dress—which had a sheer panel
between the bralette and skirt—barely covered my butt. Besides
some smudged eyeliner and my face shimmering from sweat, I
could admit that it was a good picture of us. I was still going to
kill Linh, though.

**Jas:** I hate you.

**Linh:** Don't resist this Jas.

**Linh:** We don't have to call it a date. Let's just all hang out!

"Hello?" a customer called out. *Shit.*

"Sorry! I'm coming!" I tossed my phone aside. If my mom
was here, I would have been reamed out for making a customer

wait. I rushed out and greeted the customer, who looked like she just came from yoga class. She was twisting her blond ponytail as she looked at the menu board hanging above our cappuccino machine.

"Hi. Sorry about that. What can I get for you?" I tried to sound chipper.

"Do you use fresh strawberries in your smoothie?" Yoga Girl eyed the faded smoothie poster suspiciously.

"We use frozen strawberries. That way, we use less ice when it's blended," I explained.

"Do you use dairy in it? Or do you have, like, soy milk?" Yoga Girl wrinkled her nose. I resisted the urge to roll my eyes. This was a donut shop, not a juice bar. She needed to lower her expectations.

"We use a nondairy powder. Is that okay?"

Yoga Girl agreed. Apparently nondairy powder was acceptable, but real milk wasn't. I suppose it was possible that she was lactose intolerant. Whatever. I dumped the powder, strawberries, ice, and juice blend into the blender. I placed the lid on top before turning it on, watching the blades pulverize the ice and frozen strawberries until it was the right consistency. I poured the smoothie into a clear plastic cup and topped it with a dome lid before sending Yoga Girl on her way.

Usually the donut shop was a ghost town during summer afternoons. But without fail, once one customer comes in, a string of customers will follow, like game theory or something. After Yoga Girl left, one by one they trickled in. Another strawberry smoothie. A jelly donut with a small coffee. A jalapeño ham and cheese croissant, toasted. The last customer ordered four smoothies, all different flavors. Normally, I didn't mind making smoothies, but we were down one blender. It took me longer than usual since I couldn't make two simultaneously.

When the last customer left, I looked at the clock. It was just past one. My parents should be on their way back. My mom liked to run a tight ship, and the front counter was a mess. I had to get everything in tip-top shape before they came back. I quickly dumped out the coffee grounds to make a new pot of coffee. Once I heard the water percolating, I jogged to the back to wash the blender. I wiped stray sprinkles and melted smoothie off the counters. I scanned the storefront.

*Is there anything else left to do?*

Then I saw the thing that my mom always harped on—pushing donuts to the front of the display so customers could see them. Each day, as favorite varieties sold out, it would leave empty columns here and there. My mom diligently rearranged the donuts to fill the gaps as they appeared or else they would look like leftover stray donuts scattered across the display case.

I grabbed a pair of tongs and lowered my head until I was eye level with the top row of trays. I took a moment to admire the donuts. My mom liked to place all the specialty items like the cinnamon rolls and bear claws at the top to tempt customers into buying a more expensive item. I pulled the tray toward me so I could rearrange them in neat lines, making my way from left to right. Once the top row of trays was organized, I made my way toward the middle racks. The middle racks had a mix of all the staple items: glazed donuts, twists, bars, sprinkled donuts, and old-fashioned donuts. Finally I knelt down to the bottom racks, which were mainly for donut holes because they were at the perfect height for kids to see.

While I was finishing up the last tray at the bottom right-hand corner, I saw two shadowy pairs of legs heading toward the shop entrance from my periphery. *Good thing I finished before Mom and Dad came back.* When the door opened, I heard a familiar voice, except it wasn't my mom.

"Surprise!" Linh shouted.

What. The. Fuck.

I tried to make myself smaller, curling into myself behind a tray of donut holes. Owen walked in behind Linh.

"Come out, come out wherever you are!" Linh said with a singsong lilt. I sighed and slowly straightened up. The tray of croissants on top of the display case blocked my view. Through its plastic lid, I saw the blurry shadows of not one, not two, but three people.

*Don't tell me it's him.*

I shut my eyes, praying I was in some bizarro dream, but I knew it was no use. I steeled myself as I walked toward the front counter.

"Oh my god, Linh." I forced through a fake smile as I glanced at Linh, who had an annoying smirk on her face. I stayed behind the counter to give myself a buffer from this disaster waiting to happen. "Hi, Owen." I gave him a small wave. Hiding behind his sunglasses, Owen smiled apologetically at me.

"Um, Jas. This is my roommate, Alex," Owen said, gesturing to Alex, who was busy looking around and taking in the shop. "Alex, this is Jasmine."

Seeing Alex in the flesh without a plexiglass window between us set my insides on fire, as if lava was traveling through my veins. He was wearing the most basic white T-shirt, black basketball shorts, and running shoes, yet his hotness left me speechless. Even his toned calves looked sexy. Since when were calves sexy?

Alex finally looked at me and extended his right arm to shake my hand. In a daze, I managed to extend my right arm in response. Alex's eyebrows shot up in confusion, and that was when I realized that I was still holding a pair of tongs. My reflexes got the best of me and I nearly snapped off his fingers.

"Oh my god, I'm so sorry," I said, mortified. Linh and Owen failed at holding back their snickers. I placed the tongs on the counter and wiped my sweaty hands on my jeans before extending my hand a second time. Alex eyed it suspiciously.

"I promise I don't bite," I said nervously. After a moment of hesitation, Alex shook my hand. The contact was brief. I quickly withdrew my hand once our hands separated before I did something else to embarrass myself. Why did my brain always betray me in the presence of good-looking men? It was so unfair.

Out of the corner of my eye, I saw Linh shaking her head in

disbelief. She whispered too loudly to Owen, "God, she's so bad at this."

"Okay!" I shouted, hoping to distract Alex from Linh's commentary. "So, to what do I owe the pleasure of this visit?" I said, trying to regain some composure. As I asked the question, Linh pushed past the low swinging door to meet me behind the front counter and gave me a big hug. More quietly this time, she whispered in my ear, "Stop being such a dork." Annoyed, I pinched her waist. "Hey! What was that for?"

I dragged her into a secret huddle. "What the hell are you doing here?" I whispered. "You're supposed to be in Vegas!"

"Owen pooped out after yesterday and Alex was coming back this morning anyway because he's a nerd. Come on! Let's go have lunch. I saw a new Korean barbecue place a few blocks from here. It has great Yelp reviews."

"I can't. I'm covering for my parents today." I shrugged apologetically. "Thanks for thinking of me. Do you want some donuts for the road?" I said while attempting to push Linh out. Owen and Alex watched us, unsure what was unfolding before their eyes.

The door chime caused everyone to turn around. Linh and I froze in place with my hands still trying to shove Linh's immovable body. My mom stood at the door, taking in the scene. She had changed back into her usual work outfit, except her face was still made up from the wedding. Holding our new blender, my dad walked around her and broke the silence.

"Jas, what's going on?" He stood tall as he assessed Owen and Alex.

My mom gently slapped my dad's arm with the back of her hand. "That's Linh." Then she pointed at Owen. "That white guy is Linh's boyfriend." My mom looked at Alex and waved dismissively at him. "That one, I don't know."

"Chào cô. Chào chú." Linh greeted my parents and finally walked away to hug my mom. "You remember Owen, right?" My mom offered Owen a polite smile and nod. "We came by to see if Jas can come have lunch with us. It won't be more than a couple hours." Linh clasped her hands around my mom's, giving her puppy-dog eyes.

*What are we, twelve?* I couldn't believe Linh was asking for permission to take me out for lunch.

"Who are you?" my dad gruffly asked Alex. He stood uncomfortably close to Alex, with only the blender between them. Alex was taller than my dad by a few inches, but that didn't keep my dad from staring him down.

Before I could intervene, Alex took a small step back and lowered his head to offer my dad a slight bow. "Hi, Mr. Tran. I'm Alex."

I already knew what my dad would say next. All my friends have been subjected to my dad's infamous interview questions. To say my dad was protective was an understatement. I could hang out late only with friends he approved of. Many applied, but few were accepted.

"Alex. What's your last name?" my dad asked, trying to figure out Alex's background. My mom, standing next to Linh, paid close attention to their interaction.

"My last name is Lai," Alex replied.

"You speak Mandarin, Alex Lai?" My dad's face was still expressionless.

"Ba—" I intended to save Alex from further questions, but to my surprise, Alex started conversing with my dad in Mandarin. It was fluent Mandarin too, rather than the broken Chinglish I spoke at home. I was really impressed. It was surprisingly attractive.

They spoke faster than I could comprehend, but I caught some parts. Alex told my dad that he also went to UCLA for college, but that he met Owen when they both started their jobs a year ago. When my dad inquired more about Alex's background, I learned that Alex's family was from a city a couple of hours west of Shanghai and that he went back to visit his grandma there every summer. Once my dad heard this, his expression softened and my mom's face lit up.

"Is that why your Mandarin is so good? You should teach Jas," my dad said. *Thanks a lot, Dad!*

At that moment, everyone looked at me. I didn't know what else to do but offer a weak smile. And then, of all things, my stomach growled.

My mom tapped my dad's shoulder. "Baba, stop talking so much. They need to eat lunch." She looked back at me. "You go too, Jas."

"Yes! Grab your purse, Jas," Linh said, shooing me.

I turned on my heel, walked into the back of the shop, and gathered my things. What the hell just happened? How did I go from light Instagram stalking yesterday to going to lunch with Alex today? I stopped to tighten my ponytail. Damn it! Why did I look like shit?

"Jas! Let's go!" Linh called after me. I walked back out and reassured my parents that I would be back soon. Linh and Owen were already outside. Alex held the door open for me.

"Thanks," I said as I walked past him. "Sorry about my dad."

Alex chuckled. "It's cool." He let go of the door and walked silently next to me.

We all climbed into Owen's SUV.

"Are you good to drive?" I asked Owen as he started the car.

"He's fine," Linh said. "I made sure he yacked and drank lots of water last night. Alex drove most of the way here, so Owen can handle driving a few blocks."

As I turned to buckle my seat belt, I caught a glimpse of Alex doing the same. My eyes widened, watching his arms flex as he reached for his seat belt. I quickly averted my eyes before he could catch me staring at him.

*Be cool, Jas! Be cool!*

How was I supposed to make it through lunch?

# Chapter 4

There was a fifteen-minute wait at a new, all-you-can-eat Korean barbecue joint that was seven blocks away from Sunshine Donuts. The restaurant's specialty dish was a sizzling plate of baby back ribs covered with melted cheese. After several viral videos of the plate's epic cheese pulls, crowds flocked to the restaurant. We considered ourselves lucky to have a relatively short wait. Linh took the opportunity to drag me to the bathroom while Owen and Alex waited for our table.

"Okay, Jas. Let's see what we can do about your face." Linh dug through her purse, pulling out a small makeup bag.

"I think it's a little too late for that. First, let's talk about how you ambushed me today. I'm still trying to process what's happening right now."

Linh laid out her makeup on the bathroom counter and turned around to examine my face. "Hmm. Have you gotten paler? I thought we used the same foundation."

"Well, being indoors all the time will do that to you." I swatted at the eye shadow brush that Linh raised to my face. "Linh! You're not answering my question!"

Linh tapped her brush at the edge of her eye shadow palette. "What do you want me to say? You're the one who followed Alex," she said as she assaulted my eyelids with a neutral taupe color. "He asked me about you. I showed him that picture of us at the club because your profile picture is a French cruller. Now stop moving and let me fill in your eyebrows!"

"How did you convince them to come here for Korean barbecue? Their apartment is so close to K-Town."

"Stay still!" Linh grabbed ahold of my face with both hands and started filling in my eyebrows with a dark brown pencil. "I showed Owen the video of the short ribs. You know he loves anything with cheese on it."

"What did you even say to Alex? What did he want to know?"

"Okay, we need to hurry." Linh turned me around to face the mirror to make sure I approved of her work. "Maybe some eyeliner or mascara before we head back out there."

"Linh! Just tell me, so I don't say something stupid!"

"You need to chill out. Close your eyes." I felt Linh's eyeliner pen expertly glide across my eyelids. "He just asked if I knew you and how long we've been friends. I talked you up. He obviously liked what he saw from the picture, and now I'm trying to get you looking halfway decent before he claims false advertising on me. Now open your eyes."

I looked in the mirror. It was a minor improvement, but I

basically looked the same. "This is a lost cause. Let's just go," I said. Linh dumped all the makeup into her purse and we walked toward the bathroom door. As I grabbed the door handle, Linh pulled off my hairband, causing me to take a step back. "Whoa! What are you doing?" Linh buried her hands into my hair, fluffing it.

"There. Much better. Okay, let's go, Jas," she said, pushing me forward.

Walking back out into the restaurant shocked my senses. The restaurant was packed with noisy customers. Grills sizzled from all directions, and the restaurant was blasting a mix of post-2000 pop songs and K-pop. I was so distracted that I walked past Owen and Alex, who were already seated at a booth by the window. Linh slid next to Owen and I nervously took my seat next to Alex. He smiled at us, so I returned a small smile. I didn't know what to say, so I buried my face into the menu.

*Okay, I can do this. Just relax. It's just lunch with friends. Don't be a dork.*

Our waiter arrived and interrupted my self-affirmations. He brought each of us a glass of water.

"Are you ready to order?" he asked, whipping out a small tablet. Linh answered for all of us.

"He's getting those cheese ribs," she said, pointing at Owen. "I'm getting the all-you-can-eat, option A. You too, right, Jas?" Linh looked right at Alex and pointed at me. "This girl knows how to eat."

"Oh, thanks for that," I said, shooting Linh an annoyed look.

"But yeah, option A sounds good," I admitted as I closed my menu.

"I think I'll get the same," Alex said, handing the waiter his menu. Our waiter tapped into his tablet, confirmed our orders, and walked away. There was a brief lull, which allowed me to hear the song playing in the restaurant. Linh and I recognized the song at the same time. We looked at each other and couldn't contain our laughter.

"What's so funny?" Owen asked as he sipped his water.

"Freshman year, we lived in Sproul Hall, and Linh decided we should enter the Sproul's Got Talent show. The prize was a hundred-dollar gift card to the bookstore, which I didn't think was worth it, personally," I said.

"Hey! Books were expensive," Linh argued.

"Anyway, it was so last minute. We figured we would just pick a random song to sing together, and of all things, Linh picked 'California Gurls' by Katy Perry."

"It was a total shitshow. Neither of us could sing. I put all my efforts into dancing." Linh paused to do a little shimmy. "Jas was too shy to dance and she only knew some of the lyrics, which she sang really loudly. I just remember you yelling 'Bikini on top!'" Linh snorted.

"We didn't win obviously, but random people in the building called me California Gurl for the rest of the year." I grinned, shaking my head.

Owen chuckled. "Sounds like Linh. Always getting into trouble," he said, bumping shoulders with her.

"Hey! Without me, Jas would have never left our dorm room that year. She was always studying."

Our waiter arrived and turned on the grill that centered the table. The hood range whirred above us. Plates of raw meat and banchan started to appear. My mouth watered. I was starving. I grabbed a pair of tongs and immediately started grilling the bulgogi.

"What was your major?" Alex asked me before throwing some galbi on the grill.

"I majored in neuroscience at first, doing the premed track for the first two years. I wasn't cut out for it, so I changed my major to sociology." I flipped over the meat and some grease splattered on me and Alex. Translucent golden oily spots expanded on his formerly pristine white shirt.

"Sorry!" I offered Alex a napkin, which he gladly accepted. His attempt to wipe off the grease stains was futile, but it gave me the chance to observe him while he was distracted. Linh kicked me under the table to redirect my attention to my bulgogi, which nearly burned.

"Nah, that's my fault for wearing a white shirt to Korean barbecue. So, what do you plan to do with your sociology degree?" Oh, the million-dollar question. The question that I had been asked for the last three years by my parents, my brother, Linh, and every Sunshine Donuts customer.

Luckily, it was at that moment that our waiter presented Owen with a volcano of pork covered with molten, gooey cheese. We oohed and aahed as we took out our phones and recorded Owen taking a scoop and slowly stretching the cheese. Owen was so excited about the cheese that he immediately stuffed it in his mouth, forgetting that it was burning hot. There's nothing less attractive than someone trying to blow on their food while chewing it at the same time.

While Linh and Alex were busy posting their videos on Instagram, I refocused my attention on eating. The nice thing about Korean barbecue is how communal it is. We all helped one another grill the food and shared dishes. It gave me plenty of excuses to interact with Alex. I tried not to think too much about the times our fingers touched when we passed plates. There were a few times where I felt his gaze linger on me a little longer than it should have. I wasn't sure if he liked what he saw or if he was trying to figure me out.

Owen and Alex got caught up talking about work for a while. I didn't understand what they were talking about, except that I caught Alex saying he was happy about his short commute since his next client was local. Linh and I zoned them out while we kept stuffing our faces. I couldn't tell if the guys were impressed or horrified by the amount of food Linh and I ate. When I was finally done eating, I leaned back into my seat, rubbing my belly.

"What's that on your shirt? Is that from a national park?" Alex asked me. I glanced down. I could see why he would think that, with the bronze screen print of pine trees taking up most of the front of my navy-blue shirt.

"Oh no, Jas. Don't tell me you're still listening to the National. Their music makes me want to die," Linh said disapprovingly.

I ignored Linh and looked at Alex. "I went to their concert a long time ago. It just happened to be the shirt I grabbed this morning," I said, narrowing my eyes at Linh.

"I've never heard of them. What kind of music is it?" Alex asked.

"Depressing shit! Jas has weird taste in music," Linh said as she snagged the last piece of kimchi.

"Hey! I listen to most kinds of music, except for K-pop—unlike someone here. You don't even know what they're saying," I said to Linh.

"Why do you hate things that bring people joy, Jas? I don't need to know what they're saying to enjoy it. Plus, the guys are hot," Linh said, showing me a picture of her favorite member of BTS, what's his name. "Have you not watched any of the videos I've sent you? Look how their bodies move."

I left Linh alone to drool. "Anyway, why do you ask? Have you gone to any national parks?" I asked Alex, even though I knew this already.

Alex's face lit up. "Yeah, I hiked at Yosemite earlier this year. I'm planning to go to Zion next year."

"That's cool. Do you hike often?" I asked.

"Yeah. It's a good way for me to clear my mind, especially since work can get crazy. If I have time, I'll go to Runyon Canyon. During the week, I try to hit up Elysian Park."

"That's by Dodger Stadium, right? Can you see the stadium

from there?" I wasn't a huge baseball nerd, but I did follow the Dodgers. Baseball was the perfect sport in my opinion. Unlike basketball, which always has music or horns blaring in the arena, baseball had enough quiet moments where you can have a conversation with your friends. Also, the food came to you, which was a bonus for a couch potato like me.

"No, but there's a good view of downtown. I'd recommend it," Alex said before peering out the window. "Although you're right by the hills. I'm sure there's a trail close to your house."

"Ha! I would love to see Jas hiking," Linh said, pointing her metal chopsticks at me. "You never made it up to our dorm without complaining."

"Thanks a lot, Linh," I said, kicking her under the table. Our waiter came and brought us our check. "For that, you can pay for lunch," I said jokingly. I handed her the bill, but Owen snatched it out of my hands. He offered to treat us, saying he was still celebrating the end of his last project. Alex and I immediately opposed the idea and took out our wallets. Owen was not prepared to have us gang up on him to split the bill and gave up quickly. After we paid, we headed out toward Owen's car.

I walked alongside Linh and gave her a side hug. "Thanks for taking me out to lunch today. It was nice to get out of the donut shop for a little bit."

"You're welcome," Linh said before she leaned in and whispered, "You did good today. Maybe more to come?" Linh pressed her hands together and looked up at me. She was either pleading with me or praying for me. Between the two, I'd place my bets on the latter.

I rolled my eyes and shook my head at Linh before I let her walk ahead with Owen. I was glad that Linh dragged me out, even though it was under precarious circumstances. It was really nice to be with friends, eat good food, and just be out in the middle of the day. I couldn't stop a goofy grin from spreading across my face. It was a little embarrassing, so I looked down at the crumbling parking lot floor. We were almost at Owen's car when I sensed Alex staring at me. I looked up and let him see my dorky smile. He smiled back, amused. There was that dimple again. It seemed to appear only when Alex smiled broadly. I wanted to poke it.

The four of us settled into Owen's car. Our food comas led to a quiet drive back to Sunshine Donuts. Besides Linh groaning about how full she was, the only sound I heard was the A/C on full blast. I looked out the window as Owen drove past strip mall after strip mall. The car was stopped at a traffic light when I heard the texts I had anticipated from my parents. They were usually paranoid whenever I went out and notoriously texted me about my ETA. I was surprised that they hadn't texted me sooner. I sat up straight when I saw the texts were from Alex.

**ALEX:** Didn't mean to stare earlier.

**ALEX:** Wanted to make sure you weren't a weirdo adding me on IG.

**ALEX:** I feel like I've seen you before.
**ALEX:** It's driving me crazy.

*Oh shit.* How was I supposed to respond to that? I blinked at my phone for a second before I turned to my left, meeting Alex's eyes. I let him examine my expressionless face while I stared back at his. His lightly tanned skin was so perfectly even and smooth, with tiny freckles under his left eye. His eyes squinted as he searched for clues. Even with the cold air blasting throughout the car, I felt the rush of heat radiate from my face. It started to feel claustrophobic, sitting so close together in the back seat. He still couldn't place me, but I conceded our staring contest. I could handle only so much of it before I felt self-conscious.

*Fuck it.* There was no point trying to avoid Alex's scrutiny. He was smart enough to know something was up. I started to type, "Remember buying tickets to the Stanford game?" before backspacing my way out of the hole I was digging. How was I supposed to clue him in without looking like a psycho? I quickly peeked at Alex out of the corner of my eye, aware of his exponentially growing suspicion. If I didn't respond quickly, I was going to look crazy whether I liked it or not. I looked back down at my phone and typed the first thing that came to mind.

**JAS:** Maybe if I wear my UCLA polo, it'll jog your memory

Alex stared at the message for a while. He looked up, facing the back of Owen's headrest. I imagined his synapses lit up like a pinball machine, trying to recall our first meeting. Now he knew I remembered him this whole time, but how could he possibly remember me? We hardly talked the one time we met.

We were a block away from Sunshine Donuts. Owen hurried to make a right turn before the yellow traffic light turned red. The sharp turn made me lean to my left and lose my balance. I slapped my hand down to catch myself and ended up putting my hand on top of Alex's right hand. I removed my hand immediately as if it burned. I held my breath as I glanced at Alex, who looked down at his hand and then at me with furrowed eyebrows. I saw his brain gradually put two and two together. His eyebrows began to relax. He bit his lip, trying to stop his smile from pulling to the edges of his face, chuckling to himself while he shook his head in disbelief.

Owen turned into the parking lot and parked right in front of the donut shop. "Thanks for the ride, Owen." I scooted forward and wrapped my arms around Linh from my seat. "I'll talk to you soon." I glanced at Alex, suddenly feeling shy. I didn't know what to do, so I gave him a small wave. "See you around." I hopped out of the car and walked toward the shop. Just as I walked through the door, I received more text notifications, creating a nice remix with the warbly door chime.

**ALEX:** I remember you now.

**ALEX:** But you can still wear that polo for me if you want;)

*Bleh!* I hated winking faces. They caused so much grief when I was desperately boyfriend hunting in college. I spent hours deciphering texts because of winking faces. I couldn't resist a snarky reply.

> **JAS:** Was that supposed to be flirty?
> **JAS:** Because if you liked the polo, then I question your judgment.
> **ALEX:** the polo wasn't that bad
> **ALEX:** it looked cute on you

My eyes widened as I reread Alex's last message over and over again.

"Jas! What are you doing?" my dad asked, snapping me back into reality. I found myself standing in the middle of the shop, glued to my phone. I looked around. There weren't any customers. Owen's car was already gone. I wondered if Alex saw me standing there like a doof. I got behind the front counter and tied my hair back into a ponytail. My phone buzzed again.

> **ALEX:** Call you later?

*Yes!* I screamed inside. Before I could reply, a different kind of notification appeared on my screen.

> **alex_laiiiii has requested to follow you.**

$\mathcal{M}$y dad interrogated me about the lunch and Alex. There wasn't much to tell, but it didn't stop him from asking me what I knew about his parents, their professions, Alex's job, and where he grew up.

"Ba, why would I ask him about any of that stuff? Is that what you think we talk about when meeting new people?" Learning more about your parents wasn't quite first-date material.

Assuming we'd go on a first date.

I hoped there would be a first date.

My dad shrugged. "What's wrong with that? Don't you want to know what kind of family he comes from?"

I didn't even know how to bring that up organically, but I made a mental note for it anyway, knowing that my dad would keep asking me until I found out. "What does that have to do with anyth—"

My dad held up his hand to interrupt me. "Do you hear that?"

A whirring sound rumbled from the ceiling until cool air blasted through the vents.

"You fixed it?" I looked proudly at my dad.

He basked in glory until my mom came and burst his bubble. "Ba called a shīfù to come fix it while you were at lunch. It needed a new part."

When my mom left to check on all the topping trays, my dad made a sour face behind her back. It made me laugh.

"Okay, I go home now." My dad reached into his pockets to find his car keys. "Oh! Jas. Give me your hands."

"Why?" I held my hands close to my chest, unsure if this was a trick.

"Just do it."

My dad held out his fist until I cupped both of my hands underneath his. When he opened his hand, small, gently bruised white flower buds bounced onto my palms.

"I took it from the wedding. Jasmines. You like it?"

"Uh." I held them up to my nose. "They smell nice, but . . . what am I supposed to do with them?"

He covered my hands with his. "Keep it. Put it in your room. It lasts a long time."

"Uh . . . okay. Were you supposed to take these?"

He lifted his eyebrows as he shrugged. That meant no. He didn't say anything else as he backed his way out of the shop. I guess this was our little secret.

I grabbed a small parchment bag that we used when customers ordered only one donut. I dumped the flower buds into it, closed it, and put it in my purse before I forgot about it.

Since my dad had finally left and my mom was busy, I took a moment to check my Instagram to make sure there wasn't anything weird. When everything checked out, I switched back to Alex's profile. It was much more interesting than mine. I was so enamored with his face that I didn't notice my mom peeking over my shoulder.

"He looks very handsome in that picture," my mom said, startling me. She pointed at the picture of Alex wearing a navy suit, standing with a group of his colleagues at his company's Christmas party. I didn't disagree with her. "So, is he your boyfriend now?"

"Ma! I just met him. He's just a friend."

"If he's just your friend, why you look at his pictures for an hour? You didn't even get up when a customer came in."

*An hour?*

"A customer came in? When?" I lifted my head to look around the store and felt a crick in my neck. I rolled my neck to stretch it out. My mom tapped my back, which she always did to remind me to straighten my posture. I sat up, pulling my shoulders back so that my mom would let it go.

"Jas, you need to stop looking down at your phone. I heard a girl fell into a hole in the ground because she kept looking down at her phone when she was walking. You need to pay attention."

"Okaaay, Ma," I dragged out. My mom and her stories. I was

about to put my phone under the front counter when I received a text from Alex.

ALEX: Your Instagram is boring

I literally laughed out loud. The last thing I posted was a picture of my parents and me standing next to a Rose Parade float in Pasadena on New Year's Day, one of the few days where they closed the shop.

JAS: You mean, you don't find the picture of our menu
    fascinating?
ALEX: Srsly tho. I feel cheated.
JAS: Sorry to disappoint
JAS: I wiped all of my incriminating photos.

Alex didn't respond right away. Maybe this was the wrong way to go. Sarcasm usually put me on the fast lane toward the friend zone and I needed to make a U-turn quick.

JAS: What were you hoping to see?
JAS: if you ask maybe you shall receive

I watched the ellipsis appear and disappear as Alex typed and presumably deleted his message. Each time Alex stopped typing, it made me more and more nervous. I must have misread our interactions. Maybe I shouldn't have texted him that question. It obviously made him uncomfortable. He was probably figuring out a way to get out of this conversation. I needed to give him an out, for him and to save my own face. I kept coming up with duds when Alex finally replied.

**ALEX**: Just you

*What the what? Just me?*

I had an idea. I had to execute it while I had the nerve. The timing was perfect, since there weren't any customers in the shop and my mom was in the back, washing all the baking trays. That was going to keep her busy for a while.

I untied my hair and bent forward to get some volume. I opened up my camera and put it on selfie mode to see how my hair looked. It didn't have the Beyoncé-wind-blowing-in-my-hair look I was hoping for. I grabbed a small, rainbow-sprinkled donut with vanilla icing and held it up to my nose. It looked like I had a donut goatee. It wasn't as cute as I imagined. I tried another pose, holding the donut over my left eye, extending my right arm to capture a selfie from the shoulders up. Unfortunately, the lighting wasn't too good inside, ironic for a shop called Sunshine Donuts.

I turned myself left and right, tilting my phone in different angles, trying different shots. In my last attempt, I took a bite of the donut and puffed out my cheeks.

"You look like a crazy person!" my mom shouted, suddenly appearing at the doorway that separated the front and back of the shop. I nearly choked on my donut. "Stop taking pictures of yourself. Go do some work." She turned around and took the trash out toward the back alley. I had only a minute before she came back. I sent Alex my best selfie with the donut held up to my eye. It kind of looked like my donut monocle.

**JAS:** I have to get back to work

**JAS:** So, in case I donut get a chance to text back, you know why

**ALEX:** Donut puns?

**ALEX:** Cute

Cute? What's cute? The pun? My picture? I heard my mom slam the back door, announcing her return. I tossed my phone under the counter and tried to make myself look busy. I scurried toward the eat-in area, haphazardly sweeping the floor, over-analyzing the "cute" comment. Maybe Linh would have some insight. I had to send her a screenshot to get her input. I walked back around the counter and my phone was nowhere to be found.

"Looking for this?" My mom held up my phone. "Get. Back. To. Work. Talk to your boyfriend later."

"He's not my boyfriend, but if you want him to be, I need to talk to him," I said, too eager to be convincing.

My mom shot me a cool, stern look. "He can wait. Come on. I'll help you clean up before we go." End of discussion.

With that, we started on all of our normal closing tasks early. My parents were so nervous about leaving me to run the shop alone that they didn't want me to stay a second past ten. I collected all the empty trays from our display case and washed off all the grease and icing. My mom set aside a half tray of leftover donuts for my dad, who would later crush them into crumbs and mix in cinnamon and sugar for our crumb donuts. We made sure all the equipment was cleaned and all the ingredients were stocked for my dad.

"Hái yǒu shénme ne?" my mom pondered as she looked around for last-minute things to do before she went home to get ready for the reception. My dad had just arrived to pick up my mom. He waited patiently in the car as my mom fretted around the back counter. She turned the key in the cash register and printed out the balance. She tore off the receipt and stuffed it in her pocket.

"Bùyào pà," I reassured her.

"When you close, go home right away. Don't stay late, okay?" She was about to leave when she turned back toward the register. She punched the keypad until the cash drawer sprang open. She grabbed all the large bills, leaving only enough cash for change. "Don't worry about counting the money. I'll do it tomorrow." She looked side to side to make sure no one was around to see her put the money in her purse.

Of course, she wasn't about to let me close out the cash register. She trusted nobody but herself to count every penny.

"Wait." She unzipped the side pocket of her purse and pulled out my phone, checking the screen before handing it back to me. "Here. No messages from your boyfriend."

"Okay okay!" I shooed her out. "Go have fun already!"

"Call me if you need us!" she shouted before she stepped out the door.

"Don't worry! Nothing's going to happen!"

I waved them off and waited until they drove out the parking lot before I sat on the stool behind the front counter. My body relaxed, partly because my parents weren't here to boss me around and partly because there wasn't anything to do but to babysit the shop until closing time.

At first I tried to keep myself busy. I restocked the straws, napkins, and coffee cup lids at the front counter. I reorganized the sweetener packets into a neat, color-blocked row. In between the occasional customer, I wiped down every surface. It was so boring; I began to tally the number of customers who came in and what they ordered. I was going to prove to my mom how pointless it was to stay open late into the evening.

By 8:30 P.M., five customers had come in, generating a total of $19.81 in sales. With an hour and a half left to go, there was no way we were going to make enough money to make it worthwhile to keep the fluorescent lights on. Knowing my mom, though, she would still say that a sale was a sale, and it was $19.81 going into her pocket.

The parking lot was dark, with only the shop and the liquor store next door showing any signs of life. It was quiet, except for the humming from the refrigerators and the buzzing neon OPEN sign. When my phone pinged, I jumped at it. I hoped it was Alex, but it was just my mom.

**MOM:** Everything okay?

I texted her a picture of all the nobodies that sat in our shop.

**JAS:** Yes, everything is okay. Are you having fun?

Then came the onslaught of selfies my mom took with all my aunts and uncles. Pictures of the bride and groom in their traditional gold wedding attire and Western suit and white wedding dress. I thought my mom was done sending me photos when she sent a video. I pressed play and Cambodian music blared through the speakers. Cymbals kept a fast beat over the gentle dulcimers and weaving wind instruments as a singer crooned the melody. I watched my aunts laugh as they danced, curling their fingers and rotating their wrists in unison. When they realized my mom was recording them, they egged my mom and dad to join them and the video got cut off. My mom was indeed having fun, and it was the best consolation prize.

"Um, hello? Can I get some service here?"

"Oh my god!" Startled, I slipped off the stool.

The music from my mom's video was so loud, I didn't notice the customer waiting for me. The guy was leaning on the door-jamb, arms crossed, holding in his smile as he took in the shock on my face.

I didn't know what to say. I couldn't think over the loud internal screaming in my head. I mean, this was a normal response when your ex-boyfriend shows up out of nowhere. He looked just as I remembered him, except his hair was shorter, more clean-cut than I was used to. It didn't match his laid-back personality. He still looked good, though, wearing black skinny jeans with a gray T-shirt under a light, short-sleeved button-down shirt. His Vans matched the chambray stripes on his shirt.

"Michael. What are you doing here?"

His amusement dissolved at my wary tone. "I was at the stoplight when I thought I saw you. Why are you—oh!" He stood up straight at his realization. "Are your parents here?"

Just like that, it was like we were seventeen again, afraid we were going to get caught.

"No, they're not here."

I gulped as he walked in.

"So, this is the shop," he said, taking in the washed-out posters of donuts and croissants. He browsed the minimal selection of donuts behind the glass case. I couldn't blame him for his curiosity. I never let him step foot in here when we dated secretly during high school. Still, what was he doing here? We hadn't spoken in years—or rather, Michael hadn't spoken to me in years. The fact that he approached me after the way I left things between us made me question reality.

"So, what are you doing around here?" I aimed for a breezy tone. Last I heard, Michael had recently graduated with his degree in environmental science. Not that I was keeping tabs on him.

Michael stuffed his hands in his jeans pockets. "I just moved back home. I'm starting a new job in August, working for L.A.

County, measuring the air quality. Did you know that the San Gabriel Valley has terrible air quality because we're surrounded by mountains?"

"Oh." I shrugged, half interested in this new information.

"Hey. Are you still in the yearbook group chat?"

I was, but I had turned off the notifications, so I had no idea what was going on with any of those folks.

"Yeah. Why?"

"Everyone's in town. We're meeting up for brunch tomorrow. You should come."

"I'll drop by if I can," I said noncommittally. "It's kind of short notice and I have to work and you know how my parents are."

I had no intention of hanging out with high school friends. It was another opportunity to put a spotlight on how little I had accomplished compared to my peers. I had always considered myself to be smart, but when I entered high school, I quickly found out that I had been a big fish in a small middle school pond. Instead of trying to compete with the Ivy League–bound nerds, I decided to join clubs that suited my personal interests, like the poetry club and the yearbook committee, where Michael and I spent most of our time together.

Michael stood there, analyzing my face. His mouth shifted to the left into a lopsided smirk. He knew from past experience that I could get out of work for a while if I needed to. "I'm going to tell everyone I saw you. You better show up. Eleven o'clock at Max's."

"I'll see what I can do." We stared at each other for a moment. This was the part where we usually hugged goodbye, but the front counter divided us. Michael shuffled his feet before he nodded and saw himself out. I wished for a customer to come in or the phone to ring. Anything to distract me from thinking about Michael.

I can't remember the first day we met. Just that we were always friends because he was friends with everyone. He never belonged to any one clique. He floated around campus with his chill vibe. That's why being the yearbook photographer suited him. Everyone liked having him around, and it allowed him to take photos of people being themselves.

During senior year, there were six of us who led the yearbook committee. Being the staff photographer meant that Michael spent time with everyone. Since I couldn't stay after school, I was assigned to cover lunchtime pep rallies and club meetings.

At the first pep rally, Michael nudged my arm and leaned close to my ear. "Are you going to the football game later?" he yelled over the loud cheers coming from the packed gymnasium.

"I heard the football team isn't that good this year. Plus, I have to go home after school," I yelled back.

"Where's your school spirit, Jas?" Michael asked. I shrugged, not wanting to yell back and forth. "What about homecoming?"

I shrugged again. I had managed not to go to any school dances up until that point. Not because I didn't want to or nobody had asked me to be their date. I knew money was tight and

I didn't want to have to explain to my mom why I needed to buy tickets or dresses. I especially didn't want her to ask me if I was going to the dance with a boy. Michael just nodded and resumed taking pictures.

The week after, Michael showed up to the poetry club meeting to take photos. Poetry club was a new club, which is how I rationalized why there were only eight members, myself included. We were all in Ms. Jenkins's AP English class, and honestly, half of the members were just there to kiss butt. I heard Michael's camera click a few times. He didn't stay for more than five minutes. I figured it was because we were just going over the reading list for the semester. Not quite exciting stuff.

That Friday, before heading out of yearbook, I was looking over the list of local businesses that I was assigned to hit up for sponsorships when I noticed something sticking out of my binder. It was an envelope addressed to me. In it was a note paper-clipped to a black-and-white side profile photo of me at the poetry club meeting, looking thoughtfully at the reading list. I unfolded the note and found this poem:

> *Roses are red*
> *Violets are blue*
> *Jasmines are pretty*
> *Just like you*
> *(I know this poem sucks. Will you still go out with me tho?)*
> *Michael Perez*

If I wasn't so shocked, I would have laughed at the fact that he signed his full name, like there was another Michael. Besides, I'd recognize his scribbles anywhere. I scanned the classroom, but no one was around. Michael later told me that he was nervous and didn't want to hang around to get rejected in person. At least if I rejected him over text, he would have the weekend to mend his ego.

Michael was a sweet boyfriend. I experienced several firsts with him. First football game. First dance. First make out in the photo darkroom. Michael was my first everything, but I always knew we had an expiration date.

Outside of a few school functions and the occasional date, Michael and I were primarily a couple during school hours. Getting out of babysitting Patrick took (1) a lot of justification, (2) reassurance that I would be with friends that my parents had met and trusted, and (3) usually a lie. Whenever Michael and I wanted to Netflix and chill, I told my parents I had to stay after school to meet with my calculus tutor. That usually gave me an hour or two before I had to go home. "I have a group project for class" usually worked pretty well if I wanted to stay out later, but I couldn't use that every day. Keeping our relationship a secret was always a point of contention with us.

The main reason was that my parents would only approve of my dating Asian guys. It didn't matter how many of my cousins dated or married non-Asians. Their only daughter was going to eventually marry an Asian guy. I tried to explain that to Michael, but he was so sure that if my parents met him, they would love him. He clearly didn't understand that my mom, as tiny as she was, could turn a feather duster into a lethal weapon.

I made sure to cover all my tracks when it came to Michael. He was never the wallpaper on my phone. He was not allowed to step foot in the donut shop, not even with friends. I knew he wouldn't be able to act like a strictly platonic friend in front of my parents. He knew I would never tell my parents about him. He never understood why we had to keep it a secret or why I wouldn't try to get out of the house more. On prom night, we decided to break up at the end of the semester. We told ourselves that there was no point in staying together, since we were about to head off to college.

Breaking up in advance didn't prevent any heartbreak. My mom and brother came to my graduation. My dad had to keep the shop open, so my mom live-streamed graduation from her phone so that he could watch. After the ceremony was over, my friends called me over to take group photos. Michael made his way next to me as everyone's parents held up their phones to take pictures. When the group started to disperse, Michael held on to my arm so that his parents could take a picture of just the two of us. I immediately shot him a look and jerked my arm away. My mom was right there, standing only two feet away. Luckily, she was preoccupied. She couldn't figure out how to stop live-streaming the event.

I never forgot how hurt Michael looked as he threw up his arms in defeat and turned around to redirect his parents. I tried to apologize to him afterward, but he didn't return my texts or calls. We didn't really speak to each other much after that. I ran into him occasionally during college when some high school friends got together on the weekend, but he usually spent most of the time avoiding me, which I didn't understand. As far as I knew, Michael was still dating his girlfriend, Vanessa. Regardless, it still felt awkward to be around him, so I stopped showing up to their get-togethers.

I hadn't seen my high school friends for what? Three years now? I hadn't kept up with them other than the occasional social media post. It seemed like everyone was doing great. I was the only one who had regressed. Maybe I'd just stop by. I didn't have any life updates, so it should be quick.

After closing the shop, I drove home. When I turned onto my street, I passed my dad, who was driving back to the shop. They had already returned from the reception. When I unlocked the front door to the house, I found my mom sitting on the couch glued to her phone, still dressed in the gown she wore to the wedding, exchanging photos with all my aunts on WeChat.

"How was the wedding, Ma?"

"Who was that, Jas?" My mom's voice was monotone, but I knew better than to mistake it for indifference.

"Uh . . . who was who?"

"That last customer. The one who didn't buy anything. I saw on the camera, you talked to him a long time."

Oh, shit. I forgot about the security cameras that pointed toward the front of the shop. My parents never had to check the app before because they were always there. They must have saved the password because they set those cameras up a long time ago. Thank god they don't record audio.

"Just a friend from high school," I said, casually to cover my nerves.

"I don't remember him. Who is he?" My mom continued to tap on her phone. The constant dinging sounds meant that she was playing her slot machine game. My mom would see through any cagey responses, so I decided that the best defense was a good offense.

"His name is Michael. We had a few classes together."

"Which classes?"

"AP Bio and yearbook."

"Where did he go to college?"

"San Diego State." I anticipated her next question, so I added, "For environmental science. He was just telling me that all my friends are going to brunch tomorrow. You remember Rae, right? And Kayley and Billy?" Yes, remind her of friends she liked. "I haven't seen them in a long time. I'll just go say hi really quick. You wanted me to go out more, right?"

My mom responded with a terse but emphatic *hmm*. She continued to play a couple of rounds of slots before she looked up at me. "Yeah, okay. Brunch tomorrow. Tell your friends I say hi."

*Whew.* I couldn't believe I got out of that. Since she was in a somewhat agreeable mood, I decided to shoot my shot.

"How was the wedding?" I asked again. "Looked like everyone was there."

"Yeah, everyone was there," she said, distracted.

"Did they all close their shops or something?"

My mom looked up from her phone. She knew where this was going. "Your cousin Brian close Uncle Tommy's shop. Brian just like you—still no job."

I ignored the dig. "But what about everyone else? Auntie Shelly? Uncle Tin?"

"They close their shop," she admitted. "But they're getting old and their kids are married now with jobs. You know your cousin Christina is pregnant?" She directed her attention back to her slots game.

"So what?" What did that have to do with anything?

"What you mean, so what? Your auntie Shelly and uncle Tin don't have kids to support anymore. We still have to take care of you and Pat. When you and Pat have jobs, then Baba and I close early, maybe hire someone to help."

"Why wait for that? Don't you want to go to more family parties or weddings or . . . or . . ." My mom was so drawn into her game that she wasn't listening to me anymore. That's when inspiration struck. "Or . . . those Vegas trips with Auntie Kim? Doesn't she go every weekend on those tour buses?"

My mom didn't look up, but her lip curled with consideration. "Not every weekend."

"Come on, Ma. You and Ba have to start thinking now about how to run the shop without me. Wasn't it hard today with the wedding? What if I get a job soon?"

"Ha! You haven't looked for one yet."

"I'll start looking for one!"

Judging by my mom's eyebrow raise, she didn't have faith in that promise. I had to go for the things she cared about. "But what about dates, Ma? Dates happen at nighttime. Can we at least close early?" I rifled through my purse and brought out my tally sheet. "I counted. We had six customers after you left, and we barely made twenty dollars. You can check the camera if you don't believe me."

My mom's eyebrows furrowed as she looked up at me briefly. What was this face? Was I actually winning this argument? Facts for the win! She couldn't argue with data.

She let out a low grumble. "Maybe after Fourth of July," she said, then quickly added, "Only for summer!"

I held in my excitement and commanded my feet not to do a happy dance. I was afraid if I looked too happy about it, my mom would take it away. "Thanks, Ma!"

I left my mom to her game and ran upstairs to my room. I tossed my purse on my desk and pulled off my hair tie. As my ponytail came loose, I could smell the bulgogi from lunch in my hair. *Alex.* I was so distracted by Michael and my mom that I forgot about him. I checked my phone and my heart sank.

I missed his call. Looking at the time stamp, it was around the time I was doing a final run-through of the shop before shutting off all the front lights.

**ALEX:** Sorry. Lost track of time
**ALEX:** Hope we can talk soon. Gnite

I wanted to reply, but it didn't seem like I had much room to work with. What was I going to say? "Good night but hello?" *Good flirting there, Jas!*

My brain was exhausted. What was it about running into an ex that made you feel all jumbled inside? Maybe it was for the best that Alex and I didn't talk tonight. Alex would have asked something as normal as "How was work?" and I would have said something stupid like "Ya know. Funny thing. My ex-boyfriend stopped by and I'm seeing him tomorrow. Don't worry, it's just brunch, the best meal in the universe!"

Ugh. Linh was right. I was bad at this.

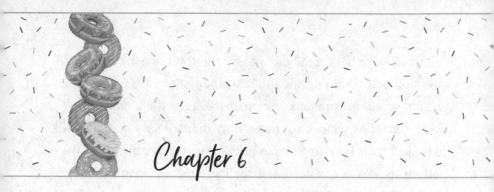

## Chapter 6

*W*hen I arrived at Max's, there were groups of people waiting outside. Max's was more Mexican American than Mexican Mexican food. It was known for its hard-shell tacos with a handful of shredded bright orange American cheese shoved on top. What it lacked in authenticity, it made up for in cheap food and drinks, ensuring its popularity among the high school and college crowd.

I purposefully came late, hoping to catch everyone at the end of their meal. The plan was to blame my tardiness on my parents and leave after fifteen minutes of small talk. I committed to this plan, leaving a smear of pink icing on my T-shirt for added effect. However, when I walked inside the restaurant, I found all my old friends sitting in a booth, still waiting for their first round of bottomless mimosas. They hadn't seen me yet and I contemplated turning around and forgetting this whole thing. There was no point in sitting through a whole meal when I could text them my non-updates.

I took a step back, ready to make a run for it, when the maria-chi band behind me decided to start their show. I yelped at the sudden sound of trumpets, which encouraged the amused sing-ers to start their chorus of gritos. They didn't need microphones to project their booming voices across the room, causing all the patrons to look in my general direction—including my friends.

"Jas! Over here!" Rae waved her arms over her head to get my attention. Only her high-pitched voice could cut through the lively music. I swallowed my dread and weaved through the tables and servers to reach them. I spotted the empty space they left for me next to Michael out of habit. Damn it. I didn't think about this.

"Hey, guys," I said, standing at the edge of the semi-circle table. I was greeted with welcome cheer from everyone—Rae Hwang, Billy Flores, Kayley Dizon, Josh Cooper, and Michael.

Rae stood up to give me a hug. "I haven't seen you in so long!" she said as she squeezed her arms around me. "You need to sit with me. I need to know everything that's been going on with you." She made everyone scooch over before she slid back into the booth and directed me to sit next to her. Well, that solved the problem of having to sit next to Michael. Except now I was sitting directly across from him. This was way worse. Michael knew it too because he averted his eyes as he took a sip of water.

"So, Jas. What's new with you? Michael said he saw you at your parents' shop yesterday," Rae said before digging into the free chips and salsa. "Do you want to order a drink?"

"No, no thanks," I replied. "I actually have to go back there soon to help out my parents. I've been working there since I graduated. It's just temporary until I find a real job." I tried to re-direct the conversation. "What about you guys? Billy, how's . . . grad school?" I knew he was in a PhD program for something science-y, but I was coming up short. I should have gone through the group chat before showing up.

Billy rolled up the sleeves of his Stanford hoodie. "It's all right. My faculty advisor is okay. I finished my first rotation of labs. I have a few ideas about my dissertation topic, but I have to get through my qualifying exam first."

"Cool." I had no idea what all of that meant. Everyone around the table gave me a brief rundown of their lives. Kayley just came home after a year of teaching English in Japan and planned on going back. I asked if she was in Tokyo, but it turned out she was in the Hacienda Heights of Japan. Josh was working toward his CPA. He was in the middle of explaining all the parts of the exam he needed to pass when their food arrived. Rae took the opportunity to interrupt Josh.

"Josh, I love you, but nobody wants to hear all that. I actually have some news," she teased. "As you may or may not know, I was handling all the social media for *Angel City Magazine,* but someone from *LA Weekly* reached out to me. They're looking for someone to improve their digital presence and they liked what I was doing for *ACM,* since *ACM* is completely digital." Rae continued to rattle off all the things she did for *ACM,* stuff about community engagement and analytics. It was no wonder why she·went into communications. She was the talker of our group.

When I turned back toward the table, I found a plate of food waiting for me. It was a charity plate, made up of random scoops of food from everyone else's plates—a single tortilla, hash browns, huevos rancheros, and machaca.

"We didn't know if you were coming, so we didn't order anything for you. But there's plenty of food. It would be a waste to order another plate," Michael explained. "It's faster, since you have to leave."

"Oh, thanks." I didn't know how else to respond. Everyone was looking at me with eyes encouraging me to stay and eat. So much for leaving early. I thought about scarfing the food down, but that would be too obvious. I ate silently and nodded attentively as the conversation topics moved to gossip about our old high school acquaintances.

This was the problem of meeting up with old friends after a long absence. Since they wanted to include me, they talked about old memories we shared or people we used to know. When there was nothing left to reminisce about, they caught each other up on things I knew nothing about because I was out of the loop.

I reached for my glass of water and took a sip. When I put the glass down, I realized that I didn't order my own drink. Everyone was still chatting. Nobody noticed, right? I pretended like nothing happened, but across the table, Michael stared at me. His eyes darted between me and the glass of water. My face flushed with embarrassment at the thought of drinking out of Michael's glass. We had done it many times when we dated, but we weren't dating now and dredging up nostalgic feelings was asking for trouble.

Michael shrugged and took his glass back. He didn't dwell on it as much as I did, but it was too much for me.

I pulled some cash out of my wallet and placed it next to my plate. This was met with objections. "Thanks for brunch, guys. I'm sorry. I have to get back to work. Good luck with school and exams and job interviews. You guys are killin' it. So happy for you guys."

I tried to make a quick exit, but Rae pulled me back for a big hug. "It was good seeing you. I missed you! Hey! If I get this new job, let's all get together again. Whoever's still around, at least. Yeah?"

"Sure," I lied. "Just let me know."

"Check your texts and you'll know!" Rae said before she let me go. That was a burn, but I deserved that.

Just as I stepped out of the booth, Michael stood up too. "I have to go to the restroom," he said. "I'll walk you out."

I didn't need to turn around to know that everyone at the table was staring at us. I didn't think anyone could ruin brunch for me, but these fools kept making it painful.

"Okay," I gritted behind my weak smile. It wasn't until we made it past the mariachi band that Michael spoke again.

"Hey. Is everything okay?"

"It's fine. I just need to go back to—"

"You have never once wanted to go back to the shop."

"Things changed. And like I said, it's just temporary. I've been looking for a job." Well, that was a stretch. I had decided only yesterday to put any effort into that, if searching for jobs on the internet and wailing over how they required a master's degree for minimum wage counted as effort.

Michael paused, deciding whether he believed me or not. "Well . . . I'll let you know if I hear of job openings. If there's anything I can do to help, just ask. I'll be around until my job starts."

"You don't have to—"

"I know, but that's what friends do. We're still friends, right?"

That was a loaded question. Were we still friends? Did we have to be friends?

Out of the corner of my eye, I caught Rae popping her head out to see if Michael and I were still talking. Right. If I wanted to still hang out with this group, Michael and I had to be friends.

"Uh, yeah. Friends."

Michael stood there, searching my face for who knows what. "Cool."

Before I could stop it, he went in for a hug. My body stiffened at first contact and I couldn't relax into it. I reached around and briskly patted his back so that he'd let me go. When I took a step back, he smiled before heading back to the table.

For all intents and purposes, it wasn't a terrible thing to be friends again with Michael. But if it was the right thing to do, was it supposed to feel unsettling?

WHEN I RETURNED to the shop, my mom was busy recapping the wedding with Auntie Helen on the phone, even though Auntie Helen had attended too. It was like they had nothing better to do during these slow days but to rehash their evening together.

I was about to walk past her when she grabbed my elbow. She continued talking to my aunt but held out an envelope that had already been cut open. She motioned for me to take it and presumably translate it for her.

I unfolded the letter, which came from the strip mall's property manager. The letter contained three concise paragraphs, which I considered to be long for something that could be summed up in one sentence.

I made a long face. My mom was not going to take this well.

Anticipating bad news, she cut her phone call short. "Why you just stand there? What it say?" she commanded. From her frustrated tone, she already knew the answer. She was hoping she'd misinterpreted it.

"Rent is going up, starting next month," I finally said.

My mom called Auntie Helen back and went on a tirade. She attacked this development from all angles.

*Who did they think they are?*

*We're the only two tenants here!*

*They better use the extra money to fix the concrete!*

When she ran out of new things to be mad at, she circled back to all the things she had already said in a long run-on sentence. She punctuated this second retelling with a few *oh my god*s and what had to be Khmer curse words.

I went to the back of the shop to let my mom cool off. I texted Linh to fill her in on the last twenty-four hours.

**LINH**: damn girl. When did your life become a soap opera?
**LINH**: so that's why you and Alex didn't talk last night. I
was waiting up for it.

I forgot that Linh went to Owen's on the weekends. I love Linh, but she was nosy as hell.

**JAS**: pls don't. you know I will tell you everything anyway
**LINH**: don't keep him waiting. Call him tonight!
**JAS**: I'll have to see how this whole rent thing pans out.
My mom is pissed.
**JAS**: Hope she won't back out of closing early.
**LINH**: you better find a job then or figure out how to make
up the difference.

Hmm. That wasn't a bad idea. I poked my head out to find my mom pacing up and down behind the front counter, likely on her fourth go-around about this. I wondered how Auntie Helen was holding up, listening to my mom repeat herself. My mom was speaking more calmly now, but it would be best to wait until she was in the right headspace to discuss ways to build the business. If I wanted things to go in my favor, though, I'd better come up with some ideas of my own.

LATER THAT NIGHT, I settled into my room after closing the shop. I wasn't sure if it was too late to call Alex. I knew that Owen had to wake up early for work and I assumed it was the same for Alex. Fuck it. I sent a quick text.

> **JAS:** hey

I stared at my phone, hoping that he'd reply right away. When I didn't see so much as a *read* update after a minute, I tossed my phone on my bed. I didn't want to sit around and wait for him to call, so I jumped in the shower. After changing into my pajamas, I checked my phone again. I had one missed call and two unread text messages from Alex.

> **ALEX:** Why you donut pick up my call?
> **ALEX:** You donut want to talk?

I smiled at the unexpected response. I wouldn't have taken him for someone who liked puns. I situated myself on my bed, leaning back against the headboard, and called him back. On the second ring, he picked up.

"So, you *do* want to talk," Alex said.

My ears perked up. I wasn't prepared to hear Alex's voice again. Two days ago, I was sitting in the exact spot, moping around, and now Window Guy was talking to me on the phone.

"Ha-ha. I shouldn't have started the donut puns," I said, lamely.

"Why not? I think it's fun. How was your weekend?"

"Um . . . good." I didn't want to talk about anything that happened since I saw him. I wanted to keep him in a separate dimension, uncomplicated by all the shit I'd been dealing with. "What did you guys do after I was dropped off?"

"Nothing really. Owen didn't get over his hangover until this morning. He finally felt up for going out. He took Linh out for dinner and he went to drop her off at home." The thought of Alex alone in his apartment distracted me for a moment.

"I can't believe you guys drove all the way here from Vegas to eat lunch with me."

"Well, I like to meet all my new followers," he teased.

"So, what's your verdict, now that you've met me?" I asked, genuinely curious.

"At first I didn't know what to think. Linh showed me your picture and then I saw you in person . . ."

I groaned, dragging my hand down my face. "Linh was afraid you'd call her out on false advertising."

"No, it's not that," he chuckled. "I mean, you looked like a party girl in that picture and when I met you at the donut shop, you were . . . how should I say this?"

"You can say it. I was a dork. I can't believe I tried to shake your hand with my tongs." I pulled my comforter up to my face, wanting to hide from my own embarrassment.

Alex laughed. "That was pretty funny. You almost got my hand."

"To be fair, I was not expecting any of you to show up."

"Yeah, I sensed that. So, I have to ask," Alex said, like he was finally getting down to business. "How do you even remember me?"

"No, no. I should ask you the same thing."

"I asked first."

I didn't respond. I wasn't going to admit to Alex that my stalking ways started three years ago.

"Well?" Alex asked, breaking the awkward silence.

"Fine. It's because you're hot," I declared quickly, like ripping off a Band-Aid. It was the first thing that came to mind and it was true. "There. That was easy. So, now you tell me how you remember me."

Alex barked out a laugh at my brazen response. "Fine. If that's how you want to play it," he said, trying to match my tone. "I remembered buying tickets from you because . . ." He paused, unsure how to proceed. Then, in a warmer, almost shy tone, he said, "I thought you were pretty."

I wanted to squeal into my pillow.

"And I couldn't believe that you worked at Pauley and you'd never been to a game!" he quickly added, inserting levity back into our conversation.

"Oh, please! I didn't have time to go to any games." Not that I would have gone if I did have time.

"By the way, when did you stop working there? I don't know if I should tell you this, but uh . . . I kind of looked for you whenever I passed the box office."

"I didn't know I had a stalker," I joked while I died internally upon hearing Alex's admission. "I only worked there for a quarter. I got slammed with classes and coming home on the weekends."

"Ah. Well, at least the mysterious disappearance of Ticket Girl has been solved."

Shocked, I paused for a second. "Wait. Did you just call me Ticket Girl?"

"*I* did not call you that," he clarified. "My friend made fun of me whenever I wanted to walk by the box office, looking for Ticket Girl. I'm sure he thought I made you up because you were never there."

"Oh my god." My face hurt from smiling so much. "I can't believe this."

"What?" he chuckled nervously.

"If I'm Ticket Girl, then I guess you should know that you're Window Guy," I confessed.

"Window Guy?" Alex laughed. "Didn't you already know my name? Why would you call me Window Guy?"

"I don't know. That's just how I referred to you whenever I thought about you."

"Are you saying you thought about me a lot?" Alex said extra flirty for added dramatic effect.

"No!" I laughed.

"Well, maybe we should do something about that," Alex said. "Hold on."

I heard Alex fumbling with his phone before it went silent. I pulled my phone away from my ear and checked to see if he was still on the line. I brought the phone back up to my ear when I heard a notification from my phone. Alex sent me a text. I sat up straight and hesitantly brought my phone in front of my face, unsure about the direction our conversation was heading. I hesitantly swiped my thumb across the screen.

When I opened the text, my jaw dropped. I pushed my glasses up the bridge of my nose. On my screen was a picture of a shirtless Alex sitting on the couch, his left hand shaped like an O surrounding his left eye. He had copied my selfie from earlier sans donut. He had such an adorable smirk on his face, but the picture itself was a thirst trap. My thumb and index finger went their separate ways across the screen, zooming in, secretly wishing that they were touching his chest in real life. God, did he have abs? Real people didn't have abs, at least not anyone I had ever met. Now I knew why Alex was so confident. He had every right to be.

"Helloooo? You still there?" Alex spoke up from the phone, interrupting my drooling. I put the phone on speaker so that I could still look at the picture while we talked.

"Hi," I breathed. I cleared my throat, trying to compose myself. "Um . . . thank you?"

Alex laughed. "For what?" He was fishing for a compliment,

as if he needed any. He knew what he had going on. I didn't want to give him the satisfaction.

"For not sending a dick pic?" I chuckled.

"You're welcome?" Alex laughed at my flippant remark. "Well, I just wanted to give you something to think about. I'm actually about to work with a new client this week and I'll be pretty busy."

"Oh." I felt a pang of disappointment.

"But I do want to see you again," Alex rushed out. "Without Linh and Owen this time. I'm pretty swamped this week and I'll be heading out of town for the Fourth of July. Do you want to try to meet up the week after? Is that okay?" I knew from my conversations with Linh that Owen and Alex worked late during the week. Linh managed to put up with it since she was busy with her job and studying for the LSATs.

"Yeah, that's fine." Then I meant to say, "I shouldn't have anything else going on." Instead, what ended up coming out of my mouth was "It's not like I have anything better to do." What was wrong with me? I winced at my poor choice of words.

"Wow." Alex feigned offense, but I could tell he was smiling. "Don't be too excited now."

"Sorry. That came out wrong," I said contritely. "Let me start over. Yes, I'd love to. Let me know when you're free."

Alex chuckled. "Sounds good. I have to get going. I have to wrap up some things for work tomorrow."

"Without your shirt on?" I unintentionally mused out loud.

Alex laughed at my unexpected response. "However you want to imagine me doing work. Shirt optional. Catch you later."

I watched as the call ended on my phone. I held my phone close to my chest and sunk into my bed. This was the best possible ending to this roller-coaster weekend. I couldn't stop replaying my conversation with Alex in my head. How was I supposed to fall asleep now with my body buzzing with thoughts of freckles, charming smiles, and abs? Couldn't forget the abs.

## Chapter 7

*B*leary-eyed, my mom went through the motions during morning rush the next day. Her mind had been running the numbers in every direction since I confirmed the rent hike. Her trademark chipper customer service persona was mostly intact, except for the moments when her face was turned from the customers' view.

When the last customer cleared out of our eat-in area, I bussed the tables, using hot towels to wipe crumbs and hardened icing off the surfaces. I collected the red plastic hot dog baskets we used to plate the donuts and took them to the back to wash. There I found my mom perched on a stool over the glazing station, hunched over a notebook. Dumping the baskets into the sink, I peeked over her shoulder to see what she was scribbling.

"What is all of this?" I asked, scanning her analog spreadsheet with numbers in neat rows and columns within their invisible borders. "Is this how you do the bookkeeping?" She didn't answer my question. "Can't we just raise the prices?"

It seemed like the most obvious answer. It had been years since my parents last raised prices.

My mom clicked her pen in quick succession. "Not so easy."

She explained that our prices were comparable to other mom-and-pop shops in the area. She was afraid it would drive away our regular customer base that they spent years cultivating. If she priced them any higher, customers might as well go to the chain donut shops that had the luxury of being situated near the main shopping areas in the city. She'd long felt that was the reason why our business had been steadily declining.

"I don't know about that, Ma," I said. Our customer base mainly consisted of early bird senior citizens who lived within walking distance of our shop. They weren't the type to go out of their way for a donut. "Don't you think it's because . . . you know . . . *they're dying*?" I whispered.

"Jas!" she scolded. Her face wrinkled at the thought, but it wasn't a false statement. A few of our customers had passed away within the last year.

"Ma, I think it's time we try something new." I took out my phone and opened up Instagram. "If you don't want to scare away our old customers, we need to find new customers."

My mom scrolled through photos of colorful, outrageously decorated donuts. "Aiyah." She huffed in exasperation. "Tài máfanle. This is too much work for Baba."

"We don't have to do anything this complicated. Like, can't we at least do Fourth of July sprinkles or something?"

She flipped open our supplier's catalog and pointed at the box of red, white, and blue flag-shaped sprinkles. It was perfect.

"Yeah, let's get this."

She shook her head. "Look at the minimum order. We can't order that much and get it delivered by Saturday."

I was getting frustrated. If my parents didn't want to raise prices on our current products, then it made sense to create something new at a higher price point. Changing sprinkles for a day was the easiest thing they could do. If they were going to be resistant to this minor change, they might not like any of my other suggestions. I had to be smart about this. If I wanted to sway my mom, I had to appeal to her frugal sensibilities.

"Does Uncle Tin or Auntie Shelly have an extra box of sprinkles you can buy off them? So, we can try them out?"

"Maybe." She glanced back at the catalog. "I can call them." She looked back at the over-the-top donuts plastered on my phone's screen. "I don't know if sprinkles will be enough."

I replaced my phone with hers. "Just call them. We can start on this first."

She called around, starting with the relatives and friends whose shops were closest to ours. Out of everyone she called, the only person who had a spare box was her own BFF, Auntie Helen, who operated the Donut Shoppe. It had a charming retro feel that Auntie Helen was able to retain when she left the original black-and-white subway tiles untouched during her recent renovation. I meant to make quick work out of this visit. However, when I entered the Donut Shoppe, I found a lanky dude hunched over his iPad at the front counter.

It was a trap.

Auntie Helen scurried out from the back of her shop. "Ah! Jasmine. How are you? Have you eaten yet?" She gestured to the display case. "Do you want something to eat?"

I swallowed a cheeky response to the offer of the same exact donuts we made at our own shop. I smiled politely and shook my head. "I've eaten. Thank you. I came to get—"

"Jasmine. This is Hansen, my sister-in-law's son." She tilted her head toward him. "Hansen, this is—" When he didn't bother to look up, Auntie Helen slapped his arm. "Hansen!" she scolded. "This is Jasmine."

He lifted up his head and gave an indifferent "Hi."

When our eyes met, there was a mutual "Can you believe our elders? There's no way this is ever, ever going to happen" feeling. Seriously, even if it were just on paper, nobody would ever believe the two of us were a couple. With his permed hair and streetwear, Hansen looked like he belonged in the cool group of his high school. I looked like I belonged in marching band.

"What are you watching?" I asked, humoring Auntie Helen with some small talk.

"I'm actually drawing." He flipped over his iPad so I could see the anime character he was working on.

"That's cool."

"Yes, yes, very nice," Auntie Helen interjected. "Fun hobby, but Hansen's here for a few months. He might apply to school or maybe work for a little bit."

Great. He was younger than me too. I was learning so much about my fake future fiancé.

"Good luck with that," I offered. Auntie Helen was hoping I'd say more, but there wasn't more I could do. I had trouble figuring out my own life, much less being able to help this random guy. "Well, I have to get back. Can I get the sprinkles?"

Auntie Helen produced a heavy box of patriotic sprinkles from under the counter. I slid the envelope of cash to cover the price of the box, including sales tax. Auntie Helen didn't bother arguing about the extra cash, knowing my mother—like a Lannister—always paid off her debts. Not a penny less.

BACK AT THE shop, I found my mother pacing back and forth behind the front counter. She clicked on her pen like she knew the answer on *Jeopardy!*

I lifted the box and placed it on the front counter. "I got the sprinkles."

She shook her head as she paced away from me. "Sprinkles might not be enough."

I tilted the box back to read the label. "It's a ten-pound box, Ma. I think it's enou—"

"No. This is for one day. We need something else, something your baba can make every day."

I wasn't expecting that, but this was good. This idea opened my mom up to other suggestions. I reached for my phone to gather some inspiration, but my mom shot that down right away.

"No. Those donuts too crazy."

"But what are we supposed to do, then?"

"I have an idea," she said. She stood in front of me, the box of sprinkles between us. Her fingers drummed the top of the box. I watched her as she devised a plan with an intensity behind her eyes. It dawned on me how risk-averse she was. As tiring and monotonous as it was, she liked the routine the shop provided her. This change gave her no choice but to adapt, but she needed to be sure.

She knelt down behind the counter and shuffled things around. When she came up, she handed me a sheet of paper and a permanent marker. "Here."

"What's this for?"

"Make a sign. We close early for the summer. Six o'clock."

I was too happy and stunned to move. I had no idea where she was going with this, but I didn't care. The idea of going home and eating dinner at a normal time sounded heavenly.

My mom pointed at the paper. "Hurry. Write it down. Then we clean up the shop so we can leave on time."

"Leave on time for what?" I picked up the marker, writing the sign as neatly as I could.

"You'll see," she said, rushing to the back to tackle the chores. She didn't let me in on her plans, muttering to herself as she kept herself busy. It was worrisome, but the thought of closing while there was still daylight out kept me on cloud nine. I finished the sign and taped it to our door: NEW SUMMER HOURS: 4:00 A.M. TO 6:00 P.M.

OF ALL THE things I imagined myself doing on my first free evening in a year, staking out a competitor's parking lot was not one of them. "What are we doing here?" I whispered, hiding behind the steering wheel.

With her notebook on her lap, she ignored me, talking to herself under her breath. She made shorthand notes on a fresh sheet of paper in the back, far away from her sales log. When a customer went inside, she sat up in her seat.

"Pay attention, Jas." She squinted as the customer browsed and ordered, muttering under her breath. "Small coffee and . . . what is that pink donut?" She scribbled it down and noted the time. "Jas, I can't see. Can you find the menu on your phone?"

"Are you serious right now? This is what we closed early for?"

"Kuài diǎn! Before another customer comes in."

I opened Yelp and browsed through the photos. "Did it have chocolate stripes on top?"

"Yeah yeah yeah. What was that?"

"Um . . . a cherry cordial donut." Seeing my mom's confusion, I explained further. "You know, those chocolates with the cherry inside? One of our customers gave you a box last Christmas, remember? They made a donut like that."

My mom grimaced. She thought they were too sweet. "How much they sell it for?"

"It is . . ." I browsed through the photos for the menu. "Three dollars and fifty cents."

"Three dollars and fifty cents?! It looks like the one we sell for ninety cents. Who spends three fifty on a donut?!"

"Um . . . that guy, Ma." I skimmed the menu. "They sell other donuts for three fifty—blueberry lemon, apple pie, bananas foster, s'mores—"

"No, don't tell me more. That's enough." She closed her eyes and rubbed her temples. She began to take longer breaths. This was more than she'd bargained for. When she found a sense of calm, she sat back up, looking around to check for prospective customers.

"What do you want to do?"

She pointed her pen at the shop. "We wait, maybe for one more hour."

*One more hour!? We're going to do this for another hour?*

"Okay . . . and then what?"

Her knees started to bounce. "Then we do every night. We check other shops, see what they sell. Then we talk to Baba."

Inherently, doing some market research was not a bad idea, but this was a little overboard. I wanted to tell her that her plan was nutty, but this was her process. She found comfort in the numbers, and I only hoped that it showed her what she was looking for before I had to spend the rest of my evenings parked in the car with my mom.

My mom continued taking notes. She wrote down everything— how old she thought the customers were, what they ordered, what time they arrived. In between customers, she had me identify items on their menu that were unique to their shop. She made me read their Yelp reviews. Hearing positive reviews of our competition didn't allay her concerns.

"What do people say about us?" my mom asked regarding our Yelp reviews.

I hesitated, knowing that we didn't have many reviews in the first place. Sunshine Donuts didn't attract the Yelp elite. I skipped the ones that Pat and I wrote and read the remaining three positive reviews. The other reviews were brief, highlighting that the shop was clean, the donuts were fresh and cheap, and my parents were friendly. I also skipped the only one-star review that complained about my parents speaking Vietnamese in front of customers like nail salon ladies. Joke's on you, dude. Khmer was their language of choice with each other, and normally they were saying mundane things like "Can you get that for me?" While the reviews were positive overall, they didn't fill my mom with warm fuzzies. She told me we were done for the day and had me drive home.

WALKING INTO THE house, I heard a notification on my phone. Alex sent me a video on Snapchat of him scrolling quickly through lines and lines of data on Excel. I tapped on my phone to see the next snap. He sent me a selfie, unfortunately with his shirt on this time. He was leaning on his left hand with an exaggerated bored expression on his face. The picture disappeared shortly after, leaving me standing in the middle of the entryway, smiling and looking at nothing in particular.

"Why you look like that?" my mom asked.

"Like what?"

"Like a crazy person . . . like a shǎ nǚ."

Dismissing her comment, I told her that Alex texted me. I wasn't about to explain the concept of sending disappearing pictures and videos.

"*Mmm*. You like this boyfriend."

"He's not my boyfriend." Not yet. Hopefully. Someday. Maybe. "He's just a friend."

She walked past me and hung her purse on the back of one of the dining table chairs and walked into the kitchen. "Come help me with dinner, Jas." She beckoned me with her metal stir-fry spatula. "If you're going to have a boyfriend, you need to learn how to cook."

"Oh my god, Ma. If I'm going to learn how to cook, it's not going to be for a boyfriend." I could use some cooking lessons for myself. I struggled to make semi-homemade meals that came out of a box. When I told my mom that people could have prepackaged ingredients shipped to them so that they could cook dinner at home, she balked at the idea, calling it wasteful and lazy. When I got to the kitchen, my mom immediately put me to work.

"Jas. Come over here and chop this." My mom pointed at the cutting board with garlic, shallots, and lemongrass placed on top. I picked up the cleaver and started chopping. I watched my mom eyeball-measure fish sauce and sugar into a mixing bowl that contained chicken thighs.

"How do you know how much to put?" I asked as my mom massaged the chicken with her bare hands.

"I just know. When you cook a lot, you know from experience." She dabbed her index finger on her tongue and smacked her lips to taste her work. "See? Just right."

"Ew! That's not safe, Ma." I made a mental note to learn how to say *salmonella* in Mandarin.

"Aiyah. You worry too much."

"Can't you write down a recipe for me? I can follow a recipe."

My mom gave me the same look as when she caught me taking selfies. "What recipe? Just watch me make it and try it next time. The more you cook, the better you'll get. I was younger than you when I cooked for my whole family. You know, back in Cambodia, you would have been married already and had kids."

I rolled my eyes. "Well, we're not in Cambodia, Ma. I don't want to get married yet. I don't even have a boyfriend yet."

My mom let out an exaggerated sigh. "You guys make it so hard. You should have let me introduce you to my friends' sons. I could have matched you with someone by now."

"Is that how you and Baba met? Grandma and Grandpa matched you guys?"

"Yeah," my mom said, like it was no big deal.

"What if you didn't like Baba?"

My dad's ears must have been burning because he walked

into the kitchen right at that moment and leaned over the stove to see what my mom was cooking. "How could she not like me?" he said. "Your ma liked me right away."

"Don't believe Baba! Your grandma thought he came from a good family and he went to school, but she did not know that he skipped school almost every day." My mom looked directly at my dad.

"Hey, I left school early to come see you," my dad clarified before turning to me. "Your ma was always at home, taking care of the house. Your grandma and grandpa were out working, so I just come for a short visit. Sometimes I brought her dessert. Sometimes I brought a flower," my dad said, trying to persuade me that he was a master in the art of wooing.

"What did I tell you? I was supposed to marry you because you gave me *one* flower?" My mom was never one to be easily impressed. It wasn't so much that she liked extravagant things. It was more important to her to see that the maximum effort was made to impress her.

"Don't listen to her, Jas. She liked it!" my dad whispered.

"Ma, why did you marry him, then? Do you even like him?" I laughed.

My mom glanced sideways at my dad and turned attention back to the stove. "Only sometimes," she joked.

In a rare move, my dad hugged my mom's shoulder and leaned in to kiss her cheek. My mom swatted him away, not comfortable with this public display of affection. I couldn't re- member the last time I saw my parents kiss. The search engine in my brain was timing out: *404 page not found.* Even though watching my parents kiss would always feel a little nauseating, I had to admit it was kind of sweet. For them to be married as long as they had been, to have come to a new country and work every day together—it would be easy to say their partnership was bonded through necessity. My parents never tolerated romantic notions like "love conquers all." But seeing them like each other and laugh together after all they'd been through, I found it hard not to acknowledge their love, even when it showed itself only in small, tender moments.

## Chapter 8

The following week, Alex and I exchanged a few texts during his lunch hour and when he was done with work, which was usually around eleven P.M. With each text, Alex revealed something funny or adorable and I couldn't get enough.

On Tuesday, he texted me a picture of his lunch—a tray of tater tots smothered with nacho cheese under a pile of pulled pork.

**Jas:** Mmm nacho cheese

**Jas:** My guilty pleasure

**Alex:** that can't be your guilty pleasure

**Jas:** why not?

**Alex:** your guilty pleasure has to be something embarrassing.

**Jas:** Oh yeah? So what's yours?

Alex typed and deleted his response for a good minute, building the anticipation of the big reveal.

**ALEX:** Don't laugh

**JAS:** I promise. Cross my heart.

**ALEX:** I sometimes like listening to Taylor Swift

**JAS:** Awwwww does that make you a Swiftie?

**JAS:** were you the cheer captain or the one on the bleachers?

**ALEX:** ...

**ALEX:** this conversation never happened

*Wednesday*

**JAS:** How did you get that scar on your arm?

**ALEX:** you really zoomed in on my picture

**ALEX:** tripped at Yosemite

**ALEX:** thought I saw a snake

**JAS:** what was it?

**ALEX:** a frog sitting on top of some rope someone left behind

My only gripe about our text exchanges was that they were so few and far between. It was difficult to keep up the momentum. The quick banter was fun, but it was hard to really get to know him over text. On most occasions, we didn't catch each other at the same time. Sometimes I fell asleep before he texted at night. I was starting to wonder if this was a preview of the type of relationship we would have. Me, waiting for our availability to finally eclipse just to exchange a few messages in passing. Worse, the initial buzz of our reunion was starting to wane. I just hoped it wasn't sliding me back into the friend zone.

THE FOURTH OF July came and went. We still opened the shop that day, hoping to catch some business from the customers that flocked to the liquor store for ice. I was anxious to see how our patriotic donuts would sell. It was a barometer for our customer base, and if they did well, maybe it would be enough to sway my dad, who didn't see the fuss over novelty sprinkles.

Much to my relief, the red, white, and blue sprinkles did their job. The donuts sold out quickly, but my parents didn't price them higher than their other donuts because it was just swapping sprinkles. My dad was unimpressed, and that sent my mom back to the drawing board, spending her evenings spying on other shops. She had me create a map of all the shops within a five-mile radius. I may have "forgotten" to include the shop that was open twenty-four hours. Two A.M. reconnaissance missions were not going to happen. Not if I could help it.

I WAS SITTING in traffic on the 105 West. I thought about the ways I planned to kill Pat for flying into LAX on a Wednesday afternoon during rush hour. I scanned the presets on my dad's fifteen-year-old Honda Accord. There was nothing good on the radio. I switched to the CD player to see what my dad had been listening to. I should have guessed that he was listening to Karen Mok. He always commented how piàoliang she was in front of my mom, just to get a rise out of her. "She's not that beautiful," my mom would say. I switched it back to radio mode.

When I reached the turnaround for arriving flights, I honked at Pat, who was busy looking down at his phone. My "little" brother was taller than me by three inches. Pat would say four inches, but the measuring tape doesn't lie. My mom was going to give him crap because he didn't shave his poor excuse of a mustache. She was going to hate his "lazy clothes," which was what she called his T-shirt and jogger outfits. I popped the trunk so he could stow away his suitcase and computer bag. Pat sat in the passenger seat and didn't bother to look up from his phone.

"Uh, hi, Pat," I said, trying to get his attention.

Still glued to his phone, he replied, "Hi, jie."

I secretly loved that Pat still called me jie—shorthand for older sister in Mandarin. Though my parents had long resigned themselves to speaking English to Pat and me, they insisted that we still used honorifics. As the youngest, Pat was simply Pat.

"How was your flight?" I drove away from the curb and headed back toward the freeway.

"Fine," Pat said, uninterested in small talk.

I sighed. I drove in silence before I asked, "How's your internship?"

"Fine."

"Can you put down your phone? I'm trying to talk to you," I said, frustrated. This was so typical of Pat. If there was a Likert scale for Pat's feelings, it would start at "Slightly Dissatisfied" and end at "Fuck This Shit."

Pat looked up from his phone. "Talk about what? How you have a boyfriend now?"

I rolled my eyes. "How do you know about him. And he's not my boyfriend!"

"That's not what Mom says. She showed me his picture. How did you land such a good-looking dude?"

"How does she even have his picture?" I asked, bewildered.

"She took a screenshot of Linh's Facebook." *Damn.* I shouldn't have showed her how to take screenshots.

"I can't believe she did that."

"Why not? She texts me about it all the time. It's really annoying. She's so excited that you finally have a boyfriend, like it's a fucking miracle. You should just tell her about Michael."

"No way. She would kill me."

"No, she wouldn't. She didn't care when I dated Emerson." Emerson was Pat's high school girlfriend. She was half-white and half-Mexican, but my parents always thought she was Filipino.

"You know it's different for guys. The only girl you brought home that Ma didn't like was Diana because she had resting bitch face."

Taken aback, Pat replied, "Really? But she was really nice!"

"How come you guys broke up, then?" I asked, knowing the answer.

Pat looked out the passenger window and mumbled, "She got tired of me playing video games."

Reflexively, I said, "*Mmm.*"

Pat pointed at me. "You sounded just like Mom right now."

I slapped away his hand. "Take that back!"

"So, *Ma*," Pat said, purposely antagonizing me, "what are you going to make me for dinner?" Pat always knew how to get under my skin.

I narrowed my eyes at him. "I'm going to kick your ass."

"Love you too, jie," Pat said, returning his attention back to his phone.

"Hold on." I reached over and made a move for his phone and tossed it in the back seat. He realized too late what I was doing and didn't dodge in time.

"Are you for real right now?" He stretched his arms back but was unable to recover it.

"I need to talk to you about something important."

"What?"

"Mom's going crazy over this rent hike. You have to help me out here. Mom finally decided to close the shop earlier so that we can have some free time. You know she has me spying on a different donut shop every night?"

Pat shook his head in disbelief. "You know Mom and Dad will do what they want to do. They don't like change."

"I know but I think she might come around to switching up

our menu. They're overwhelmed with all these new ideas. We don't have to do anything too complicated."

"Why do you care so much? Let them figure it out."

"Because . . . Mom told me that they always planned to hire someone once we started our careers. They don't worry about you because of your internship. Your life is figured out. It's me that's holding up their plans. Can you imagine if they hired someone? You and I would never have to go in ever again and—"

The sound of Pat cracking his knuckles interrupted my train of thought. I looked at him out of the corner of my eye. He moved on to fiddling with the A/C vents.

"So . . . I was thinking, while you were home, you and I could test out some new donut flavors. They won't let us mess around if they are there, so I was thinking, we tell them that we'll watch the shop for them and they can take a day off or two. I hope they take the bait since they've never gone on vacation. If that doesn't work, maybe we can have them leave in the afternoons when it's slow. Do you think that will be enough time?"

Pat held out his hand. "Let me stop you right there. This is a stupid plan."

"I know this isn't how you wanted to spend your week off, but don't you want to help out Mom and Dad? *Our* mom and dad who walked across the jungle—"

"Save your breath. I know the story—"

". . . with a small bag of possessions to get to the refugee camp in Thailand . . ."

"I know, I know! Stop the guilt trip, okay?" Pat crossed his arms, unfolded them, and crossed them again.

"What's wrong with you? Why are you so antsy?"

He fidgeted in his seat, silent, just like that time he had to come clean about the car accident—a fender bender—that he got into two months after he got his driver's license.

"What is it? What did you do?" I pressed.

"I had to push my internship to fall quarter," Pat muttered. "It starts in September."

If we weren't already stuck in traffic, I would have slammed the brakes. "Wha . . . I'm confused. I thought you had a summer internship."

"I kinda forgot to follow up with the recruiter and . . . I guess I didn't accept on time."

Pat had done a lot of stupid things during his nineteen years of life, but this was by far the most moronic mistake. He forgot to reply to an email! This was my parents' pride and joy?

I slapped his arm with the back of my hand. "Are you fucking serious? So, what have you been doing this whole time?"

"Chill out, jie. Class just ended a couple weeks ago. I've been hanging out with my friends."

"Are you serious?!" I repeated. "Mom and Dad are going to kill you. You know how many people they told about your 'Gugo' internship?"

"Technically, I still have one. It's just starting later than they thought."

I scoffed. "No wonder you were able to come home for the

Fourth of July. You're not even doing anything right now! How were you going to explain being free for two months?"

"Well, I wasn't planning on telling them anything. I'm gonna go back to Santa Cruz."

I gasped at his deceitful plans. "You have to stay and help me. Come on. For Mom and Dad." Pat began to protest. "And I am not beneath blackmailing you."

Pat let out an incredulous laugh. "With what? They'll get over it."

"You think so? You think they're going to tell our aunts and uncles, 'Just kidding! Pat did not go to "Gugo."'"

"They will live," Pat insisted.

"How about when I tell them about the time you got suspended for smoking weed after Academic Decathlon? Or all the signatures I had to forge for you when you got caught ditching school? You know how much crap you're going to get for that?"

"Can't be worse than when you . . ." Pat stopped himself. He knew it was a low blow.

"No, it's not worse than that," I said solemnly. "But don't you think we owe it to them then? For being fuckups?"

"How are you going to explain that I'm staying longer?"

"I'll think of something. They don't know how internships work anyway." I tapped my fingers on the steering wheel as I thought. "First, we have to bring more business to the shop. I'll get a job ASAP. If I can even get an interview, you can go back to Santa Cruz."

"How are you going to find a job that fast?"

My fingers rapped on the steering wheel. "I'll think of something."

When I strolled in at six the following morning, I anticipated our usual rotation of customers, fulfilling the same orders they asked for every day. I even applied a little makeup since the A/C worked now. I didn't think much of it, but it turned out to be the tipping point for my regular customers to share some long-held opinions about my appearance.

At first, I thought it was a fluke. It started with Carol, the vice principal of the elementary school across the street. She liked to say that she planned to retire this year, but she had said that for the last five years. Every month, she held professional development meetings, which required three dozen donuts to keep the staff engaged.

"Jasmine! You look positively radiant today. Did you sleep well last night?" Carol asked as I tucked in the top of the last box. I was taken aback by her comment because I actually stayed up late the night before, texting Alex.

The best comment came from Sam. Fortunately, he brought a dollar bill to pay for his coffee this time. When I reached out to grab the crisp dollar from his hand, he tightened his grip. My confused eyes met his after our brief tug-of-war.

"Your mom told me you have a boyfriend now. Is that why you have a pep in your step these days?" Sam—who could pass for a frumpy Michael Douglas with a bad hip—never looked so serious, but the glint in his eye blew his cover.

I couldn't believe my mom was already starting to tell customers about Alex, but I didn't want to call her out. "I do have a boyfriend. I'm lookin' at him right now."

Sam let go of his dollar and winked at me. "Don't tell the missus." I shook my head and laughed when I rang him up.

I guess I did have a pep in my step, but my mom shouldn't have told customers about Alex yet. I wasn't sure if we'd ever go on a date. Alex told me that this project was the biggest one he had worked on in his entire career and the team he was on was full of overachieving workaholics. He let his colleagues know that he already booked his trip to China next month. Other than preplanned trips, his coworkers never seemed to have any downtime. They even worked through lunch and dinner. Not to mention most of my time got eaten up by our after-hours spying and reviewing job postings for positions I was not qualified for.

After the morning rush passed, I wiped down the counters and gathered the coffeepots to rinse in the back sink. I had two in each hand when the front door swung open.

"Hello! Delivery for a Jasmine Tran."

The carafes nearly slipped out of my hands. The deliveryman placed a clear cylindrical vase filled with dusty pink roses and succulents on the front counter and held out an iPad. "Can you please sign here?"

I freed my hands and quickly scribbled my signature with my finger, staring at the flowers in awe. I picked up the envelope that was placed in the middle of the bouquet and carefully lifted the flap, not wanting to wrinkle it. I slid the card out and marveled at the precise penmanship.

*Jasmine,*
*I hope you still don't have anything better to do tomorrow*
*because I'm looking forward to taking you on our first*
*date. Thanks for putting up with my busy schedule. Hope*
*this makes up for it.*
*—Alex*

I heard my phone ring just as I finished reading the card. I picked it up without looking at the caller ID.

"I can't believe you," I said, touching the soft petals.

Alex chuckled. "So, you got the flowers? I'm glad you like them."

"You didn't have to. A text would have sufficed."

"So, I take it that's a yes, you're free tomorrow? I hope so because my mom's coming into town next week and this was the only day that was open."

"Well, I think I can squeeze this into my busy schedule." The longer I stared at the flowers, the bigger they seemed. "You really didn't have to send flowers."

"I would have brought flowers to our date, but where we're going, you won't want to carry flowers around."

I caught the grassy, floral scent as I swooned from anticipation.

"Are you going to tell me where we're going?"

"No. It's a surprise. Can I pick you up around five?"

"Yeah, if you don't mind picking me up from the shop. Can you at least tell me what I should wear? Should I dress nice? Is it casual?" I asked, digging for clues.

"It's pretty casual. I'm sure anything you pick will be fine." That was not helpful at all. "I gotta go. I'll talk to you later."

My mom sneaked up next to me and assessed the bouquet of flowers. Her glasses hung on the tip of her nose. Her gold chain bracelet scraped against the vase as she turned it around. She gave a noncommittal "*hmm*" before walking toward the back of the shop. Glancing around me, I couldn't find a place to put this vase without it being in the way. I didn't want to hide it in the back of the shop, surrounded with stainless-steel appliances and stacked bags of flour. It deserved to be out in the open for everyone to appreciate.

I pulled out my phone and took a picture of the bouquet. I added a *Thank You* sticker on it and sent it to Alex. I also sent the original photo to Linh. She texted me back right away.

LINH: Jas and Alex sitting in a tree

I shook my head disapprovingly at the unsurprising response from Linh. Considering this was my first real date since we'd been friends, I braced myself for more ribbing.

JAS: Shut up
LINH: You're welcome
JAS: For what?

I looked back up at the bouquet. A fat pink rose tipped over and busted open upon impact on the front counter.

> **JAS:** the flowers were your idea, weren't they?
> **LINH:** 😇
> **LINH:** did your mom like them?

That bitch. So that's her angle. It was genius, though, to win my mom over at the same time.

> **JAS:** yes she did
> **LINH:** I may have made some suggestions for tomorrow too...

Oh no. On the one hand, Linh knew me well enough where I should trust her to give Alex recommendations that I would have liked. On the other hand, Linh was sneaky, and for all I knew, she could be setting me up for skydiving or dancing lessons.

> **JAS:** Where is he taking me
> **JAS:** he told me to dress casual
> **LINH:** don't be too casual!
> **LINH:** when you get home, text me some outfits
> **LINH:** gotta make sure you look hot tomorrow

I wasn't sure how I was supposed to pull off hot and casual at the same time. I was about to pick up the vase when my mom signaled me to put it back down. She held out her phone and took her own picture. "I have to send this to Auntie Helen or else she won't believe me." My mom tapped on her phone, sending off her text. I pressed my lips, annoyed by Auntie Helen's lack of confidence in me.

"Alex is going to pick me up tomorrow at five. I promise I'll get everything done so you don't have to do anything when you close."

My mom frowned. "What are you talking about?"

"Alex . . . my 'boyfriend'?" It wasn't like my mom to forget.

My mom waved her hands to stop me. "I know. But why you talk about closing tomorrow? You go home early and get ready." My mom tilted her head as she examined my outfit. "You need it."

"Thanks, Ma!" I tried for enthusiasm, but it still came out a bit sarcastic. Truthfully, I was excited to go home early. It had been a while since I dressed up for anything outside of coming to work. I finally moved the vase to the back of the shop. My dad eyed the flowers as he finished wiping down his workbench.

"Don't put those here," he said when he saw me walking in his direction. "Put it over there." He pointed to the empty space on the chrome wire shelf where we stored boxes of coffee cups and straws.

I nudged the boxes over to make room for my bouquet. Surrounded by brown cardboard, my pink flowers looked terribly out of place. My dad walked over and placed his hands on his hips when he stood next to me. "Is it from the same boy?"

I gave my dad a quizzical look. "Who else would it be, Ba?"

"We need to meet him. Invite him over for dinner," my dad said in an unusually businesslike manner.

I laughed. This had to be a joke. From what I gathered from the many TV shows I watched, meeting the parents came much later—months, years even—into the courtship, when things were really serious. I turned to my dad, who couldn't comprehend what I found so funny.

He looked like he was actually serious about this.

The laughter died on my lips and panic took over.

"No, Ba. I haven't even gone on a date with him and you want him to come over for dinner?" I said incredulously. "Absolutely not."

There was no way I would subject Alex to a dinner with my parents. There were only two possible outcomes. The first was that my parents would scrutinize every aspect of his life as if they had been FBI agents in a previous life. *Name. Date of birth. Internet search history.* They'd swab his mouth to send samples for DNA analysis. The second possibility was much worse. They might actually like him, even love him. Then they would want to know if I wanted lobster as one of the ten courses served at my wedding reception. I would have to decide soon lest I lose the auspicious date that my mom's fortune-teller chose based on Alex's and my birthdates. The logical part of me knew that the dinner would result somewhere in the middle of these two extremes, but I didn't care. I couldn't risk anything that would send Alex running for the hills. He would probably prefer running for the hills than being judged by my parents.

My mom chimed in. "Con, invite him for dinner. How about next week?"

"No." I balked. "Most people don't introduce their boyfriends to their parents until it's serious."

"That makes no sense. I'm not going to let a stranger take you out alone. No. We have to get to know him first," my dad argued.

"He can't come." In my panic, I started grasping for straws. "His mom is visiting next week."

My dad shrugged. "Have him bring his mom, then."

"No, no no no no no no. NO!" Things were spiraling out of control. This was exactly why I never told my parents about my past dates. They were already intruding on my time with Alex and now I might meet his mom too? "Please, Ba," I begged. "You can meet him another time."

"Invite them," my dad grunted as he gathered his things and headed home.

"At least ask them. It will be like when your grandparents introduced Uncle Tin to Auntie Shelly and her parents," my mom reasoned.

"That was to arrange marriage! This is not the same."

"So what? We meet his mom; we see if he comes from a good family. You can tell a lot about someone when you know their family, so ask him." She moved on and mumbled to herself a list of ingredients she needed to buy. I nudged her with my elbow.

"Don't go too crazy with dinner," I pleaded. "We don't know if it's happening yet. It's not a big deal."

"Not a big deal? It's the first time you bring a boy home." My mom shook her head at my apparent nonsense. "Tell them to come hungry."

"Ma." I gently rubbed my mom's arms, like I was petting a racehorse before it took off full speed ahead. "Seriously. Don't stress over it."

"Don't worry, con. I won't scare him away. He might be your only chance!"

I rolled my eyes and left my mom to her dinner planning. I took one last look at my pretty flowers before I dragged myself back to work. If only he had just texted . . .

## Chapter 9

*A*lex had waited in front of my house in his car for the last fifteen minutes. Even though my mom offered to let me go home early to get ready for my date, we were slammed with a big group of teenagers who all wanted smoothies just as I was about to walk out of the shop. I didn't want to leave my mom hanging like that. Now I was running way behind, only halfway done with curling my hair into beachy waves. Sweat started to bead on my forehead. I wasn't sure if it was from the curling iron or the ninety-degree heat outside. Alex must be dying in his car. I texted him before he melted away.

**JAS:** hey. so sorry.

**JAS:** I need another 10 minutes.

**JAS:** do you want to come inside?

**JAS:** fair warning. my dad is home.

It wasn't long before I heard the doorbell ring. I made out my dad's and Alex's muffled voices as they greeted each other. What kind of small talk might my dad exchange with Alex? Alex laughed heartily. What could he possibly be laughing at? *Oh no. No no no no no.* I curled my hair as fast as I could, ignoring the stick-straight pieces I missed, and blotted the sweaty sheen off my face. I nearly tripped running down the stairs.

When I swung around the banister at the last step, I found my dad showing Alex the wall in our family room that displayed every award I had ever received since kindergarten. This wall was largely ignored except when my parents wanted to show off to distant relatives whenever they stopped by. Alex nodded politely as my dad pointed at my blue ribbon from my eighth-grade science fair and the framed copy of my AP score report when I passed four AP tests.

Alex turned around and I understood what Linh meant by hot yet casual. Alex was wearing a solid olive-green T-shirt with slim gray jeans that fit him to perfection. Judging by the smile on Alex's face, he liked my outfit too—a flowy off-the-shoulder white top and skintight light-washed jeans. I didn't get a chance to enjoy his attention when I saw what he was holding.

"Sorry for making you wait. We're leaving now, Ba." I tried to release the picture frame from Alex's grasp.

"Wait a minute." Alex tightened his grip and turned the frame around. "Is this you?" He bit his lip to hide his smile.

I crossed my arms as I looked at my hideous eighth-grade

portrait. "Puberty was not kind to me, okay? The braces didn't help, either." I had zits all over my face, which hadn't caught up to my nose.

"Well, this picture alone made it worth the wait." Alex placed the frame back on the faux marble end table and followed me to the hallway, where I grabbed a pair of strappy brown leather sandals. "Um, you might want to wear those." He pointed at my black-and-white-checked Vans slip-ons while he put on his black sneakers.

Confused, I asked, "Where are we going? If we're going to do a lot of walking, I'm going to change."

"No, don't change. Just trust me."

My left eyebrow arched as I laid down my sandals and put on my slip-ons.

My dad sneaked up behind Alex and patted him on the back. In Mandarin, he told Alex not to keep me out too late.

"Okay okay okay, Ba!" I practically pushed Alex out of the door before my dad said anything else. Alex led me to his car and opened the passenger door for me. I climbed in and almost slid off the leather seats. I pushed myself up before Alex made it around to the driver's seat.

When Alex slid inside, I said, "I'm so sorry I made you wait out here and then for making you wait in there."

Alex turned the key in the ignition and warmed up the car before driving off. "Don't worry about it. We should sti'l get there on time."

"You're still not going to tell me?" I glanced at Alex, hoping to get some clues. Alex shook his head, keeping a strong poker face.

The car pulled up to a four-way stop. He turned to me and his eyes slowly scanned my body. I squirmed in my seat, unaccustomed to getting checked out.

"You look—" he started to say when the car behind us honked. Alex cleared his throat and turned his attention back to driving.

"I look what? It's better than the blue polo, right?"

With a sideways glance, Alex sneaked another look. His mouth pulled into a lopsided grin. "Much better," he said. He turned up the volume of his car stereo when he merged onto the 60 West Freeway.

I eyed his preset radio stations. I shuddered at the Odesza song that was playing. It made my skin crawl.

Alex kept his eyes on the road. "Linh told me you might do that."

"Do what?" I asked, worried what kinds of things Linh could have told Alex.

"Judge me by my music selection. I believe her exact words were 'Jas is a music snob.'"

I pursed my lips. "Don't believe everything she says. I'm not a snob. Besides, I listen to most genres. I really don't care if you like Taylor Swift."

"Oh yeah? What's your favorite band?"

I hated when people asked me this. My answer fluctuated with my mood. "What are we talking about here? From the last ten years? British bands? Mid-aughts alternative? Indie?"

Alex seemed to consider these parameters. "You sure you're not a snob?"

"Let's just say that I have discerning taste."

"What if I play this?" Alex pressed a button on his steering wheel and suddenly a Chinese pop song from what sounded like a girl group projected from the speakers.

I slumped into my seat. "You can't be serious." I might not have clear favorites, but Chinese pop music was not near the top of my list.

"Come on. You don't think it's catchy?" Alex started to sing along, hamming it up like we were on an episode of "Carpool Karaoke." "Is it because you don't know what they're saying?"

It was too cute, and the disapproving look on my face melted away.

"Maybe," I admitted. "How do you even keep up with what they're singing?"

Alex turned down the music. "I just can. Probably helps that I grew up in China."

I gave Alex a double take. "Really? Till when? I just assumed you grew up around here. Like, in SoCal."

"Well, I was born here, but my mom's a geology professor and she taught at a few different places when she graduated with her PhD. She thought that it would be better for me to stay with my grandma in China until she found a full-time job. That's when I moved out here to Arcadia, which wasn't the best place for me to learn English. There are so many Chinese kids there."

"Oh." I never would have guessed. "So, how did you learn then?"

"I watched *Friends* reruns. It was always on TV."

"Oh my god." I laughed. I turned my attention back to the road. For a Friday night, traffic was surprisingly light by L.A. standards. I lowered my sun visor, but the sun hovered just below it, so I flipped the visor back up.

"Do you want my sunglasses? They're in the glove compartment." Alex reached over and popped it open. I reached for his sunglasses at the same time he did and my fingers brushed his knuckles as they retreated. The gentle touch lasted only a second, but I instantly turned into a ball of nerves. I lifted Alex's Ray-Bans off his open palm and put them on. The frames were a little too wide for my face, but I was relieved that I didn't have to stare at the sun for the remainder of our drive.

Alex caught my hand as it descended on my lap. Red brake lights lit up the road as traffic came to a halt. He tilted his head, his warm gaze staying on my face as a slow smile appeared on his.

"Looks good on you," he said. I seemed to forget how to exhale as I stared at our hands, commingling with each other.

"Thanks," I managed to say.

"Could you *be* any more nervous?" Alex teased, successfully lightening up my mood with his Chandler impression.

It was actually a little uncomfortable holding hands. I couldn't figure out if it was because his hand was bigger than mine or he was squeezing too hard. Either way, Alex released my hand after I wiggled my fingers, allowing blood to circulate into them once again. Before he could return his hand back to the steering wheel, I curled my fingers and slowly ran them up and down his palm and under his fingers. Alex's hand stilled, unsure what was happening. On the second pass of his hand, Alex's hand relaxed, letting me take the lead, when I gently laced my fingers back into his.

I leaned back into my seat and closed my eyes as I tried to calm my nerves. Every switch in my body was flipped up. If holding hands felt this good, anything more was going to overload my circuits.

The clicking sound of the signal to change lanes interrupted my train of thought. My eyes popped wide open as he exited the freeway. When we passed Union Station, I had a sinking suspicion.

"Are we heading to your apartment?" I asked warily.

"Yes and no. I'm just parking my car there and we're going to Uber the rest of the way." Alex gave my hand a reassuring squeeze.

"You know, I would have driven here if I knew we were hanging out around this area."

Alex shook his head. "What kind of guy would I be if I made you drive into L.A. on a Friday night for our first date?"

Maybe I'd been out of the dating game for too long, but that was the most romantic thing anyone had ever said to me. I felt like a freaking princess in a sporty compact sedan.

Alex parked his car in the private lot behind his apartment

building—a renovated brick building with converted loft-style apartments to appeal to young professionals—and reached into the back seat to grab his lightweight black bomber jacket.

"When did you move in with Owen?" I asked as we walked to the corner to wait for our Uber.

"Last month. It's much closer to the office than my last place. How long have you known Linh and Owen?"

"Linh since freshman year. She didn't meet Owen until the year after."

"They're fun to hang out with," he said as his hand found its way back to mine, which sent a rush of fizzy feelings through my body like a freshly poured glass of Coke.

"What?" I asked to cover the hitch in my breath. I felt myself inch closer as I added *Likes my friends* to the growing list of things to like about Alex. Maybe we were standing too close because I couldn't decipher why his eyes lit up on me. When I thought he'd clue me in, the rolling crunch of asphalt alerted us to our Uber driver's silver SUV pulling up to the curb.

"Can you tell me now where we're going?" I asked as Alex held the door open. Alex shut the door and walked around the car to sit behind our driver, Saul. I looked disappointedly at the chasm created by the empty seat between us.

"Oh yeah. About that." Alex patted the side of Saul's seat. "Don't tell her where we're going. It's a surprise."

Saul tipped his cabby hat in agreement, even going as far as lowering the volume on his phone so I wouldn't hear his GPS. I tried to bribe Saul into telling me where our final destination was. I jokingly threatened to give him a 1-star rating, but he remained tight-lipped. Instead, he offered us a variety of snacks and water while he made questionable shortcuts to avoid bottlenecks. All I could gather was that we were heading northbound once we drove past the golden twin dragons at the entrance of Chinatown.

When Saul turned onto some side street, going uphill, Alex glanced sideways to see my reaction. I dragged my eyes away from the window and looked at Alex, who waited eagerly for my response.

"Are you taking me hiking?" I asked, catching the sign pointing to Elysian Park. "I thought you said we weren't doing a lot of walking. I would have changed."

Alex narrowed his eyes and tilted his head. "No, we're going to the Dodger game," he said, gesturing toward the stadium. "Are you sure you passed all those AP tests?" he teased. I shoved his shoulder before I could stop myself.

"Ow!" Alex yelped.

"Sorry. It's a bad habit," I said, smiling weakly at my explanation. Pat and Linh had grown accustomed to my hitting over the years. Nowadays, they anticipated getting hit and managed to dodge my hands half the time.

"So, what do you think?"

My face broke into a wide smile. "I haven't been here since high school. I wonder who's pitching tonight. I hope it's Ferris."

Pleased, Alex gave me his dimple-making grin. "I don't know who that is, but I'm glad you like it."

It was almost six-thirty by the time Saul dropped us off at the edge of the parking lot. Staring at the uphill concrete expanse, I was grateful that Alex advised me to switch shoes. I felt the urge to stretch since I hadn't exercised in so long, but I didn't think it would be attractive. Alex took effortless long strides as we climbed toward the stadium, passing row after row of parked cars.

"So, Jas. I've been meaning to ask you," Alex said, walking a few steps ahead of me.

"Yeah?"

"So, your dad said your family's from Cambodia? But you speak Chinese?"

I knew where this was headed. Everyone I've met has asked me the same questions. I took a couple of quick steps to catch up to Alex. "Yes and yes," I said simply.

"But you're Vietnamese, right? Or how does that work?"

"My parents escaped the Khmer Rouge and stayed with relatives in Vietnam for a while. They changed their last name there to blend in. Then they came to the U.S. as refugees. But my family's roots are Chinese. That's the . . . short version . . . of the story. You're lucky . . . I saved you . . . from getting the long version . . . from my dad." I huffed and puffed, powering through the end of my condensed family history.

"Do you need to take a break?" Alex stopped suddenly, causing me to bump into him.

"No, I'm fine," I gasped.

"Here." He pulled me off to the side, so we weren't holding

up the people walking behind us. I fanned my face with both hands when I really wanted to collapse as if I'd just finished a marathon. Alex put his hand on my shoulder and lowered his head, like a coach giving a pep talk. "Are you going to make it up there?"

"Yes. Just give me a minute. It's just hot."

Hot was an understatement. Though dusk was approaching, the dry heat and still air offered no reprieve. Alex released my toasty shoulder and looked behind us, assessing the distance to the stadium.

"Okay. Let's go," I said after I caught my breath.

"Wait." Alex pulled out his phone from his back pocket. "Let's take a picture."

"Why? So, you can remember standing in the middle of the parking lot with me?" I blotted my sweaty face with the back of my hand.

"No. It's my first time coming here." Alex put his arm around my shoulder and drew me closer. I immediately stopped protesting and leaned into him, feeling his soft shirt underneath my hand as I hugged his waist. Alex held up his phone and captured us with Dodger Stadium in the distance.

I lifted Alex's sunglasses away from my face and rested them on top of my head to look at the photo. It was unfair how perfect Alex looked, with his disarming smile and his soft hair that magically stayed in place. Even the tiny squint of his eyes worked in his favor. I, on the other hand, looked hopelessly smitten.

Once we made it into the stadium, we headed toward the

concession stands. Alex couldn't come to his first Dodger game without getting a Dodger Dog. We were on our way to get micheladas when I led Alex to a booth that sold a mishmash of apparel and souvenirs.

I greeted the attendant. "Hi. He needs a new Dodger hat." I turned to Alex, appraising the circumference of his head. "What's your hat size?"

"What are you doing?" Alex asked, as a means to say that this was all unnecessary.

"We're sitting on the first-base side, right? You're gonna want a hat. Trust me."

The attendant guessed Alex's hat size and handed over three different options. I chose the classic cobalt-blue snapback with the white L.A. logo and smashed it on his head.

"Sorry to ruin your perfect hair," I said. "Does it fit okay?"

Alex handed me the Dodger Dogs so that he could readjust the hat. "Yeah, it fits," he said as he wiggled the bill until it was perfectly centered.

Before Alex could reach for his wallet, I shoved our food back into Alex's hands and gave the attendant my credit card.

"We'll take it," I said. The attendant swiped my card before Alex could protest.

I winked at Alex. "Looks good on you," I said, copying his words from earlier.

"Thanks," he replied, expressing his gratitude and admitting defeat.

After we bought our drinks, I followed Alex to our seats.

I wasn't paying attention to where we were going as I put all my focus on walking down the stairs without spilling my beer. When Alex turned into our row, I stopped on the stairway to see where we were.

"Alex. We're sitting here?" I looked up at the cheap seats hovering above us, my mouth gaping. "I've never sat this close to the field before." Alex stood in the middle of the empty row and shrugged.

"It's my first game. Can't watch from the nosebleeds," he said smoothly. A knowing smile stretched across his face. If his hands weren't full, he would have patted himself on the back.

I carefully walked down our row and lowered myself onto the warm seat next to Alex. The sun touched the entire east side of the stadium. Had I known we were coming here, I would have applied sun block. I lowered Alex's sunglasses back down on my face.

"Cheers." Alex held up the large plastic cup holding his michelada.

"Cheers." I tapped his cup with mine, knocking some of the chili powder off the rim. After I took a small sip, I placed my cup in the cup holder and pulled out my phone. I took a few pictures of the field, still in awe of where we were sitting.

"Hold on," Alex said, stopping me from putting away my phone. He tapped my screen and switched my camera to selfie mode. Alex put his left arm around me. "We have to document our first date."

The way he said it, so nonchalantly, made it seem like it

would be the first of many. I tried not to read into it as I held up my phone and snapped five pictures of us that pretty much all looked the same.

"So, why do you like baseball?" Alex asked as he bit into his hot dog. "Did you play in high school or something?"

"No. I did not play any sports in high school. Couldn't you tell from the walk up here?" I said, causing Alex to chuckle. "No, the first time I came here was during middle school." My face lit up from the memory. "There's nothing like hearing the crack of the bat and watching a grand slam in the bottom of the ninth. Everyone stands up, screaming. You high-five every person you can reach. I was hooked after that."

"How are they doing this season?"

"I'm not sure. I haven't been keeping up as much. We have one TV at the shop, but my mom hogs it to watch Chinese dramas."

Alex nodded while he crumpled the foil wrapper. "Have you worked there for a long time?"

"Ever since I was little," I said, taking a long sip of my beer. "Ooh! Someone's throwing the first pitch."

"You know you're going to have to tell me more than that. All I really know about you is that you eat like a pregnant lady, you're smart, and you're funny. I had to stop reading your texts during meetings."

"Was that supposed to be a compliment?" I scoffed. "There's not much to say. I'm just helping my parents out while I figure out what to do with my life. What about you? Did you always know you were going to be a consultant?"

"I didn't even know what consulting was until college. My mom was disappointed I didn't study a science like her."

"What about your dad? Did he care?"

Alex shrugged as he looked toward the field. Coolly, he replied, "Can't say. Never met the guy." Alex's jaw clenched briefly before he changed the subject. "This song reminds me of you."

Not wanting to press a sore spot, I rolled with it. I stopped and listened to the organist play his rendition of "Despacito." Alex read the confusion on my face.

"You don't remember? This was playing in your office when I bought tickets from you. I swear, I couldn't escape that song that year."

Impressed, I replied, "I can't believe you remember that." I paused. "So, out of curiosity, how come you didn't ask me out back then?"

I wondered about this before. I wanted to think that if Alex and I had dated in college, things would have turned out differently. I wouldn't have wasted so much energy chasing other guys only to get my heart broken. But then I remembered what a wreck I'd been; maybe it was better that he didn't know that version of me.

Alex dragged out an unexpected throaty, reluctant sound. It made me regret asking him the question. After a moment, Alex finally said, "I was dating someone at the time. It didn't work out, obviously. Believe me. Had I known how things would have turned out, I would have asked you out then."

This piqued my interest. "What do you mean?"

"She cheated on me," Alex said bitterly. "Whatever. Let's not talk about exes." I didn't know what to say. I was curious, but I didn't want to ruin the mood even further by delving into it. Fortunately, Alex veered our conversation back to safer first-date territory. "Quick. Tell me your top three pet peeves."

"Um . . . dance remixes of slow songs. When someone leaves just a little bit of water in their water bottle or glass. Deep V T-shirts on guys. You don't have any, do you?"

His nose crinkled as he mentally assessed his wardrobe. "What if I did?"

"Well, it was nice knowing you," I deadpanned. Despite my aversion toward the V-neck, I was sure Alex would make me a convert. He could be wearing a garbage bag and it would be next season's "must have" item.

Alex laughed. "Wow. Brutal."

We took a break from Q&A to enjoy the game. As the game progressed, Alex asked me to explain some baseball rules, only half of which I confidently answered. Google helped me with the rest. When the sun finally set behind the stadium, Alex watched as I slipped off his sunglasses and hung them on the front of my shirt.

"Hey. Eyes up here," I said, pointing at my own.

Alex extended his left arm behind my seat. "I don't know what you're talking about. I'm trying to watch the game," he said, feigning innocence. The announcer named the next batter, who approached home plate. The batter's walk-up song, Taylor Swift's iconic "Shake It Off," blasted across the stadium. I pressed my lips together to stifle my snicker.

"You promised not to laugh," Alex said as a gentle reminder.

"I'm not," I said. At least not anymore, since his fingertips began to mindlessly trace the edge of my top, grazing around my collarbone and effectively shutting me up.

A collective "Oh!" boomed from the crowd as the batter struck out. The players on the field jogged back to the dugout as the game headed to the top of the fifth inning. I looked up on the big screen to check on the score when it transitioned into a heart frame with a cheesy saxophone soundtrack.

My eyes widened at the screen. Alex—who had been leaning back for most of the game—scooted forward to the edge of his seat.

There we were, staring at our stunned selves on DodgerVision, with everyone surrounding us cheering us on. "Kiss! Kiss! Kiss!"

Feeling the mounting expectations from the crowd, Alex turned to face me, his expression asking for permission. My eyes widened; my body was temporarily paralyzed by the thousands of fans who watched for my next move. I looked down. My lips parted at the thought of kissing his mouth.

Next thing I knew, Alex turned his cap around and leaned forward while his hand held my face, drawing me closer. My hand pressed flat on his chest, bracing for impact. When I felt the warm press of his lips on mine, my mind went blank, as if nothing else in the world existed. I relaxed my grip on his shirt and reached around his neck as he deepened the kiss. Gradually, I became aware of my surroundings, like how our seating arrangement and the stupid armrest made it virtually impossible to press my body against his. How I felt rather than heard Alex groan on my lips because the crowd roared and the group of drunk guys behind us howled like wolves.

When we came up for air, we still found ourselves on the big screen. Suddenly comprehending our very public display of affection, I leaned forward, propping myself up with my elbows on my knees. I shielded my eyes with my hands, embarrassed by the show we gave to our audience. Alex didn't seem to mind as the drunk guys behind us gave him high fives. When the crowd settled down, Alex gently pulled my hands away from my face.

"Hey. Was that okay?" he asked. Alex took his hat off and ran his fingers through his hair. Was he nervous? He put his arm around me and rubbed my shoulder. Warmth spread across my face. I lowered my chin, resisting the urge to touch my tingling lips.

"Did you forget fireworks or something? You had to get thousands of fans to cheer you on?" I joked.

"Are you saying you didn't feel fireworks?" Alex tried to keep his tone light, but I heard the hint of concern in his voice. A knot formed in the pit of my stomach. The last thing I wanted to do was to ruin our movie-worthy kiss.

"I'm sorry. I meant—"

I paused. Sarcastic responses ran through my head, but they didn't seem appropriate. What purpose did they serve other than to protect my ego? To look cool?

Fuck being cool. I was never cool anyway.

I looked at Alex square in the eyes. "That was the best kiss of my life," I breathed before a shy smile crept on my face. Alex's expression mirrored mine.

"Does that mean I have to try and top that kiss?" His eyes glimmered with excitement at the challenge.

My thumb ran across his dimple before circling back to wipe off the remnants of my lip gloss at the corner of his mouth.

"I won't stop you."

## Chapter 10

*I* sat alone at a dim hipster bar a few blocks away from Alex's apartment, staring at a list of "libations." Alex and I left the stadium after the seventh-inning stretch to avoid traffic. The Dodgers were down by five runs anyway, so it seemed pointless to stay. It was just past nine and the night was still young, so Alex suggested coming here. The bar crowd was full of twentysomethings looking to blow off steam from their nine-to-five jobs with artisanal cocktails and board games.

My phone was going off like crazy. It was the yearbook group chat. Rae got the job at *LA Weekly* and everyone was texting their congratulations.

> **JAS:** Congrats! When do you start?
> **RAE:** Thx! I just put in my two weeks' notice and I start
> the Monday after.

> **RAE:** let me know if you guys know anyone. I want to refer
> my replacement.
> **JOSH:** What about Jas?

What about me? I didn't know a thing about social media or journalism.

> **RAE:** Oooh! Let me know if you're interested. I can fill you
> in and put in a good word.
> **JAS:** I'll think about it
> **RAE:** Don't wait too long. My boss is trying to find my
> replacement fast
> **MICHAEL:** You should go for it

This was too much to think about. It was tempting, since I was coming up with nothing with my job search. Over the last week, I applied to random entry-level jobs only to get rejected within a day or two. It wouldn't hurt to get more info from Rae. When I last checked *Angel City Magazine*'s website, I thought the headlines were interesting.

ON THE SCENE: ZERO WASTE REFILL STATION POPS UP IN
    LOS FELIZ
PROPOSED DOWNTOWN HOMELESS SHELTER DRAWS
    PROTESTS FROM NIMBYS
REVIEW: THE GLASS VINES GO ACOUSTIC AT THE WILTERN

It was certainly more appealing than the internship at Linh's law firm, which I applied to only because she kept sending me more emails as the deadline approached.

As if she knew I'd been thinking of her, I started to receive multiple texts from Linh. I switched out of the group chat to see all the questions she sent, asking me about my date. Every other text was an emoji—hearts, a kiss, a pair of eyes. The last ten were eggplants. I rolled my eyes. I quickly swiped her texts away when Alex returned from the restroom, taking his seat beside me.

"Who's sending you eggplants?" Alex asked like this was a normal conversation starter.

"Linh. Who else?" I snorted. Satisfied with my answer, Alex noticeably relaxed, leaning against the bar counter.

"I wasn't sure if you were dating anyone else," he said, glancing at me before he tried to get the bartender's attention.

"If I was dating somebody else, Linh wouldn't have thrown you at me." I swiveled my stool toward him. "What about you? Are you dating anyone else?"

"Honestly, I haven't dated anyone in a while." I must have made a face because he asked, "Why are you looking at me like that?"

"I find that hard to believe." It's a wonder that nobody else snatched him up already.

"Well, work keeps me busy, so I haven't been actively looking. But if you ask me . . ."—his voice lowered along with his gaze—"I think I'm doing all right."

The bartender came to take our order. The gold accents on his navy suspenders gleamed under the Edison lights. Alex asked for water, since he was driving me home later. Based on the bartender's recommendation, I ordered a Negroni and watched him mix my drink. For the final flourish, he twisted an orange peel and dropped it in my glass. The smell of citrus tickled my nose as I tilted the glass back for my first sip. The cool drink was delicious, but it was no match for the heat of Alex's eyes.

His fingers brushed my hair back over my shoulder.

"It was in the way," Alex said, answering the curious look on my face. Before I could respond, he leaned in and gently kissed behind my ear. His nose traveled down my neck and I felt another kiss on my collarbone. Somewhere in the mix, I forgot how to breathe. The sound of crashing Jenga blocks jolted me out of my haze, nearly causing me to spill my drink.

"Hey. Easy there." I laughed nervously.

Alex lingered at the crook of my neck. "You smell like vanilla frosting."

*Oh boy.* I took another sip of my drink.

"What is happening right now?" It'd been so long since my last cocktail. The Negroni broke the filter between my brain and my mouth. My baffled tone caused Alex to retreat.

"I'm sorry. I didn't mean to make you feel uncomfortable."

"No, it's not that," I said hurriedly. "I mean, that felt good." My voice lowered. "Very good, but—" I hesitated. I pursed my lips, trying to contain the words that threatened to spill out.

"But what?" Alex asked.

The dam broke and I began to ramble. "I don't want you to get the wrong impression. This is our first date. I know we're close to your apartment. I don't just do *that* with anybody. I don't know where this is going. I haven't dated anyone in a long, *long* time. I've had my heart broken before. So, I don't want to play games. I'm not trying to play hard to get. I know that's not romantic, but I just need to know where you see this going."

Alex blinked a few times, processing everything I just said or possibly trying to recall the location of the nearest exit. "Uh . . . I thought it was pretty obvious," he said, watching for my reaction.

I swirled my drink around my glass to distract myself from my awkward outburst. I know I said "Fuck being cool" and all, but that fleeting moment of courage came and went.

"Jas, I like you."

I turned back to the bar and put my glass down. Alex swung me around until I faced him. Feeling self-conscious, I looked at my knees, which knocked his. Alex tipped my chin up so I could see his sincere eyes.

"And if it's okay with you," he added, "I'd like to keep seeing you."

"Okay," I managed to say before it became harder to breathe.

"And if we're putting it all out there, then I'd have to say that I hope you don't want to date anyone else, but I'd understand if you did. I know you've had to accommodate my schedule."

"Oh," I said softly. "Well, there's no one else."

"So, are we okay?" Alex held both of my hands on top of my

knees. "Because I don't know about you, but I think I can kick your butt at darts."

I smiled, relieved that I hadn't completely humiliated myself and grateful that he handled my fragile feelings so gently. I knocked back the rest of my drink before taking his hand, following him to the corner where two dartboards hung on the wall.

"Since I had a drink, you have to cut me some slack," I said.

Alex gathered the darts from the board and handed some to me. "Sure. Ladies first."

I stood at the marker on the floor, about six feet away from my target. I adjusted my stance, right foot ahead of left, about shoulder width apart. I brought the dart close to my right temple, squinting at the bull's-eye. Out of the corner of my eye, I saw Alex, amused, watching my every move.

"You know, you can take a picture. It'll last longer," I said cheekily, right before I launched the dart. It landed very close to the center circle. Alex nodded as his lips pressed into a small "not bad" frown. On the outside, I shrugged it off, while on the inside, I felt like hot shit.

Unfortunately, my beginner's luck was short-lived, since every dart I threw afterward bounced off the wall. Alex fared better than me, though I wasn't paying attention to the score. My eyes were too busy looking at the cute way that Alex's tongue stuck out when he lined up his shot and how his biceps flexed when he threw the dart.

"What do you want to do next?" Alex said as he threw the last one. "Besides checking me out?"

"I don't know what you're talking about. You think too highly of yourself."

*"Mm-hmm."*

I might have been more convincing if I didn't gravitate to his open arms so easily. Together we swayed too slow for the indie-pop track that was playing throughout the bar, but fast enough for me to get swept up in the moment. He smelled too good for someone who just sat for hours outside in the sweltering heat. I tilted my head up just in time to see him lean down for a kiss. Feeling uninhibited from my drink, I stood on my toes, meeting him halfway, letting his lips coax mine. My hands made their way toward his face, eventually curling around the nape of his neck. His hands traveled in the opposite direction, inching lower and lower down my back, pressing me closer, until suddenly . . .

*Bzzz. Bzzz. Bzzz. Bzzz.*

My vibrating phone zapped Alex's hands away, bursting our little bubble.

"I didn't know you had a security system down there," Alex joked.

"Sorry." I checked my phone. I should have known that it was my mom.

**MOM:** Jasmine

**MOM:** It's late

**MOM:** You work tomorrow

**MOM:** I'm waiting for you

I grumbled while I swiped the message away and returned my phone into my back pocket.

"Is everything okay?" Alex asked.

"That was my mom. I'm sorry. I have to go home." I couldn't believe I just said that. It wasn't even ten. Even Cinderella had until midnight.

Alex looked equally disappointed to end our date so soon, but he understood. We walked out of the bar after Alex closed his tab. On the way to his car, I found myself leaning closer to Alex, seeking warmth from the cool summer evening.

"Are you cold?" Alex asked. He shrugged off his jacket and hung it on my shoulders. It wasn't that cold, but it would have been foolish to refuse. I weaved my arms through the sleeves and let his residual body heat envelope me. If I could live in this jacket, I would.

Once we made it to his car, I returned his sunglasses to their rightful place. With a mellow dance track playing, Alex drove me home with zero sense of urgency. All five lanes on the 60 Freeway were clear, but we were coasting at sixty-five miles an hour, like he didn't want the evening to end. In darkness, he radiated a quiet composure that made me feel like I could be myself around him. That he could handle all that came with dating me. Time to put that to the test.

"Before I forget," I said, "don't freak out, but my parents want you to come over for dinner next weekend. I know you said your mom will be visiting. She's invited too."

"Uh . . ." Alex leaned an arm against the window and covered his mouth with his hand. "I don't know, Jas."

"I know it's a lot to ask, but my dad insisted," I said apologetically.

"Don't get me wrong. I'm down, but . . ." He paused for a moment. When he spoke again, his voice was hesitant. "Let me check with my mom. She's in town for a conference. It should be over by Sunday, but I don't know if she'll come. Can I let you know?"

"Yeah, I'm sure it'll be fine," I said in a rush, so he knew there was no pressure. "I mean . . . you know my schedule. It's exactly the same. *Every. Day.*"

"You hate working there, don't you? I noticed that you don't like talking about it."

I shrugged. "I've been working there a long time. It's not exciting or glamorous. My parents didn't even start paying me until this year. It's almost like, why did I even go to college if I was going to end up back there?"

"Well, it's not like you can't do something else. What are you passionate about? What are you interested in?" It was like Alex put on his consultant hat all of a sudden.

I looked out the window. "Look. You're not the first person to ask me this. The TLDR version is that I'm not passionate about anything and I don't have any experience outside of the shop."

"Not true, Ticket Girl," Alex countered.

Irritated, I replied, "That was only for one quarter. I barely made it through college. I didn't have a plan except to graduate.

I chose my major because I didn't want to stay an extra year. I honestly don't know what to do."

"Do your parents care what you do?"

I shook my head as the car came to a brief stop at the exit. "No. At this point, they literally don't care, as long as it's stable and pays okay."

Alex threw up his hands in disbelief. "Then what's the problem? You can do anything."

"Where would I even start? You can't get a job without experience, but then you can't get experience unless you have a job. The system is rigged."

Alex gave my knee a gentle squeeze. "I don't think you give yourself enough credit. You're good at lots of things."

"Like what?" Making air quotes with my fingers, I asked, "'Eating like a pregnant lady?' What could I do with that?"

Alex thought about it for a second. He snapped his fingers when he came up with his idea. "You could record those mukbang videos of yourself eating a ton of food and then post them on YouTube."

I gagged at the thought. "Ew, gross! I can't stand it when I hear other people chewing food. I don't understand how anyone can watch those videos."

"Says the person who watches pimples being popped. I couldn't look at my lunch today after you sent me that video. It was like she squeezed a rotten hard-boiled egg out of that lady's scalp."

"You don't find them oddly satisfying? When she gets all the gunk out in one shot?"

Alex grimaced as he turned onto my street.

"Hey. Pull over." We were about half a block away from my house. My mom was probably looking out the front window, waiting for me to get home. Alex complied and parked the car. "Just forget the last few minutes. It's not a big deal." Alex wanted to respond, but I cut him off. "I just wanted to say thank you." I smiled at him. "I had a great time tonight."

My phone started vibrating again. My mom barraged me with texts, which meant that she was pissed. I glanced at the clock. She was only going to get five hours of sleep before she needed to get up to open the shop. Because of me. Any hope to recover the romantic vibes we had before all the job talk came up was lost.

"That's my mom. I better get home," I said, lamely. I couldn't believe our date was going to end this way.

Alex tilted my chin up so that our eyes met. The blue glow from his dashboard illuminated his earnest face.

"Hey. I had fun tonight too." He leaned over the center console and kissed the corner of my mouth before planting a soft kiss on my lips. "See you next week, maybe? When I win over your parents?"

I traced his jaw with my fingers. His confidence was endearing, though misguided. "Well, you better take me home soon before my mom starts docking points."

NONE OF THE lights in the house were on. I gently closed the door and locked it behind me. I stepped out of my shoes in the hallway and reached for the banister. I got as far as the first step when my mom called me from the living room.

"Jasmine, guòlái."

*Shit.* "Ma, you didn't have to wait up for me."

"Nǐ wèishénme bù huídá? (Why didn't you respond to my messages?)"

The fact that she spoke entirely in Mandarin didn't bode well for me. If I didn't want to make her more upset, I had to respond in Mandarin too. Well, as best as I could. I walked over to my mom, who was sitting on the sofa in her pajamas, half asleep.

I checked the time on my phone. "Ma, gānggāng ten-forty. (Mom, it's only ten-forty.) It's not even late. After you texted, wǒ lìkè huí jiā. (After you texted, I came home right away.)"

"Nǐ wàngle wǒmen xūyào zǎoqǐlái? (Did you forget that we have to wake up early?) Míngtiān hěn máng. (Tomorrow will be very busy.)"

"Měitiān hěn máng. (Every day is busy.)" I slumped my shoulders, knowing where this conversation was heading.

My mom sighed heavily. "Exactly. Now I'm going to be tired tomorrow," she said, switching to English. She knew when to spread the guilt extra thick like it was smooth peanut butter.

I knew saying sorry wouldn't mean anything, so instead I said, "I'll come and open the shop with you." Realizing an opportunity presented itself, I added, "What if you and Ba take the day off? Pat and I can open the shop tomorrow."

My mom threw a skeptical look. "Are you sure? You think Pat will wake up?"

"I'll make sure he does."

My mom nodded and slid her feet into her slippers. She walked up to me and patted my shoulders to turn me toward the stairs. "You tell your boyfriend about dinner next week?"

"He's not my boyfriend," I insisted. "But yes, I asked. Maybe Sunday. Is that okay?"

"Yeah, no problem," she said, her voice as light as her steps. After getting everything she wanted out of that conversation, she was going to bed in the best of moods.

In the safety of my room, I started to change out of my clothes. I forgot I was still wearing Alex's jacket. I hugged myself, hunching my shoulders like a turtle retreating into its shell, trying to catch a whiff of his scent, before taking it off. My skin felt sticky after baking in the stadium. I took off my shirt and glanced in the mirror. It looked like my body was color-blocked, with a clearly defined line separating my pink, sunburned neck and shoulders from my pale torso. Great.

I went to take a shower and changed into an old oversize T-shirt and shorts. When I returned to my room, I unlocked my phone to set my alarm to 3:30 A.M. I turned up the ringtone. I was going to need all the help I could get to wake up that early. The crescendo of beeps ended with a loud *ping-ping*. It was a text from Linh.

> **LINH:** your date must be going well if you're too busy to respond

 156

**Jas:** it was good. but i'm already home

**Linh:** !!

**Linh:** how did it go?

**Jas:** i'll have to tell you later

**Jas:** gotta open the shop tomorrow

**Linh:** boo

**Linh:** ooh alex just got back

**Linh:** i'll just ask him;)

I wondered what Alex would say about our date. It was mostly good, with some precarious moments. I bit my thumbnail in anticipation.

**Linh:** he said a gentleman doesn't kiss and tell

**Linh:** but there was kissing right???

**Jas:** 🙈

**Linh:** you're the worst

**Linh:** ooooh!

Linh littered her texts with heart emojis.

**Jas:** what?

**Linh:** check Instagram

I swiped my phone and tapped on the app's icon. At the top of the feed was a picture of Alex's Dodger hat, sitting on his immaculate black desk. He posted it three minutes ago, with the caption "Would have stayed for extra innings #firstgame #newfan #hookedonbaseball."

I screamed inside. I fell back into my bed and stared at my phone, beaming.

How was I supposed to go to sleep now?

## Chapter 11

$P$at wasn't thrilled about getting up at the crack of dawn. He ended up sleeping on top of a sack of flour in the back of the shop for the first hour while my dad worked around him. My dad was reluctant to leave the two of us alone. Most of his concerns were directed at Pat.

"If you forget the prices, there's a menu down there." My dad pointed below the cash register when Pat woke up.

I shooed my dad out before our regulars came in. "What are you and Ma going to do today?"

He shrugged. "I don't know. No one told me about getting a day off! I'm going to sleep."

"Do something fun," I pleaded. "Take Ma to lunch. She'll like that."

"We'll see. Good luck, you guys!"

Once he left, I instructed Pat to set aside a few plain cake donuts and glazed donuts. We needed some for our test batch. Since he was home, I tasked him with coming up with some new flavor ideas, based on some of the data my mom collected. We knew our dad would not go for fancy, complicated flavors that would take too much time to make. That meant we weren't going to get up to the $3.50 price point, but we couldn't do anything too simple or else we wouldn't make much more money than we did now. We had to strike a happy medium.

We worked through the morning rush or, I should say, *I* worked the morning rush while Pat dithered around amidst the chaos. He was so slow at packaging a dozen donuts that I left him at the cashier to ring everyone up. Most of our regulars paid with exact change, making Pat's job super easy.

Once the crowd died down, I bugged Pat for his ideas. I was anxious to get started. He pulled out his phone to show me some pictures of donuts we could use for inspiration, a.k.a. copy. I scrolled through a short list of options.

"Is that it? I can't even tell what they are." The donuts weren't too different from what we currently sold, other than their brightly colored icing.

"These are priced at $2.75 at that shop near the high school. The flavors are more unique, though. That purple one is ube."

I shook my head. "Dad's not a pastry chef and he doesn't know what ube is." I thought back to some of the shops I spied on with my mom. "The easiest thing to do is to try new toppings. Or . . ." I looked back at Pat's phone. "Like this one." I pointed at a white iced donut that had a simple chocolate drizzle accent. "Dad could do that. We just have to pair it up with the right flavor." I began typing out a shopping list on Pat's phone.

"Here. Go to the restaurant supply store and buy new trays for toppings and some piping bags. Then go to the grocery store to pick up all this stuff."

Pat's eyes widened as he read the list. "You want me to buy all this?"

"Yeah. Go now. Once you get back, we're going to need all the time we can get."

Pat came back two hours later. I helped him unload everything onto the workbench, trying to create some sort of organized system.

"So, I got everything. This stuff, I get," he said, pulling out a box of Froot Loops. He reached to the bottom of the shopping bag and held up a jar of black sesame seeds. "But what the heck is this for?"

"I don't know yet. Testing out an idea."

"Are you sure you know what you're doing?"

I put on an apron and tied a knot in the back. "Yeah," I said with the kind of false confidence that came from watching hours and hours of competitive baking shows. "We got this."

I put Pat in charge of helping customers while I worked in our newly anointed test kitchen. I grabbed a new tray and poured the Froot Loops on one side and crushed Oreos into the other. With a spatula, I smoothed out the tray of white vanilla icing. I twisted a plain donut into the frosting and then dipped it in the crushed Oreos. It didn't look half bad. Dad would have made it look much neater. I placed the Oreo donut on a rack and made a Froot Loop donut.

Pat came back to check on my progress. "Hey, those look good."

"Yeah, this was the easy part." I shook the jar of sesame seeds in his face. "You ready for black sesame donuts?"

"Are you fucking serious? Like the black sesame candy Grandma would have with her tea?" Pat stuck his tongue out in disgust. "Are you an old auntie?"

"Hey! They make black-sesame-flavor boba. I think we can make it a donut."

Pat watched in horror as I dipped a donut into the sesame seeds. In my head, I envisioned a nice even layer of black sesame seeds, dotted equidistant from one another, like the inside of a dragon fruit. However, when I turned it over, it looked more like a black, sandy paste.

I held it up to Pat's nose, which he promptly crinkled. "Wanna try it?"

"Nope."

"Chicken." I took a big, daring bite, which was the wrong move. The thick coating of sesame seeds left a dry mouthfeel, causing me to cough when I tried to swallow it.

Pat turned his head away, unable to watch. "All right. That's a dud."

"No, wait," I said as I coughed into my elbow. "It kind of tastes okay. Too sweet, though. I just have to approach this from a different angle. Try different proportions." I put the donut aside and assessed my remaining ingredients. I scooped out some vanilla icing into a small mixing bowl and tossed in a few tablespoons of sesame seeds. I searched the entire work-bench until I found salt on the shelf above. I threw in a pinch and mixed it together as it blended into a light gray color. When it had the right consistency, I twisted a plain donut into it and once again, offered it to Pat.

He accepted the donut tentatively, examining it with his lip curled as if I had offered him a poison apple. He nibbled at it and let it melt in his mouth. I waited with bated breath until he finally shared his verdict.

"It's kind of good. It could use more salt." He looked at it thoughtfully. "Can it be less gray?"

I took a small bite and agreed with his assessment. "All right." I clapped my hands together. "We are getting somewhere. Here's the plan. Keep a lookout on the front. I'm going to keep mixing different flavors. Let's regroup and pick the top five options. Sound good?"

Pat nodded and departed from our imaginary locker-room pep talk.

"Wait. One more thing, Pat."

"What is it?"

"Can you get me a glass of water?" I started bouncing on my feet, my sugar high taking off. "There's sesame seeds stuck all over my teeth." I displayed all of my speckled teeth in a wide smile.

Pat rolled his eyes at me. "You're so embarrassing, jie."

I toiled at the workbench like a mad scientist, fueled by the influx of sugar. However, my enthusiasm came crashing down.

Taking bites out of multiple donuts with incompatible flavors made my stomach churn. There were fails, like clogging the pastry filler machine in an attempt at making a peanut-butter-and-jelly-filled donut. Some showed promise, like the coconut-pineapple donut, topped with toasted coconut flakes. The pineapple made the icing soggy, though. In the end, after all that work, Pat and I agreed on our five varieties: Froot Loops, cookies and cream, black sesame, matcha green tea, and a Neapolitan donut, made with a swirl of our existing vanilla, strawberry, and chocolate icing.

There were enough plain donuts left in our display case to make three of each kind. I started working on them when Pat asked a very good question. "So, jie, how do you expect these to sell?"

I frowned as I twisted a donut in my green matcha icing. "Uh . . . we make a sign?"

He looked out at our empty storefront. "That might work . . . *if* there were people to read the sign."

"I didn't think that far ahead." Honestly, all I envisioned was putting the donuts among the rest of them, hoping the next customer that came in would be intrigued by our exciting new offerings. As I finished each donut, I arranged them on a tray rack to allow the icing to set. Once all the donuts were iced, I took a step back to look at my hard work.

"What do you think? Do they look like the ones on Instagram?" I wiped my forehead with my apron.

Pat smacked my arm. "Duh, jie. We should post it on Instagram, so it could go viral."

"I don't think it works like that, Pat." I picked up the tray and handed it to Pat. "But I think I know someone who can help. Take these out to the front. The lighting is better out there."

I called Rae, and she came within thirty minutes. She was happy to help and happier when I told her she would be paid with free donuts. Rae gave me a big hug when she barreled into the shop.

"Jas! I was drooling when I saw the cute donuts!" She let me go and treated Pat to a squeeze. "Pat! I haven't seen you in so long!" She stepped back and held him at arm's length. "Since when did you get so tall?"

I forgot what a flirt Rae could be, and judging by Pat's blushing face, he fell for it. I needed her to reserve her effervescence to attract people *into* the shop, not for those of us who were already here.

"So, Rae. I just created an Instagram account for Sunshine Donuts and took a few pictures of the donuts. Can you help us make it look cool or something?"

Rae gave the shop an appraising look. "These donuts look great, but no offense—cool is not your brand."

"Excuse me?" I was about to rescind my offer for free donuts.

"Sunshine Donuts is more like cute homey mom-and-pop style. We can work with that!" Rae detected my skepticism and held out her hand for my phone. "I'll show you."

With my phone in her possession, Rae's thumbs worked their magic. For the pictures of our new donuts, she wrote descriptive captions, interjecting well-placed buzzwords like *handcrafted* or *seasonal*. She stepped outside into our parking lot to take a picture of the storefront and included a lovely short narrative about how our family-owned business has operated for the last twenty years.

"Too bad your parents aren't here. It would have been cute to take a family photo of you guys at the shop."

"Uh, maybe next time," I said. "So, how do we get followers?"

"Both of you should follow the account and share it with your friends. It's a local shop, so spreading the news throughout our networks might work best. I'll do the same."

Pat and I did as we were told. I wasn't sure how much good it would do. We didn't have many followers, unlike Rae, who had a huge following of acquaintances.

I watched as Rae littered her captions with hashtags. "So . . . is this what you do for work?"

"Kind of," she said. She looked up at me with a gleam in her eyes. "Why? You thinking about applying for my old job? You should do it."

"I don't know. I don't know anything about social media or digital anything."

"Honestly, my *ACM* job is not rocket science. They'll train you. *I'll* train you. As long as you're willing to learn and if you like what *ACM* is about, then you'll do fine. I'd rather someone I like take over my job than some random person."

"Why are you leaving then?"

"I just . . . outgrew it, ya know?" She shrugged. "I was ready to try something different."

That was a feeling I could relate to, now more than ever. If I had to spend what little time I had away from the shop watching other people's donut shops, I was going to lose it.

When we were done with our posts, I asked Rae, "So, what's next?"

"We wait," she said simply. She looked at the donuts we plated for pictures. "You should keep these on display on the front counter. I can help you make a sign."

I smirked at Pat. "A sign sounds like a *great* idea."

He returned an unaffected blink. "I'll go find some paper and a pen."

I heard the door open and I quickly put on my brightest smile for the customer. I was eager to see what kind of reception our new donuts would get. It was a good thing Rae was still here. She could assist me with promoting them.

"Welcome to Sun   " My customers looked like a couple of freeloaders. "What are you guys doing here?"

Kayley and Michael took note of my surprise.

"Rae texted us about free donuts," Kayley said, her eyes popping when she saw the new display.

I knew it. Freeloaders.

"These look so good," Kayley said.

I slapped her hand when she reached for one. "Wait. I have some in the back you can sample."

"She means the ugly ones," Pat said, showing up with a hap-hazard sign that read !!NEW DONUTS!!

Rae snatched the sign away, shaking her head with disapproval, and made Pat hand over the marker to fix it. "I told them free donuts after they check in and promote the shop on their accounts too."

I came back out with some of the test donuts cut up into bite-size pieces. My friends circled in on them like vultures. Rae took selfies with all of us, posting them all on the shop's Instagram account.

Kayley licked green icing off her fingers. "The matcha one is my favorite."

The positive feedback made my heart swell. I made these cute-ass donuts.

*I did this. I. Did. This. I DID THIS!*

"Who do this?!" I was so wrapped up in my own self-congratulation that I didn't notice my dad coming in.

Pat swiftly pointed at me, that narc. Knees bent, my dad stood in front of the glass display case, squinting at the tray of brand-new donuts. My friends retreated back and sat down at a nearby table, forming a little peanut gallery. My mom came around behind the front counter and lifted her glasses while she scrutinized my work. She picked up a sample of the black sesame donut, sniffed it, and popped it into her mouth.

"Why are you back so soon?" I asked as my mom chewed.

"You make this?" When she swallowed, she frowned. "Too

sweet for me." She turned around to peek into the back. I ran past her and blocked the entryway.

"If I knew you were coming back so soon, I would have cleaned up," I explained. "Why *are* you here, anyway?"

"Why not? It's our shop." She recollected her day. After my dad got home and took a nap, they went out to lunch and ran errands. "Then I check the camera and see all your friends. I see *that*." She pointed at the donuts. "I want to see for myself."

"What do you think?"

Her head bounced as she tossed thoughts around. "It look almost like the ones from the other shop. Baba can make it look more clean. Where did you buy the stuff? Show me the receipt." Pat handed the receipt over. My mom unfolded it, holding it tautly with both hands like she was reading a scroll. She mouthed the prices as she ran down the list. "Why the tea so expensive? Is it a big pack? How much you use?" She looked over my shoulder.

"Uh . . ." I wasn't sure how to tell her that I dumped the entire bag in the small batch of icing.

A customer came in right then, buying me some time. My mom stayed behind, watching closely while Pat assisted the customer. I'd never seen him before. He casually mentioned that he was a regular customer of the liquor store next door and had always passed our shop, but it was his first time coming in. He scanned the display case until he rested his eyes on the new donuts. He ordered a half dozen and didn't hesitate when Pat told him the total price.

I jumped in as Pat rang the customer up. "If you like them, can you leave us a Yelp review? If you show us the Yelp review next time, we'll give you a free medium coffee."

"Okay." He grabbed the bag of donuts. "Thanks."

When the door closed behind him, my mom grabbed my shoulders from behind. "He pay sixteen dollars and fifty cents?! For six donuts?!" I turned around and saw my mom's appalled face. No doubt she was thinking about all the things she'd rather buy with $16.50. She glanced at the receipt again. "Where did you buy all this?"

It was my turn to point at Pat. "Ask him."

She folded the receipt and stuffed it in her pocket. "We're going to need more. Pat, you take me." She glanced at me. "You stay here with Baba."

"No, he should go home and rest." *Wait. Where is he?*

A clang came from the back followed by the sound of trays being stacked on top of one another.

"What you do to the filling machine?! Sïle, is this peanut butter?!"

I winced and jogged back to the workbench. "I'm sorry, Ba. I'll clean it up. You need to go home and sleep." I stacked all the mixing bowls that I used for my experiment and hooked the filling machine under my arm and took them to the sink.

My dad stood beside me as I sprayed the icing away. Wagging his finger at me, he said, "This is the last time you touch my stuff." I flipped the lid on the filling machine and scraped out the brown-and-red slop. My dad shook his head in disbelief. "Hmph! Peanut butter . . ."

"Jas! Your friends are leaving!" my mom called out.

I rinsed my hands and walked my dad out. My mom was on the phone, calling different vendors with Pat nearby to read the list of ingredients on the receipt. I boxed up a dozen donuts for Kayley and Rae before we hugged goodbye.

"Thanks for everything today, Rae. I owe you."

"Don't worry about it. Send me your résumé, okay? ASAP!"

My mom looked on curiously and covered the cordless phone receiver with her hand. "Jas. You sure you're going to be okay . . . *by yourself*?"

"Yeah." They weren't going to be out long. What was she so worried about?

"I can stay for a while . . . if that helps," Michael chimed in suddenly, still sitting at the table in the corner.

I froze. Of all things, that was the last thing I expected Michael to say. Boyfriend Michael would never, but I guess Friend Michael would. Pat, who was standing behind my mom, widened his eyes at me. *I don't know where this is going, either, dude!*

My mom put on her polite customer-service smile. "Michael, right?"

"Yes," he said, taken aback by the recognition. He pursed his lips, suppressing his smile. "I won't be in your way," he said to me. "You know, to help you keep an eye out if you still need to clean stuff up."

"You really don't need to," I said, after gathering my wits.

My mom finished her phone call and rested the phone on the counter. She glanced at her watch. "We need to go." Her eyes darted between Michael and me. "We'll be back soon." When she and Pat walked past me by the door, she gave me a pointed look. A warning. She knew something was up.

I needed to rein this in. After they drove off, Michael leaned back in his chair, smiling broadly at me.

"What are you smiling at?" I stepped toward the front counter when I heard Michael stand up. I swung around and pointed at him, pinning him to that spot from across the room. "You need to stay there."

Michael reluctantly lowered himself back into his seat. "You told your mom about me."

What was that? Disbelief or hope in that statement? No no. This was messing with my head. I had to get ahead of this quick. "I had to." I pointed at the cameras that perched on the ceiling corners. "She saw you the last time you came by. I told her that you were my *friend*." I made it around the front counter and planted both hands flat on the cold stainless steel. I looked him square in the eye. "You really don't need to stay."

Michael leaned his elbows on the table. "I was told I would get free donuts for my services." He gestured to the empty table before him. "Services were rendered, but I don't have donuts yet."

I tilted my head, narrowing my eyes at him. Was this guy for real right now? How could he sit there and act like we were the same two people who sat in fourth-period class together? Or was I reading this all wrong and making it a big deal when it shouldn't be? Was this what it was like to be friends with an ex?

He matched my expression, mocking me.

"Come on. I'll let you know if a customer comes in. Make sure no one bothers you."

I stared at him, making sure he was sincere about it. I reached under the counter for a red basket and lined it with parchment paper. I grabbed a pair of tongs and threw in a maple bar—Michael's favorite. I slid it across the counter. A truce. "I shouldn't be long." There wasn't much to clean up except for that filling machine. That was going to require some meticulous scrubbing to get the peanut butter out of its nooks and crannies. "Just shout from there if I don't come right out."

He stepped up to the front counter and slid the basket toward him. "You got it."

I left him standing there as he took a bite. I went right to work, sweeping deviant toppings off the workbench. I washed icing off the bowls and trays I used. In between tasks, I popped my head up to the small window in the wall that separated the front and back of the shop, checking for customers. All I would see was Michael sitting back in his seat, browsing his phone or eating his donut in prim bites. Honestly, how could he eat so slow? It was all I could think about as I chipped at the peanut butter gunk stuck inside the filling machine. It was the reason why we used to run late to fifth period. Well, except for the times we were making out in the—

*No! Abort! Abort! Don't go there.*

I was getting nowhere with this stupid machine. I slammed it on the counter, which, incidentally, made the last remaining peanut butter and jelly ooze out of its tubes.

"Jas?"

"Everything's fine," I replied to Michael, assuming he was curious about the loud noise.

"Good to know. Um, the phone's for you."

The phone? I washed my hands and walked out to the front. Michael held the shop's phone out to me, his face unreadable. I gripped its antenna and slid it next to my ear, keeping a wary eye on Michael.

"Hello? This is Jasmine."

"Hey." It was Alex. *Why was he calling the landline?*

I wasn't sure why that was the first question I thought of. Perhaps it was from the feeling that two worlds that were not meant to overlap were somehow colliding, like everything was blurring together while hanging upside down. Alex was in my ear, but I was looking at Michael and none of it made sense.

I turned around and walked into the back of the shop to get some air. "Hey. What's going on?"

"I tried your cell, but it kept going to voicemail. I thought you'd want to know that I can make it to dinner next week. I got ahold of my mom. She wasn't sure if she could make it. I gave her your address just in case, but I wouldn't count on her coming. So, I hope your parents will be happy with just me."

I smiled, relieved I didn't have to meet his mom yet. "I'll be happy with just you."

"I have some time to chat." I could hear Alex's smile.

"I can't. I'm the only one at the shop right now."

"What about the guy who picked up the phone?"

I lowered my voice. "What about him?"

"Is he a new employee?"

"Uh . . . no." I looked out the small window. Michael finally finished his maple bar and bussed his own table. "He's my friend." It was the truth. Michael and I were friends. Nothing more. It was a fact.

"Okay then. I'll let you go." Then, after a beat, he said, "I miss you."

He said it, firm and clear. It was enough to get my heart rate going. There was something vulnerable about it, though. Like he was testing the waters.

So, I said, "I miss you too." Because it was true. I was laying down all kinds of facts today, and in case he needed more, I added, "Can't wait to see you on Sunday."

"Me too. Talk to you soon."

I walked back out to the front to dock the phone back into its charging station and found myself alone, with an empty red basket on the front counter.

Michael left without saying goodbye. Why would he do that? It didn't feel right, so I texted him.

**JAS:** sorry I didn't get a chance to thank you before you left.

**JAS:** Don't text and drive!

Because I said that, it took a while before he replied back.

**MICHAEL:** No prob. Thought I should leave before your
    mom got back
**MICHAEL:** Like old times;)

Oh hell no. What was I supposed to say to that? I couldn't frame any of my thoughts into words and I was ready to send a bunch of alarmed, embarrassed, and exploding brain emojis when he ended our conversation with this:

**MICHAEL:** jk jk ttyl

He better jk! What the heck was wrong with him? Did he think we were at the point where we could laugh at our past?

I sat down on the stool, propping my face up on the front counter. I felt the ache travel up my back and down my legs. I hadn't sat down during this marathon of a day, but it was worth it. It was the push my parents needed to make the necessary changes, not only to make rent but hopefully feel secure enough to finally hire someone. Phase one of my plan was in motion. It was time to work on phase two.

## Chapter 12

*I* muddled the lemon slice in my iced tea while Linh sat across from me at Lucky Island Café. Nothing like eating Hong Kong–style comfort food while Linh helped me pad my résumé. Normally, our leisurely eating would annoy the waitstaff, but we were one of three tables seated in the dining room. They had no one else to wait on but us.

Linh pulled my laptop closer and pointed at the big empty space at the bottom of my résumé. "I thought you finished your résumé."

"I did! I didn't know what else to write. There are only so many things I can say about working at the donut shop."

She read through my bullet points.

- Sell donuts seven days a week
- Clean donut shop
- Restock items as needed

"Seriously? You can't say this." She deleted everything off my résumé except for my name and contact information.

"Hey! Why'd you do that? That's what I actually do at my job."

She ignored me as she typed a new—much longer—bullet point and turned the laptop toward me to review her work.

- Conducted market research to gather consumer data that informed the development of new products aimed to double the profit margin.

I glanced at Linh over my glasses. "You know this is a lie."

"How is this a lie? This is what you and your mom did all those times being sketchy in the parking lot. And the donuts are selling out!"

That part was true. It took a few days for the social media campaign to get traction. During that time, I went into the shop early to tweak the recipes with my dad. It turned out, for the black sesame donut, less was more, and my dad figured out how to keep the flavor without the muddy gray color. The matcha donut was the biggest hit, selling out every day this past week. My mom choked at the price of matcha powder, but she found comfort when new customers flocked in and paid three dollars each for them.

"It's not exactly the truth," I countered.

"It's not entirely a lie, either. It's . . . it's *based* on the truth," she maintained.

I blinked at Linh. "You know, you're going to be a scary good lawyer."

Linh smiled at the dig, thinking it was a compliment. She hounded me for what she considered more impressive-sounding tasks like negotiating with vendors and creating—nay—*launching* a social media marketing campaign. Some were more truth-like than others. When we moved on from the donut shop, she asked, "Why didn't you include your experience at the ticket office?"

"I was only there for three months."

Linh pointed at the blank white gap on my screen. "You don't have anything to lose but empty space." She typed it in, making it sound better than I could have.

- Processed ticket transactions for large-scale Division 1 sports events including football, gymnastics, and volleyball.

Seriously? That was a lot of words just to say that I sold tickets.

"Did you do anything else in college?" Even after we played around with the margins and the font, there was still about three inches of blank space left.

I reviewed the brief job description Rae texted me. On top of managing *ACM*'s social media accounts, this job included event planning, identifying trends through analytics to inform *ACM*'s broader marketing strategies, and promoting their brand and community engagement. "I don't have experience doing any of these things." I felt so pathetic. What did I even do in college besides analyzing all the bad things happening in the world?

"Didn't you help set up those movie screenings?" Linh asked.

"Unofficially." Thinking back, I couldn't believe I was so desperate to find a boyfriend that I helped Justin all those times. I cringed at the thought.

"Who cares? Let's put it under Volunteer Experience." Linh continued typing. "Did you do any research projects?"

"Yeah, but for research methods. It's not relevant at all." I thought back to my coursework. "Well, I guess I could put that." Might as well since we were throwing in anything I could pass off as my qualifications. "I did learn stats and how to analyze data sets."

"See? Now we have something we can work with." Linh furiously typed and managed to fill up most of the page. I might actually be hirable. "You have a couple more lines to go. How about some interests? I saw it on Owen's résumé. It could be something to show your personality."

I shrugged. "I have the personality of a couch potato. What can you say that wouldn't make me sound like a loser?"

Linh turned toward me and waited until I met her eyes. "Come on, Jas. If you're going to talk to me like that, how are you going to talk about yourself during the actual interview? You might think I'm exaggerating about your work, but you can't deny that you did these things. If you don't own it, who will?" She looked back at the blinking cursor on my résumé.

When she had her lightbulb moment, she typed quickly and finished with a hard tap on the Enter key. "There."

I read the list of interests she added for me. "Are you serious?" I tossed her a skeptical look. "You're going to put 'Marvel movies, baking, and Dodger baseball' on my résumé? It sounds like a dating profile."

"So what? Owen has 'Playing Texas Hold'em' on his résumé. Plus, *Angel City Magazine* is a lifestyle magazine. It's all relevant."

I scrolled through my updated résumé. It was as good as it was going to get. I saved the file and emailed it to Rae.

"Now what?" I asked.

"Now you have to practice saying how amazing you are, and after that, we raid your closet to make sure you have something to wear."

I groaned. "I guess that's one thing I'll miss about working at the shop. I won't get to bum around in T-shirts and leggings anymore."

"A big-girl job requires big-girl clothes. Welcome to adulting," Linh said as she dug into her baked pork chop rice.

"Yaaaaay," I said weakly.

I let Linh grill me with interview questions. Even though it was just practice, I quickly became overwhelmed. I didn't know what I was going to do next week, let alone five years from now. How was I supposed to come across as confident when I still didn't feel like I amounted to anything? I was as basic as they come. Like Helvetica, but in human form. Linh made interviewing look so effortless.

"Jas, just be yourself," Linh said. What a cliché load of crap.

"That's what I've been doing and look where that got me. I might be better off pretending to be you." I polished off my plate of sizzling udon covered in XO sauce.

"You don't have to pretend to be me." Linh pushed my laptop in front of me, zooming in on my résumé. "You really did all of this. Why can't you see that?"

I slammed my laptop shut and stared at the tablecloth. "It's hard to talk positively about something that I *had* to do, you know? Am I happy that I helped bring more business to the shop? Yeah, but it's a means to an end. Even this job—which I'm not qualified for—is just a way to get out of the shop, but I know I can't say that when they ask me why I'm interested in working there or what my passion is. What *is* my fucking passion, anyway? Breaking out of the shop without my parents questioning all my life choices? Which is fucking ironic considering all my life choices have revolved around the things they wanted. It's all bullshit."

I looked up to Linh's wide, concerned eyes. During my rant, the restaurant had filled up. Nosy aunties and uncles were staring at me. I guess I spoke louder than I thought.

Linh rubbed my arm to comfort me. "Have you told your parents any of that?"

"*Pfft.* I wouldn't know how to begin explaining any of that." This was where the gap in our language competency divided us. Whenever I tried to express how I felt—in Mandarin or English—it sounded like I was whining about trivial things. My parents weren't heartless, but the trauma they had endured hardened them in ways I didn't fully understand.

There were times when they recounted stories with dry eyes, like how my aunt Shelly escaped the labor camp. Yet on other days, my dad would turn away whenever I wore an army-green military-style jacket, deriding the concept of military as a fashion aesthetic under his breath. There were constant reminders—whether they said it or not—of their sacrifices, of their lives interrupted. It was easy to see why they pushed for what they thought were surefire ways toward stability and success. So, it seemed like the right thing to do was to do what they wanted. When it was hard to do that, it was easier to lie.

"It might be worth trying." When I was unmoved, Linh added, "You can't keep lighting both ends of the candle doing everything they want. The only person who gets burned is you. It's what got you here, isn't it?"

The passing comment about my senior year was enough to make my stomach double over. Why would she press this issue when she knew I was living with the consequences since graduation? She knew how hard it was on me. She'd witnessed it all firsthand.

Sensing that I'd had my fill of truths for the night, Linh changed the subject. "Are you ready for dinner on Sunday?"

"Yeah. I thought Alex would be nervous about meeting my parents, but he seems fine." He was unusually calm about it.

Every time I tried to prepare him for my parents, he brushed off my concerns, instead asking questions about me like my birthday, my favorite ice cream flavor, and if aliens invaded the Earth, which superhero would I want to be. Sailor Moon, obviously.

"I may have told him a few conversation starters for your parents. To get the ball rolling."

"Linh . . ."

"It's going to be fine. You wait and see. You're going to thank me."

Oh no. Where was this going? "Will I?"

"Yes, you will. You're going to be overcome with gratitude. So much so that you will want to take me to the airport when I leave for NYU."

Aw, man. Why do I always get stuck with chauffeuring people to the airport? "What about Owen?"

"He's going to be out of town for work." Linh pouted. She clasped her hands and gave me her best puppy-dog eyes. "Please."

"Fine." I gathered up my laptop and paid for the check. "This is how you know I love you."

I POURED A twenty-five-pound bag of powdered sugar into the commercial Hobart mixer, causing a cloud to puff up toward my face. My dad called, reminding me to make more vanilla glaze. I reassured him that I would do it. That was three hours ago, when my mom left to prepare for tonight's dinner with

Alex. She didn't tell me what she had planned, but it must be elaborate because she sent Pat out to pick up more groceries.

Now it was an hour until closing and I had to haul ass if I wanted to get home before Alex arrived. I measured water and vanilla extract and added them to the mixing bowl, setting it at the lowest speed. Over the noise, I heard the door chime and rushed to the front counter from the back of the shop.

"Hi! How can I—" Alex's smile stopped me in my tracks. I crossed my arms as if it would cover up my sugar-dusted clothes. "What are you doing here? I told you to meet at my house at six-thirty."

"I wanted to come early. See if I could help out. I almost went to your house, but I figured you'd be here." Alex didn't look like he was here to wash grease off the trays. He was wearing a light gray button-down shirt and dark jeans. It projected a nice-boy image aimed to ease any concerns from my parents, but the fitted silhouette had a different effect on me.

I swung the door open to let him in behind the front counter. "And what did you think you'd help me with?"

"I can show you if you want."

He crossed the threshold, angling his face toward mine, his hand on my waist. It was so smooth. So easy. So naive. Words couldn't describe the delicious sensation of Alex's parted lips pressed against my palm.

Alex's eyes popped open over my hand, which held his face away from mine.

"There are cameras all over the shop. You behave yourself," I warned. "This is a place of business."

"Yes, ma'am." He couldn't hold back his lopsided smile as he mocked my serious tone. It was so annoyingly cute that all I could do was shake my head and return to the task at hand.

I picked up a clean apron for him as we made our way to the back of the shop. Alex lowered his head as I hung the strap around his neck, like I was giving him a gold medal. Before I could tie the straps around his waist, Alex wrapped his fingers around my wrists and held them in place until my hands rested on his shoulders. He folded me into a warm embrace for a slow, tender kiss.

"I've been waiting over a week to tell you that," he said in a register that sounded like it was reserved only for me.

"Okay." I took a deep breath as my heartbeat picked up. No, wait. That was the paddle whipping the glaze. I snapped out of my dreamy stupor and tied the apron around his waist. "Message received. We have to get back to work."

Alex frowned. "That's it?"

What did he want? A round of applause? I narrowed my eyes at him. "Yes," I said, emphatically. "I have less than an hour to finish this and close the shop. And then there's dinner. So, chop-chop!"

I flipped the switch to turn off the mixer, scraping the sides of the bowl with a spatula, before turning it back on for its final spin. While we waited for all the sugar to get incorporated, I poked his biceps. Ooh. Firm.

"You might want to stretch."

I lowered the mixing bowl when the glaze reached the perfect consistency, bending down to scrape every last drop from the mixing paddle. Alex took my advice and stretched his arms, which brought the hem of his light gray button-down shirt up to the edge of his dark-washed jeans. If that wasn't enough of a tease, he began rolling up his sleeves, revealing his capable forearms. I couldn't pinpoint what about it made it feel scandalous. I dragged my eyes away before he made it to his elbows.

What was wrong with me? Calves, forearms, and elbows. Oh my!

I pointed at one of the handles, instructing Alex to grab one side of the bowl while I held the other. With our combined strength, we lifted the heavy stainless-steel bowl and set it on top of our icing station. I slid the cover back, exposing an empty angled vat.

"How would you have done this if I wasn't here?" Alex asked.

"I would have scooped it into a tray and then dumped the tray in here. This is much faster, so thank you." I peeked past the bowl. Alex was mesmerized by the ribbon of glaze pooling below. "Are you all right over there?"

"I just want to swim in there."

I scraped the sides of the bowl to speed things along. "Pretty sure that violates FDA regulations."

After that was done, Alex helped me carry it to the sink so I could spray it down. While I was at it, I rinsed the remaining empty trays. Before I could tell him to stand away from the splash zone, Alex picked up a towel to help me dry.

"Is this how you imagined spending your Sunday evening?" I shouted as I blasted water over the plastic tray.

"No, but I can't complain," he replied during a quiet moment.

I gave him a sidelong glance. He needed to reserve his charms for dinner. "What would you have done otherwise?"

Alex shrugged as he wiped down the last tray. "Usually, I'd catch up on some emails to get ready for the workweek. Maybe watch TV. Not as exciting as being a secret agent conspiring in the takedown of Big Donut." I rolled my eyes at his hyperbolic description. "Is there anything else I can help you with?"

There were plenty of things I could think of, but none of them had anything to do with closing the shop.

"Hmm," I mulled as I dried my hands with a dish towel. "You see that stool over there?" I jutted my chin toward the front counter. "I need you to sit over there and look pretty."

Alex laughed as he reached behind to untie his apron. "Seriously?"

"Yes, seriously," I mimicked. Like it was such a hard task. "Restocking things is not a two-person job. Besides, you're distracting."

Alex took off his apron, mussing up his hair in the process. As if he was trying to prove my point, he ran his fingers through his hair in a way that needed to be saved as a gif to be replayed forever. It wasn't the fact that it was *his* hand in *his* hair, although both of those things were pretty great. No, it was the way his eyes flicked up to mine, catching me openly gawking at him, lost in thought wondering how easily he could take off more articles of clothing. His lips curled into a smirk as he tossed his apron aside.

"I didn't know I was that distracting." His eyes danced like a crackling flame. He took a step forward and another until I backed myself up against the sink. His hands landed on either side of me, surrounding me, as he lowered his head. "I'm sorry," he said, his voice dipping in a way that did not convey contrition in the slightest. "Am I in your way?"

I tried to level a disapproving look, but who was I kidding? If the hitch in my breath wasn't already a dead giveaway, my fingers glided up the trail of buttons on his shirt, itching to undo them. When my hands reached his face, Alex leaned impossibly closer, hovering his tempting lips over mine.

"Hello?" a man shouted over the warbly chime that was starting to sound more like a dying cow every day.

Damn it. I pushed Alex—who looked more amused than displeased—off me and readjusted my ponytail.

"You." I pointed at Alex and then at the chair. "Sit."

"Can I at least get a donut?" He had the audacity to look at me with pleading eyes like he was so innocent.

I wasn't feeling particularly generous after our spell was broken. "No. My mom plans to stuff you with food, so don't ruin your appetite."

Alex pouted as he took his seat. Served him right, though his disappointment didn't last long. He settled into a comfortable position, his left arm hanging off the front counter, getting a side view of all the behind-the-counter action. Putting Alex in the corner proved to be a lost cause. Sitting didn't preclude him from exchanging glances as I walked back and forth between the front and back of the shop or greeting customers with his charming smile. One woman couldn't take her eyes off him, but I don't think Alex noticed. Not when I felt his eyes follow me as I bent down to get the sprinkled donut that lady was pointing at.

I wasn't doing anything out of the ordinary—this was actually my job—but there was something about having Alex's attention that made me feel confident. So, I made a split-second decision that if he was going to watch, I might as well give him something to look at.

I placed my hands on my slightly bent knees, arching my back before I slowly cat-stretched up to close out the order. Part of me felt a little ridiculous, trying to be sexy in my torn jeans and unisex Two Door Cinema Club T-shirt that did nothing for my figure. But when the customer left, leaving me alone with Alex once again, seeing the look on his face made the extra effort to stand up worth it.

Alex leaned his back against the wall with his right foot on the bottom rung of the stool. His hooded eyes traveled up to my face while I hung back at the register a few feet away.

"What?" I asked as I printed today's sales and shut down the register.

"I saw what you did."

I gave him a halfhearted shrug and shut off all the lights. "I don't know what you're talking about."

Though it was dark inside the shop, the setting sun cast a soft orange glow through the floor-to-ceiling windowpanes, illuminating Alex's playful lopsided smile. "Oh, okay. I see how this is."

"What?" I prodded again, leaning my hip against the front counter beside him, pretending to look at my nails.

"You're not as sweet as you look."

I glanced up, meeting his heated gaze with a smirk. "I never said that I was."

Alex's eyebrow quirked as he chuckled to himself, taken aback by my response. The feeling was mutual. I wasn't sure how he brought this side out of me, but whatever it was, it was palpable, with the buzzing from our neon sign giving us sound effects.

"Thank you for helping me," I said, pushing myself up. "Sorry if I was a little bossy."

"That's okay," Alex said as he sat up, perching on the edge of his seat. "I liked watching you work."

"I was aware," I started to say as I inched closer. "You know," I added conspiratorially, "you can't really see this spot on the security tape."

That was enough for Alex to hook a finger into one of my belt loops. With one swift pull, I stumbled forward. I wrapped my hands around his neck as I crashed into him. Alex caught my gasp with his hungry kiss. He made deliberate moves—the slip of his tongue, his hand pressing the small of my back until I practically straddled him. He was in complete control while I was left breathless.

"So," I managed to say in between kisses. "I take it you're a butt guy."

His splayed hands gave me a quick squeeze. "You have a good butt." Then he nipped at my bottom lip. "Your mouth's not so bad, either."

Alex's assessment of my butt and my mouth—neither of which I had ever considered on the good/bad spectrum—were the two sexiest compliments I'd ever received. I'd never been one to take compliments well, so I did what I normally did in such cases. I replied with gratitude and reciprocated a compliment to deflect attention. This strategy seemed to backfire because Alex rolled in his lip as he looked up at the ceiling with a befuddled expression.

"Did you just say I have sexy calves?" His eyes twinkled as he laughed. "I don't think anyone has ever said that to me before."

Well, shit. What was I supposed to say to that? That I couldn't think straight because it took all of my energy not to roll my hips into his?

I scrambled off him before I lost my damn mind. What the hell was I doing, making out at the shop? It was the craziest thing I'd done in a long time. I straightened my shirt and smoothed my hair so I didn't arrive home looking like a lusty-eyed monster. "We should go before they come looking for us."

## Chapter 13

*Y*ou're not worried about this at all, are you?" I watched Alex grab multiple gift bags and a large bouquet of flowers out of his car. He walked toward me with a confident stride.

"I'm telling you; parents love me."

"You don't know my parents," I warned. "They are going to break you."

Alex laughed. "Okay. Let's make a bet. If I win your parents over, you have to go hiking with me next weekend."

"Fine, but if they break you with their questions, you have to take me to that ice cream place by your apartment. The one where the cones are churros. You're gonna want to eat your feelings."

"Deal," he said with great certainty. We shook on it. I reached for the flowers, but Alex pulled them away. "These aren't for you," he said matter-of-factly. He proceeded to walk toward the front door, leaving me and my dropped jaw on the driveway.

After introducing himself to Alex, Pat called out, "Hurry, jie. Mom needs help with dinner."

"Let me change—" I started to say when I reached the front door.

"Jas! Kuài diǎn!" my mom yelled from the kitchen. I quickly took off my shoes and wished Alex luck. I headed toward the enticing aroma. My eyes widened when I stepped into the kitchen.

"What the heck, Ma?"

Plates of food lined the kitchen counter—fried rice, shaking beef, stir-fried vegetables, and bundles of vermicelli rice noodles fanned around a yellow plastic colander. My mom ignored me, too busy stir-frying rice cakes with shredded pork.

"Finish that," she ordered, pointing at the mortar and pestle.

I walked over and saw chunks of boiled catfish on a plate. My forehead furrowed. I lifted the lid of a pot that was simmering on top of the stove and saw the bubbling lime-green-colored curry soup.

"Ma, why did you make num banh chok? There's already so much food."

"It's Pat's favorite," my mom said impatiently. "Just finish it."

I poked my head out of the kitchen and saw that my dad had already opened a gift bag, which had oranges and a gold canister of tea, covered with the most intricate design. In exchange, my dad handed Alex a bottle of Heineken. *Damn it. He might win the bet.* Turning my attention back to dinner, I tossed the catfish in the mortar and beat it to a pulp. The loud pounding sounds drew Alex's attention. He walked into the kitchen with the bouquet of flowers, handing them to my mom.

"Hi, Āyí. These are for you."

My mom quickly plated the rice cakes and wiped her hands on her apron. She smiled politely and thanked Alex as she took the flowers from his grasp. She pushed her glasses up her nose and turned the bouquet around. She kept a cool face, but I could tell she was impressed. *Fuck! I'm screwed.* In Mandarin, she told Alex to sit down and relax and shooed him out of the kitchen.

"Are you sure I can't help?" Alex eyed the mush that I plopped into the soup. "What are these? Fried onions?" He pointed at a pile of golden-brown spirals.

"Those are banana blossoms. It goes on top of this noodle soup." I ladled the soup for him to see before pushing him out of the kitchen. "Now go."

When my mom started to put on the finishing touches, I headed to my room to freshen up. I didn't want to look like a mess sitting next to Alex. My hand hooked onto the banister when Alex caught up to me.

"Jas." He looked stressed. Did my dad already crack his confidence?

"What's wrong?"

"My mom just texted. She's on her way."

"Oh." I definitely needed to change if I was going to meet Alex's mom. "That's fine. My mom made tons of food. When is she arriving?"

The doorbell rang, and between Alex and me, I couldn't tell who was more afraid. I crept up to the peephole and saw a middle-aged Chinese woman in a fitted dark gray suit with a symmetrical, blown-out coif. If it weren't for her understated makeup, I would have mistaken her for the real estate agent that had ads plastered on every bus stop in the city.

Realizing Alex's mom had been standing outside for an extended amount of time, I swiftly opened the door. "Hi . . ." *Shit. How do I address her? Did I miss this from Chinese class? Uh . . . skip it. Introduce yourself.* "Wǒ jiào . . ." *Shit shit shit. English name or Chinese name? English name or Chinese name?* Alex's mom was looking at me like she hoped she was at the wrong house. I had to hurry this up. "Wǒ jiào Jasmine. Qǐng jìn, qǐng jìn." I opened the door wider as I welcomed her in.

Alex put down his beer and greeted his mother. They spoke in a different dialect, which I assumed was from his hometown of Hangzhou. He struggled to keep the tone light as they bickered back and forth. Unsure when they would hash things out, I slowly backed away and inched toward the stairs. Alex caught my arm before I escaped.

"Ma, this is Jasmine," he said, pulling me toward his side. "Jasmine, this is my mom, Dr. Xiuying Lai."

"Hi . . . er . . . Nǐ hǎo . . ." I said tentatively as I racked my brain for the right way to address her. "Bómǔ!" I cringed, knowing I shouted it out like I was answering a pop quiz question.

She laughed politely. "Nice to meet you, Jasmine," she said slowly, like it was more for my sake, not so much an indication of her English skills. She was a professor, after all. Oh, I was blowing this and we hadn't made it past introductions. Thankfully, Alex saved me from further embarrassment.

"Why don't you go get ready? I'll introduce my mom to your parents."

"Are you sure?"

"Yeah, it's fine." He guided his mom farther in. Over his shoulder, he whispered, "But please don't take too long."

I ran upstairs and changed into a burgundy maxi dress that I had set aside because I anticipated pigging out today. That was out of the question now that Alex's mom was here. A part of me was telling me to play the part of the nice, demure girl my mom always wished for. I looked in the mirror and prepared a self-effacing expression for when my parents said something nice about me. I attempted a bashful head tilt into my shoulder, but it read more uncomfortable than coy. Maybe this was one of those situations where the elders would talk about and for us. Then all Alex and I had to do was sit and look like the model children they would make us out to seem. That would take the load off us. I wanted to text Alex for some advice, but they were still talking downstairs. I didn't have time to waste, so I hurried down to rejoin them.

Everyone had gathered around the dining table by the time I arrived. Alex glanced at me out of the corner of his eye, briefly admiring my new outfit as I took my seat between him and Pat. My mom placed the fried rice in the middle of the table. Alex must have told my dad that he helped with the icing today because my dad was explaining to Alex and his mom how he flings the icing across a rack of donuts to glaze them. Hearing them converse in Mandarin made me feel self-conscious.

Upon seeing me, my dad announced, "Okay, Jas is here. Let's eat!" He reached for a serving spoon when my mom slapped his hand and subtly gestured at Alex and his mom. In Khmer, my dad whispered to my mom that he already welcomed them earlier and that he didn't need to make a formal announcement. My mom scolded my dad, so he added, "And welcome, Săosăo, Alex. We're happy to meet Jas's boyfriend." My dad glanced at my mom and made sure she was satisfied before he offered the serving spoon to Alex's mom.

My cheeks reddened. "He's not my boyf—"

"Oh!" My mom urgently waved her hands. "Săosăo, do you want what Pat's eating?" Pat had already started slurping his noodles, half of which were still hanging from his mouth like a noodle curtain. My mom was out of her seat and made it to the kitchen before Alex's mom could stop her.

Meanwhile, my dad and Alex's mom struck up a conversation in Mandarin. He asked her what she did for a living. When she answered, saying that she was a college professor, I heard my dad code-switch to a more formal accent. Pat noticed it too, so he followed suit and took smaller bites of his noodles. Everyone was on their best behavior.

Alex's mom asked my parents how long they had been living here. My parents explained that they'd lived in the United

States for almost thirty years, but in this house for the last twenty.

Alex leaned in close, keeping his attention toward the table. "I'm sorry about this," he whispered. "I'll explain later. By the way, I told my mom that you don't speak Mandarin, so don't worry about that, okay?"

"Thanks." I wasn't sure if I was supposed to feel embarrassed, annoyed, or relieved, but it did make things easier.

My mom came back and placed a bowl of num banh chok in front of Alex and his mom. His mom examined it first, dipping her spoon into the soup for a taste. She didn't go in for more. Instead, she helped herself to some of the other dishes in the middle of the table.

"Jas, I made you a bowl too. Eat this first while it's still hot," my mom said before I could get a bite of rice in. She ran back in and brought a bowl out for me. I ate the noodles first before I upset my mother. I didn't want her to think the noodles weren't good when I knew they were.

"And, Jasmine, you live here too?" Alex's mom asked.

I nodded. "*Mm-hmm.*"

She turned to my parents and said something that made my parents reply, "Oh?" They both gave Alex a questioning look.

I leaned toward Alex. "What did she say?" I asked softly, hoping only he would hear.

"I'm sorry, Jasmine," his mom answered. "I forgot you don't understand what we're saying. I told your parents that it's nice that you live at home. Alex moved out for college and never looked back."

Alex wouldn't look at me as he pushed his noodles around with his chopsticks. "Ma . . ." he said through gritted teeth.

So much for letting the elders talk for us. I chimed in. "Bómǔ, Alex said you were in town for a conference?"

Alex's mom paused from grazing her food. "Yes. I moved back to Hangzhou two years ago to take care of my mother. I was lucky to secure a job nearby at Zhejiang University. I was at a research conference at UC Riverside for the last five days."

"Oh. That's a far drive. We're happy that you came today," I said as sweetly as possible.

"Alex didn't give me much choice. He was working all week and this was my only chance to see him. I skipped dinner with my colleagues to be here."

Oof. I didn't mean to dig Alex into a bigger hole. Unsure how to respond, I did the next logical thing and stuffed my face with noodles.

"So, Jasmine. Alex tells me that you went to UCLA too," Alex's mom said, resting her chopsticks next to her untouched noodles. "And that you were premed? Which medical schools are you applying to?"

"Hmm?" My mouth was full so I couldn't ask Alex what the hell she was talking about.

"Uh, that's not what I said, Ma," Alex clarified, finally finding his voice. "She *was* premed, but she's currently helping out at her parents' shop while she's . . . um . . . exploring her options."

That sounded like some positive spin, but was he covering for himself or for me? That, I wasn't so sure.

"What *options* are you exploring right now, Jasmine?" Alex's mom asked with an edge in her voice like a knife blade scraping against my skin.

"Didn't you apply for a job at a law firm?" Alex interjected. "Or to shadow that veterinarian?"

What kind of bullshit was this? Yes, I tried to apply for the internship at Linh's former law firm, but they had filled it by the time I applied. The "shadowing a vet" was an inflated way of saying I applied to volunteer at the local humane society. I thought it could be a way to add something to my résumé. My heart sank, knowing that he felt the need to mislead his mom about me. Was he that worried about what she thought about me or . . . could it be that he didn't think that highly of me, either?

He turned to face me, letting his eyes slide toward his mom, signaling to follow his lead. I couldn't explain, but something about his request to carry on this charade flipped a switch in me. Lord knows I wasn't above lying when I needed to, but this was different. It was one thing for my parents to criticize my life choices, but they were my parents. It came with the territory. I didn't expect it from my not-boyfriend.

Fuck it. If Alex's mom was going to find a reason to pick apart everything anyway, I might as well go with the truth.

I cleared my throat. "Actually, I applied for a job at a magazine. A friend of mine referred me, so there's a good chance that I'll get to interview for it."

"Oh?" she said. My parents looked up from their bowls too, equally intrigued. Catching their reaction, Alex's mom asked, "You didn't know about this?"

"Oh, we know she's been applying for jobs." My mom laughed nervously through her counterfeit smile. Oh, I was in for it later. My mom did not like being blindsided.

"So, what kind of magazine is it? Would I know it?"

Everyone around the table turned and faced me, waiting for my answer.

"It's *Angel City Magazine*. It's a local digital magazine." As I said the words *local* and *digital*, I felt Alex's mom turn up her nose a touch higher.

"Hmm," she said, her lips curled like she had a bad taste in her mouth. "Never heard of it. So, you're going to be a journalist? Is that what you studied when you quit the premed track? I heard media is not a stable industry right now."

My parents didn't know anything about journalism or the word *media,* but *not stable* was all they needed to hear to sound the alarm in their heads. "Is that true?" my dad asked, his voice low with concern.

Everything I knew about the job I learned from Rae. With the evening stakeouts and helping my parents grow their business, I hadn't had much time to do more research about the company. I got the impression from Rae's Instagram that her job looked fun, but I knew that wouldn't blow over well with this crowd.

"Um . . . the magazine is fairly popular," I claimed, based on the number of followers on *ACM*'s Instagram account. "No,

I didn't study journalism, but my friend referred me, and she wouldn't have if she didn't think I could do it, so I'm interested to see where it goes." That much was true. Whether it was the right thing to do was to be determined.

No retort came from Alex's mom. She arched an eyebrow at Alex, who stewed in his seat. My ever-hospitable mom couldn't bear the tension and steered the conversation to more banal topics like the weather in Hangzhou this time of year and inquired about Alex's mom's research, even though it was painfully clear that it was going over both my parents' heads.

With no stakes in this game, Pat politely excused himself from the table. My parents seized the opportunity to parade him as a trophy son, talking about his internship. Pat shot me a worried look, but I waved him off, telling him to escape while he could. I was afraid that Alex's mom would question why Pat would be home if he was supposed to be interning right now, but I should have known she would redirect it to Alex.

"It's nice that your son made the effort to visit you even as busy as he is. That's a good son you have there."

This pushed Alex over the edge. He spoke to his mom in their own dialect, having an open side conversation at the table, exchanging exasperated and frosty words. My parents began having their own secret conversation in Khmer, keeping their voices low. I was left stranded on this sinking ship.

Alex's mom wiped her mouth with her napkin, flustered. "I'm sorry. I have an early flight tomorrow, so I must leave." She stood up and as if she suddenly remembered her manners, she added, "Thank you for dinner. It was delicious." Those were empty words when her plate and bowl were still full of food.

My parents stood up and thanked Alex's mom for coming. They walked her to the door, offering her a bottle of water and some fruit to take for her drive home, which she declined. They stood at the doorway, chatting for a bit.

Alex and I remained in our seats. Once he was sure his mom was far enough away, he leaned his elbows on the table and hung his head in his hands. "I'm sorry. That was my fault."

"Yeah, no shit, Sherlock." I stood up and started clearing the table.

Alex winced at my sharp tone. "Jas. Let me explain."

"I don't want to talk to you right now." I stacked empty bowls and balanced chopsticks on top and disposed of them in the kitchen sink. I returned to the dining room, where Alex started to clear the table. My mom rushed in behind him. She swatted his hands and took the plates from him. My dad appeared next to him, pulling him aside to the living room. I wasn't sure what my dad wanted to say to Alex, but my dad spoke only in extremes. His words were either sparse or long-winded. Alex was in for it whether it was good or bad, and I didn't feel like saving him. I picked up the dishes of leftover food and placed them on our kitchen counter while my mom began washing dishes.

Cutting to the quick, she muttered under her breath, in her pidgin language, "What an awful woman." Okay, she had sprinkled in a few choice words, but that was the gist of it. I didn't disagree.

"The way she looked down on our family, like nothing we did was good enough." She breathed hot air from the fire burning in her stomach. She grimaced when she picked up Alex's mom's bowl, still full of noodle soup, and dumped it in the garbage disposal. "Tā méiyǒu lǐmào."

I couldn't argue over that. Alex's mom *was* rude. I stood beside my mom to rinse the dishes. "Ma, she didn't say anything about you guys."

"But she said it about you, and that means us too." She shook her head. "See? This is why we meet parents first. Now we know."

"Know what?"

"You can't marry that boy. Can you imagine that woman as your mother-in-law?"

The plate I was holding nearly slipped from my hands. "Whoa! Who said anything about marriage?"

"If it's not about marriage, what's the point? Why spend any more time with him? He can't stand up to his own mother!"

I shushed my mom. "Not so loud, Ma. What if he hears you?"

"Hmph!" She threw down the sponge. "I don't care. You tell him to go home."

I dried my hands and stepped out of the kitchen. I peered into the living room, but nobody was there. Where did everybody go? I faced the front door and noticed that Alex's shoes were still by our shoe rack. If he was still here, then where was he?

I took cautious steps up the stairs. Halfway up, I noticed the door to my parents' room was closed. My dad had gone to bed, trying to squeeze in a few more hours of rest before leaving for the shop. After a few steps more, I heard the sound of video games coming from Pat's room. His door was slightly ajar. I leaned close to the wall to get a better look into his room. With headphones on, Pat was completely immersed in his game. By himself.

I jogged up the rest of the stairs and fought the urge to barge into my own room. I turned the knob quietly, not wanting to draw attention. It still startled Alex, who was standing at my desk, where a gift bag sat on top.

I closed the door behind me. "What are you doing in here?" I whisper-hissed.

"I forgot to give you this," he said of the gift. "And I couldn't leave without apologizing."

I stayed firmly in place. "I don't want to hear it. I'm so mad at you."

"Please." He turned my desk chair around, requesting that I sit. I didn't want to, but there was a pained sadness in his eyes, a softness in his face that I couldn't deny. I reluctantly closed the distance between us and sat down.

He knelt beside me, balancing himself on my armrest. "I don't know where to start," he said, letting out a steadying breath. "Um . . . I'm sorry about my mom. You probably gathered that we don't have the best relationship. We don't communicate well. When I texted her the address, she kept saying she didn't want to miss seeing her colleagues. She never gave me a clear answer, so I assumed she wasn't coming. If I had known, I would have better prepared you."

"Oh? You mean to get our stories straight about the lies you told her about me?"

He covered my hands with his, staring at them. "I'm sorry about that. I know that was bad." He didn't say more for seconds, debating what to say next. And when he did, his voice was gravelly. "When I came here to the United States, it was the first time I spent any real time with my mom. She rarely had a chance to visit me in China. She was practically a stranger. I don't think she knew what to do with me or knew how I fit into her life. It doesn't help that I resemble my dad. He left my mom the second he landed a job after grad school. It's a struggle, having a relationship with her. Sometimes I don't know if it's best to keep my distance or to try harder. When you invited her to dinner, I honestly didn't want to tell her, but I didn't want to lie to you, either. So, to protect you, I thought the best thing I could do was to . . . present your situation in the best possible way."

My heart broke for him. I knew that every person had a unique dynamic with their parents. I wouldn't know what to do if my mom treated me like that. Still, it hurt that he felt my "situation" required damage control. I cradled his face with my hands. He leaned into them, looking at me with contrite eyes. We stayed like this for five . . . ten seconds. Faint explosion sounds from Pat's video game filled the silence between us.

"I'm sorry," he said again.

"I'm still upset. You really screwed up. My mom's not happy."

"I know." Alex groaned as he stood up. "I got an earful from your dad too."

"What did he say to you?"

"I'll spare you the details, but basically"—Alex offered his hand to help me up—"I was told to grovel."

"Good advice," I said. Out of the corner of my eye, the gold gift bag glittered on my desk. I stuck a finger into the bag and tilted it toward me.

"After all that's transpired tonight, I'm having second thoughts on the gift," he said warily. "Linh thought you'd like it."

Now I had to know what it was. I reached under the tissue paper and pulled out a book. I flipped it over to see the front cover. *Finding Your Passion Is Bullshit!*

I stifled a laugh as I thumbed through the pages. "Inside joke," I explained when I caught Alex's puzzled face.

"Ah," he said. "So, I guess I owe you ice cream," he offered now that the mood was lighter.

I had forgotten about our silly bet. "Let's call it a draw."

He nodded and turned to the side, letting his eyes wander around my room. "This wasn't how I imagined your room," he said as if he was just noticing it. "It's girlier than I expected."

I admit, my room was stuck in time. Few things had changed since high school. White string lights zigzagged across the ceiling. Tsum Tsum figurines lined up in front of my college textbooks on my bookshelf. My mauve comforter lay askew on my bed.

Alex stepped up to the large corkboard that hung on the wall and scrutinized the concert ticket stubs pinned to it. "I've never heard of half of these bands." He extended his arm, gesturing at me to hand over my new book. I offered it to him and watched him make space for it on my bookshelf.

"Ooh . . . yearbook," he said, cracking it open.

Who did he think he was, going through my stuff? I wasn't sure why I felt the need to lunge for it, but when I did, Alex spun out of my reach.

"Hey! What's wrong?" When he found my senior portrait, he pointed right at it. "You look exactly the same." He thumbed through the rest of the pages and came across random pictures of me. There was one where I sold nachos for the poetry club fundraiser and another at a beach cleanup event. He pointed his finger on a different page. "This guy . . . he was on your shop's Instagram account. He's in a lot of pictures with you." His eyes landed on the caption. "Lovebirds Michael and Jasmine cheering on their friends at Academic Decathlon."

"He's my ex-boyfriend," I said, stating the obvious. I shut the yearbook from under him and stuffed it back into my bookshelf.

"You guys been spending time together?"

I didn't want to have this conversation with him because I didn't owe him any explanation. On the flip side, I didn't like what his curious tone was hinting at, either.

"No, we have not been spending time together. He came—with other friends—to help me promote the shop. We're barely on speaking terms—if that's what you're worried about."

"It's not that," he backtracked. "Your dad kind of mentioned that I was the first person you brought home."

"They don't know about him," I explained. "I wasn't allowed

to date in high school. Now can we drop this? I thought you don't like talking about exes."

The topic of exes ruffled Alex's feathers. "My ex is irrelevant. She's completely out of the picture. This guy—"

"This guy is none of your concern," I said, losing patience. I gestured back and forth between us. "We just met, and even if I was seeing someone else—which I'm not—you don't have a right to be jealous. And another thing. If this is your idea of groveling, you're doing a shitty job."

I glared at him while he dragged his hand down his face. This was a delightful cherry on top of this trash-fire evening. Seeing we had nothing left to say to each other, Alex turned toward the door, but I ran up to stop him. My parents had expected him to leave a while ago, so I had to make sure the coast was clear. I peeked into the empty hallway before stepping out with ninja-light feet. When we made it downstairs, I scanned the first floor to find any sign of my mother. We heard her frustrated sigh all the way down from her room upstairs, likely replaying the night's events with Auntie Helen.

I gave Alex a pointed look. That sigh said it all. I opened the front door, ready to give him the boot, but he wrapped an arm around my shoulders, pulling me toward him. With my face pressed against his chest, I heard his heart beating as fast as mine.

"I don't want to leave like this. I'm really sorry."

"I know," I said into his shirt. "You need to give me some space, okay?" I tilted my head up to see his reaction, but we were still standing close. Close enough for our noses to touch. Close enough for traitorous feelings to draw me in for a parting kiss. At first it was gentle and melancholy. When Alex tried to deepen it, like he was pleading with me to remember how good things were just a few hours before, I pushed him away. This was the opposite of space.

"You should go before my dad wakes up," I said softly as I stepped back, opening the door wider. Alex hung his head, chin to chest, for a moment before he left.

## Chapter 14

*E*veryone was in a sour mood the next morning. My mom was still fuming over last night's dinner. My dad was not accustomed to the increased workload of making and decorating more donuts. With only a week of selling our new donuts under our belts, we hadn't figured out how much to make. Some days we sold out, and other times we had trays left over at the end of the night. Because of that, my dad wasn't ready to commit to making big batches of the new icing flavors if they were not going to be used up while they were fresh. All that to say, when I was summoned to come in early to help my dad prepare small batches of icing, I was not thrilled.

"Not so much," my mom said, looking over my shoulder as I dipped a donut into a tray of Oreo crumbs.

I flipped over the donut and pressed bigger shards around the center. "This is why customers pay more money. We have to give them what they want." A half a cookie's worth of crumbs couldn't possibly put us in the red.

She turned to look at my profile, her glasses snagging my hair. "Why your eye like that?"

My eyes looked like muffin tops, spilling over the crease. I stepped to the side and smoothed my hair with the back of my hand. "I didn't get enough sleep." I didn't want her to ask me if it was because of Alex, so I added, "Didn't plan to wake up early today."

"*Hmph,*" she said. "I wake up this early every day. You're younger than me. You should have more energy!" She lifted my hand as I was about to grab another donut and massaged her thumb into my palm. "Look at these soft hands and look at mine." She let go of my hand and flipped hers over to reveal her knobby fingers. "Mine work more than yours."

I understood the subtext. I should have been able to keep up and toughen up. To her, it was a simple observation, a matter of fact. To me, it was yet another unnecessary reminder that my life, my work, would always pale in comparison to those of my parents. I knew this very well. It didn't bear repeating. Wasn't that the point, though? Wasn't that the narrative for every immigrant and refugee who had come to the United States? To come and build a better, safer life for yourself and your family? If the measure of success was that I was living a more comfortable, easier life than they had, then why was I simultaneously penalized for it? These questions rang in my head, but they were better left unspoken unless I wanted to add *inconsiderate* and *ungrateful* to my list of shortcomings.

I acknowledged her statement with a nod and iced another

donut with a light coating of Oreos. The act of obedience was purely a move to avoid further nagging and not out of any sense of duty. Satisfied, my mom left me to finish my work. With her back turned, I promptly took another donut and smushed it into the Oreo crumbs, drilling it to the bottom of the tray.

My dad stood opposite me at the workbench, gently twisting donuts into pink icing, then dipping them in a tray of sprinkles. They were picture-perfect. I waited until he finished the whole tray before I took out my phone and snapped a photo for our Instagram.

"Aiyah." He didn't see what the fuss was about or understand why people took pictures of their food. "You should take pictures of yours. They look better than before."

"Thanks, Ba." I would hope so. I'd had more practice since the first test batch.

He sucked his teeth while examining my work. Reaching into his apron, he pulled out a stack of Post-its and slid off the pen that was propped behind his ear. After a quick scribble, he presented me with the Mona Lisa of yellow smiley faces.

"You keep it up, they'll look as good as mine someday." He picked up his tray and took them out front.

I followed closely behind him and slid my tray of donuts next to his inside our glass display. Since my dad seemed more agreeable than my mom and there was a lull before our morning rush, it felt as good a time as any to bring up *ACM*.

"I don't know about that, Ba. What if I get Rae's job?"

Both of my parents blinked at me.

"What do you mean? If it's not stable, then it's not worth it," my dad said.

"Rae worked there for a year. I think it will be fine."

"How much does it pay?" Of course, my mother asked this question. "More than minimum wage?"

"Yeah." Just by a tiny bit. They didn't need to know that.

My dad crossed his arms. "What are you supposed to do after?"

"After what?"

"After . . ." He searched for the right word. "After . . . you know. If you're good at this job, do you get to be somebody's boss?"

"Uh . . . I don't know. It's a small company." That tidbit didn't help my cause.

"What would you do after?" he asked again.

"After what?!" I couldn't figure out where this was going.

My dad huffed at the slight raise in my voice. "After you leave or lose your job. What would you do after?"

"I don't know! I don't even have this job yet to think about what I would do after!"

My dad shook his head. "Nà bù zhídé." *It's not worth it.*

I felt my blood boil, slowly making its way up my chest and up my face. The heat reached my eyes, making them sting whenever I blinked. Why did everything have to have an end goal in mind? What was the problem with doing something for the sake of doing it? How would I know if I liked something if I didn't try it?

The door chime rang in quick succession as our regulars

started filing in, officially putting our standoff on pause. Both my parents put on their warmest smiles, greeting customers. My dad walked around me to finish up the last tray of donuts. I couldn't work up a smile, but I maintained a professional demeanor as I fulfilled orders. At least I thought so until my mom side-eyed me when I banged the coffee filter too loudly as I dumped out the grounds.

Faces and voices blurred together, but though I was angry, my brain automatically recognized each customer and which donuts to box up for them. When a customer modified their usual order, my arm quickly changed paths to grab the right items. I didn't think I could feel worse, but it was depressing how attuned my body was to this shop.

Maybe *ACM* wasn't worth it, but neither was this.

OVER THE NEXT few days, my parents and I orbited around each other, trying to maintain a business-as-usual attitude. Our conversations were clipped, limited to the most essential things that needed to be communicated. It was hardly tolerable, since we saw each other all the time at the shop. When we arrived home after closing, I went straight to my room, resuming my old routine.

For Movie Monday, I watched the latest Spider-Man installment. For New Music Tuesday, I listened to the Taylor Swift album that dropped out of nowhere. For Reading Wednesday, I semi-flipped through the book Alex gave me. It reminded me that Rae suggested that I post more on social media in case her boss—potentially my future boss—wanted to get a sense of my personality. So, I posted a picture of my evening's activity and added the caption "Next on my reading list!" I wasn't sure if it was doing any good, but it couldn't hurt, either.

By Thursday, my parents and I reached a breaking point, so when I suggested that they take the day off, they readily agreed. Pat managed to crawl out of bed and opened the shop with me, but the kudos ended there. He still didn't know any of our regulars or their orders and he was slow as hell because he had to check our prices half the time. We bumped into each other twice during the morning rush, the last time causing me to spill hot coffee on my shirt. Now he was sitting at the front counter, looking down at his phone.

I threw a towel at Pat's face. "Come on, Pat. Help me mop the floor before any customers come in."

Pat continued tapping on his phone. "Hold on, jie."

"Right now, Pat." I attempted to confiscate Pat's phone. Before Pat yanked it away, I caught a glimpse of the screen. "Wh-What was that?"

"Nothing." Pat slid his phone into his back pocket. "Where's the mop?" he asked, breezily.

"Were you texting Alex?" It had been four days since he came over for dinner. It had also been four days since we last had an actual conversation. We exchanged brief "hey, how are you" texts here and there, but nothing like the flirty banter of before.

Pat avoided eye contact and dragged the mop handle, rolling

the yellow mop bucket with it. "I asked him a few questions, okay? It has nothing to do with you two."

"That's not why I asked." *It's kind of why I asked.* "What could you possibly talk to him about?" I grabbed the floor scraper and started scraping knobs of hardened icing off the floor like it was a game of shuffleboard.

Pat splattered water around the eat-in area when he dropped the mop on the floor. "It's not a big deal. Just asked him for some career advice."

"Why? He's not in tech."

Exasperated with the inquisition, Pat replied, "I know, jie. I asked him if he knew anything about tech consulting."

"Why would anyone want to hire you for that?" I snorted. "You don't know shit."

Irritated, Pat stopped directly in front of me across the counter. "Thanks, jie."

The caustic tone in Pat's voice caught me off guard. This was our normal repartee. Sure, I was giving him a hard time, but a verbal elbow to the ribs was how we showed each other that we cared. He knew I was joking, didn't he?

"So, what did he say?" I asked more gently, hoping to bring the conversation back to neutral ground.

Pat released a heavy sigh. "That I'd still need a decent GPA to go into consulting and that I'd make more money if I was a software developer. He wasn't sure about tech consultants, but he mentioned that in his area, there's a lot of turnover, so I don't know."

"I didn't know you were considering other options."

Pat slumped his shoulders as he resumed mopping. "Just wanted to know what else I could possibly do."

I cringed as I watched him inefficiently push the mop around him with no rhyme or reason. It was a good thing he was book smart because the boy lacked common sense. I took pity on my smart/dumb brother.

"Hey. I'm sure things will turn out fine," I said reassuringly.

"How's your job search going? I'm running out of time. Mom and Dad barely bought your explanation last time. What are you going to do if this extends longer than you expect?" Pat kicked open the yellow WET FLOOR sign and stuck the mop into the bucket, sloshing dirty water as he rolled it inside to mop behind the counter.

"I was planning on telling them that you're doing some work remotely," I said as I rearranged the donuts and placed them closer to the front of the display. "They don't know how computers work anyway, so it sounds plausible."

"Well, please get hired soon. Do you know that Ba would text me when I'm in Santa Cruz saying how you do nothing after work? I'm tired of this shit."

"Are you serious?" I balked. "They already give me enough crap. They shouldn't bug you about me."

"Well, they do! They're more ready for you to leave than you think. You should have done this a long time ago. We'd hear about it less, that's for sure."

That wasn't true. My mom had harped on me about finding a

boyfriend since college. When she still thought highly of Alex, she shifted to bugging me about *keeping* a boyfriend. Whenever there was downtime at the shop, I had to ignore my mom as she droned on and on about how I should look, how I should learn to cook, and how I should be more graceful.

I walked up to Pat, who was leaning on the front counter, taking a break. "I'm glad Alex was able to answer your questions. How's he doing?" I casually asked.

Pat tilted his head and narrowed his eyes. "He's *your* boyfriend. Why are you asking me?"

"He's not my boyfriend," I asserted.

Pat rolled his eyes and stood up. "Whatever. I'm not getting in between you two." He pointed at me. "Just don't mess things up in case I need him to hook me up with a job."

I flipped him off. "What kind of brother are you? Aren't you supposed to beat him up if he doesn't treat me right?"

Pat gave me a pointed look. "I think we both know that you're the scary one in the relationship. You could beat him up without me." I wanted to punch him, but it would have proved his point. Fortunately for Pat, he knew when to back off.

"For what it's worth, he seems like a nice guy, and for some reason, he likes you." Pat glanced at me out of the corner of his eye before walking into the back of the shop.

"And how would you know that?"

Pat dragged the mop bucket with him toward the sink in the back to dump out the murky water. I stayed put at the doorway, so he yelled, "Well, when I told him I was working at the shop today, he kept asking questions like—" Mocking Alex's deep voice, Pat continued: "'How's it going at the shop today?' 'Is the shop busy?' 'Does the shop miss me?'"

"He did not say the last one," I bristled.

Pat laughed. "Okay, he didn't, but you get the idea." He brushed my shoulder as he walked past me. As if Pat could hear the rush of thoughts and questions in my head, he added, "Don't overthink it, jie. Now show me how to use the cappuccino machine again."

LATER THAT NIGHT, I was browsing Netflix for my usual Thirsty Thursday routine. I ran through my pre-Netflix checklist. Headphones? Check. Bag of popcorn? Check. A can of Coke that I stole from the garage, our makeshift warehouse of extra inventory? My favorite extra-soft avocado tank top? Check and check. Before I slipped on my glasses, I stuffed a handful of popcorn into my mouth and brushed the buttery residue on my fingertips onto my shorts. I kept scrolling down, browsing different titles, but nothing seemed appealing. I started coughing when a kernel got caught in my throat. I turned away from my laptop, not wanting to get soggy, chewed-up popcorn bits all over my keyboard. When I finally dislodged the kernel and my coughing subsided, a ringing noise caught my attention.

I turned back to my laptop and saw that Alex was trying to FaceTime me. Needing to collect myself, I took a swig of Coke.

I wanted to take a quick look in the mirror, but I didn't want to risk missing the call. The first thing I thought when Alex appeared on the screen was, *Wow. His room is so neat.* He was sitting at his desk inside his bedroom. I didn't have time to examine his surroundings because all I could see was Alex's floppy hair and unstylish wire-framed glasses.

"Oh my god. You look like such a nerd!" I laughed. It wasn't his best look, but it was adorable to see what he was like behind the scenes. I wondered what hair product he used, since it always looked so touchable.

"It's only nine o'clock," I commented, catching the time at the bottom of my screen. "This is the earliest you've called or texted me on a work night."

"Yeah, I met up with a current intern at UCLA today. I got paired up with him as his mentor."

"That's cool. It must have been nice to be back on campus."

"Yeah, but you know how traffic is. I left work early and still got there late. It's funny. I was in his shoes only a year ago." Alex looked intently at me through the screen. I guess the small-talk portion of our conversation was over. "Hi. It's good to see you." His voice was softer and more cautious.

"Yeah." My eyes darted between the screen and the camera, unsure where to look. I ultimately decided to look at Alex. He was a sight for sore eyes. "So, I don't recall setting up FaceTime on my Mac."

"I may have changed your preferences when I was in your room. By the way, your desktop is really cluttered."

"Hey! It's not that bad." Alex's eyes squinted. I looked down at my shirt. "It says, 'I don't want to guac about it.'"

Alex chuckled. "No, it's not that. I wasn't sure if it was my screen or if you look extra red tonight."

"Oh! Well, I was choking on a popcorn kernel right before you called and—" I gestured at my chest. "Pat spilled hot coffee on me this morning. I'm sure it'll be fine tomorrow."

"Ouch." Alex gave me a concerned look and then glanced at the corner of the screen, spotting my bag of popcorn. "I remember you telling me about your usual Thursday night plans, so I figured it was a good time to call. How are you?"

"I'm fine. How have you been?" I propped my feet up on my chair, hugging my shins. I rested my chin on my knees. It was then that I realized that I wasn't wearing a bra. I reached for the jacket hanging on my chair and tried to subtly put it on. Alex's face lit up, though he tried to restrain his smile.

"I was looking all over for that jacket."

I hugged myself. "Sorry. I forgot to give it back to you on Sunday."

Alex leaned into his right arm, running his fingers through his hair trying to keep it out of his face. "I wish I could do Sunday over. Are your parents still mad?"

"Less than before, but yeah."

"I'm sorry." He looked at me and then down at his keyboard. "I've missed you."

"I've missed you too," I admitted. It was hard not to miss him. Alex and I shared more than a mutual attraction. After Sunday's revelation, I saw him as someone trying to figure out himself and his place in his family, just like me. How could I not have a soft spot for that?

"Wanna meet up tomorrow?"

"What did you have in mind?"

"I was thinking about going for a hike. You up for it? I found a trail that's not too steep."

It wasn't my idea of fun, but he loved hiking so much that I was willing to give it a try.

"Or . . ." Alex said, sensing my reluctance, "it doesn't have to be that. We can do something else."

"No. It's fine. I just . . . have to figure out how to get out of work." This was going to be tricky now that my parents didn't think too fondly of him anymore. I didn't have school to use as a cover. "I'll have to get back to you on that."

"Okay. Let me know. Otherwise, I won't see you until I get back from China."

I forgot he was leaving for China this weekend and he'd be gone for two weeks. If I missed him after four days of sparse texting, how were we going to handle two weeks apart in different time zones?

"What are you going to do during your trip?"

"Mainly spend time with my grandma and . . . my mom." Not wanting to open that can of worms, Alex quickly continued. "My team has a handle on things while I'm gone, but I'll check my email from time to time, so I won't be out of the loop when I get back. And a friend of mine from AKPsi works in Shanghai, so I might try to meet up with him."

Ah, he was in the business frat. Typical.

"Sounds fun," I said as I trailed my finger back and forth across the space bar. "Are you going to bring something back for me?"

"Maybe." Alex tried to play it cool, but he just looked so adorkable. "Let me guess. You want me to bring you snacks." He knew me so well already.

I smiled innocently. "If it's not too much trouble."

Alex rolled his eyes. "Salty or sweet snacks?"

"Salty, hands down," I answered quickly.

"Really? I would have picked sweet. And you work in a donut shop!"

"Exactly. Can you imagine if I had a sweet tooth? We'd have nothing left to sell."

Alex pouted. "I was so sad that I didn't get a donut on Sunday."

"I'll bring you one tomorrow for carb loading. You'll need it to drag me up the hill."

He laughed, settling into a wide grin. "You can handle this. I promise."

"And for the groveling."

Alex nodded as his expression sobered. "Yes. That too." He looked into his camera, so on my screen, it felt like he was looking directly at me. His mouth pulled into a sly smile, like he was laughing at his own private joke.

"What's so funny?"

"I was wondering if this counted for Thirsty Thursday."

My answer was swift.

"You wish." Considering that his shirt was still on, it definitely didn't count for Thirsty Thursday.

By the end of our call, it felt like things mostly went back to normal. I looked at the time. It was too late to start a show. Instead, I decided to look up the time difference between California and Hangzhou. *Damn. Fifteen hours ahead.* By the time I was off from work, it would be morning in China, so there was a limited time frame where we could chat. How would we communicate while he was gone anyway? Could we still FaceTime?

Out of habit, I looked at all of Alex's social media handles to see if he posted anything new. The only update was on his Instagram account. It had a simple caption: "Back on campus!" In the picture, Alex wore a tailored dark gray suit jacket, a white dress shirt, and a black tie. His face had a bright, wide smile and his index finger pointed straight up. To the untrained eye, perhaps he was saying UCLA was number one or directing attention to Pauley Pavilion, which was in the distance behind him. I zoomed in and looked closer. He was pointing at the ticket office.

## Chapter 15

*I* kicked a rock at the entrance of the hiking trail three miles away from my house. Alex was waiting for me where the gravel met the dirt path. I dug in my feet, satisfied with the crunchy sound under my shoes, while he checked some details on his phone. With a tinge of dread, I patted away a dusty spot on my black leggings, which I'd never worn as workout attire.

A couple jogged around us and disappeared under the bright, rising sun. When Alex suggested hiking right when the trail opened to avoid the afternoon heat, it threw me for a loop. I had to think of a last-minute excuse that necessitated leaving the house at seven A.M. The best I could come up with was that I forgot to renew my driver's license and I needed to go early to wait in line. My mom nagged me about being more responsible about those kinds of things, and Pat was annoyed that he had to go open the shop with her. To cover my tracks, I met up with Alex at the trail instead of getting picked up. Otherwise, my dad would have questioned how I got to the DMV with my car still at home.

I yawned as Alex double-checked his backpack. Unlike me, he came prepared for the journey.

"Do you normally bring so much stuff with you?" I peeked inside and mainly saw water bottles and granola bars. I handed him his donut—a glazed twist that I picked up on the way from the shop—which he promptly put inside the front compartment.

"No, but I don't usually hike with someone, either," he said with a sheepish smile. He pointed toward the map of the park. "There are different trails here, so if you want to take a shorter one, we can. Let me know how you're feeling and we can play it by ear." Alex zipped up his backpack and swung the straps over his shoulders.

I adjusted my baseball cap and took a deep breath, looking ahead at the trail. "Sounds good," I said, trying to maintain a positive attitude.

"And if it helps . . . if at any point, you find a good spot for me to grovel, just say the word. All right?" He stuck out his pinkie in good faith, so I linked mine with his.

"Deal."

We walked for about half a mile, mostly in silence. It took us a while to warm up to being around each other again. As we walked along, Alex looked like he was deep in thought that I didn't want to interrupt by chatting. I wouldn't have been a good conversation partner anyway because my body was rejecting me for agreeing to this hike.

Even though it was his first time at this trail, he did his research and knew where we were going. I decided to follow his lead, especially since he was the more experienced hiker. When I slowed down to admire the yellow wildflowers covering the hillside, I was afraid that Alex was bored that I was going at a snail's pace, but he didn't seem bothered at all. We stopped when we reached a fork in the trail.

"Jas, if you want to stay on the flat path, we should turn left here. It'll look similar to what we've seen—trees, tall grass." Alex gestured at the golden, dry grass surrounding us. "If you want to see the view of the city, we should stay on this path, but fair warning. It's a little steeper." Alex looked down at my old but rarely used running shoes. "You should be okay in those. What do you want to do?"

Alex was such a good sport for what was sure to be a boring hike for him.

It *would* be nice to see the view.

Alex smiled when I started walking straight ahead. "I was hoping you'd pick this one. You won't regret it."

By the time we completed the first mile, my tank top clung to my back. It was seven-thirty and already it was seventy-eight degrees. I lifted my hat and wiped the sweat off my forehead. I chugged half of my water bottle.

"How long is this trail again?" I asked, trying really hard not to sound like I was dying.

"Almost five miles. It's supposed to take about two-ish hours to complete." I could tell Alex was trying to figure out if I was going to make it. "Whenever you want to turn back . . ."

"No. It's fine. I promised you I'd hike with you, so I will do it even if it kills me." Which it might.

"Okay, but we can also take a break whenever you need to," Alex reassured me.

As we continued walking, I felt the incline in my calves. Now I knew how Alex got his calves. I glanced down at his legs and let my eyes trail up his black basketball shorts and his drenched gray tank top. Alex caught my gaze and his eyes smiled at me. He walked closer toward me and bumped my shoulder. I grimaced as I pulled apart our sticky arms.

"Ew! Gross!" I said, rubbing the sweat off my arm.

"What? It's just sweat." Alex put his arm around me and pulled me in for a bear hug. Alex may be good-looking, but this did not make the experience any less disgusting.

"Eeeeeeewwww! This is so nasty!" I said into his tank top while walking backward in his sweaty hold. "Let me go before I fall down!" Alex stopped and released me from his hold. I had to shake off the heebie-jeebies. "Uggggh!"

Alex swung his backpack around, dug under the water bottles, and pulled out a small terry cloth towel for me. I gratefully took it and wiped my damp face. Alex was very amused by my discomfort. He looked around while I finished wiping my arms.

"Hey. If you want to keep going, we're about half a mile from the halfway point. That's where we'll see the view, and from what I read online, it should be downhill for the rest of the trail or—" Alex pointed to my left, where a paved path led to the adjacent park. "We can head over to the park and sit at a picnic table and split the donut."

Option two was so tempting. The park remarkably had lush green grass. Trees provided ample shade over the picnic tables. My achy feet begged me to sit. I hung the towel around my neck and polished off my water bottle. I patted the small dry spot on his shoulder.

"Let's go. We have a view to catch," I said, walking ahead of Alex while he zipped up his backpack.

Alex jogged over and caught up to me. "You're taking this very seriously," he said, sounding pleasantly surprised.

"Well, this is important to you," I said sincerely. Alex smiled and held my hand, gently swinging it between us. I waved my right hand at the yellow wildflowers and the trees surrounding the path. "And I had to see what the hype is about. Too bad they're not willow trees."

Curious, Alex asked, "Why willow trees? What's so special about them?"

"Didn't you know that willow trees are magical? Like in *Pocahontas,*" I said like this was a known fact.

Alex laughed. "You're so weird," he said jokingly.

"Are you saying if you saw Grandmother Willow right there, you wouldn't want to tell her your hopes and dreams?"

"If I saw a face in a tree talking to me, I would run away as fast as I could." Alex chuckled.

We kept walking at a steady pace with nothing but the seemingly endless dirt path ahead of us. "So, how does this trail compare?" I asked.

"It's okay. It's pretty easy for me. What about you? I have to say, you're holding up better than I expected."

"Thanks?" I laughed. "Yeah, it's not as hard as I thought it would be. I bet it's nice to hike here in the spring when it's not as hot."

"And it's really close to your house." Alex squinted as he looked down the trail. He jogged ahead and turned to his left. He waved me over. I couldn't muster the energy to jog, so I walked over as fast as I could. When I caught up to him, he put his arm around my shoulder and turned me around to face the view overlooking Hacienda Heights. "See? It's literally in your backyard."

I looked across the rows and rows of rooftops. My suburban hometown was as cookie-cutter as it gets, yet seeing it from up here in the morning sun gave me a new sense of appreciation for it. I felt so peaceful standing up here, away from the noise of the daily grind. I leaned into Alex and closed my eyes. A welcome cool breeze gave us respite from the burning sun.

Alex looked at his watch. "We made decent time. It's just over an hour. Let's head back down, and how about we go eat dim sum after?"

I hugged his waist. "You read my mind." Feeling accomplished for making it farther than I ever thought I possibly could, I stood on my tiptoes and planted a kiss on Alex's cheek.

Before my heels hit the ground, Alex replied with a kiss of his own that was different from all the times we kissed before. It was the slow, hypnotizing kind that made me forget about sunburned shoulders, sore calves, and a fear of heights. It was patient in its persistence, convincing me that whatever we had was more than attraction. I couldn't hold the hope blooming in my chest at bay that maybe this time, with this man, things would be different.

*Don't rush into it. Not like last time.*

I broke our kiss, trying to shake off that errant thought. Alex's clear eyes searched mine.

"Is everything okay?" Alex asked.

My stomach growled, giving me the perfect excuse. "Let's go eat." I started walking back on the trail before I said anything I'd regret.

Alex regarded me cautiously afterward. I couldn't blame him for feeling uncertain after I ruined an otherwise lovely moment. We were both in our own heads for the rest of the hike, which turned out longer than we expected because we missed a sign and walked into a different trail. The detour extended our hike by an extra thirty minutes. When we arrived at my favorite dim sum restaurant, there was a forty-five-minute wait and a line out the door. Alex offered me a granola bar to tide me over, but I slapped it away from my face. My hangry side didn't have time for granola bars, and I was on a time crunch.

Rather than waiting, I suggested that we go across the street to Mr. Tim's Diner. Like all good diners in the L.A. area, the menu was split between traditional American fare and Mexican dishes. It was par for the course as far as hole-in-the-wall places go. The menus were sticky, the terra-cotta booths were squeaky, and the food was amazing. When we walked in, the kitchen staff was blasting Maná before switching to current Latin pop songs.

After our waiter took our orders, I looked out the window and mindlessly swirled my water with my straw. My head was swimming while my heart was trying to break out of my rib cage. How could I feel so strongly for Alex so soon? Like it was too much, yet not enough at the same time? Objectively I knew Alex was better, more deserving than the last person who returned my affections. But no matter how much I tried to forget, old hurts remained as a reminder to guard what was most precious to me.

"Penny for your thoughts?" Alex asked.

I stopped swirling my water and rested both of my arms on the table. "I was just thinking about . . . how focused you are when you're hiking." I smiled weakly. "You don't have to tell me, but you looked like you had a lot on your mind."

Alex fiddled with the straw wrapper as he contemplated his response. When Alex finally spoke, his voice was low and measured. "Most of the time, I try not to think about anything. And today"—Alex looked up at me briefly before looking back down at the straw wrapper—"I thought how nice it was to have your company."

"You're just saying that."

"No, it's true. To be honest—" Alex hesitated.

Now I knew what people meant when they said they could see the wheels in one's head turning. Alex looked tense as he thought about what to say next. When his sad eyes locked with mine, I couldn't look away.

"Growing up was tough for me. When I came here, I didn't know the language. My mom was always working and I knew I wasn't planned. She made that clear. I didn't have any other family and I had no friends." He glanced down at the table, clearing the hoarseness from his voice. "I was angry and lonely for a long time. It wasn't until middle school that I became friends with some parachute kids. I'd finally found other people like me, coming from China, virtually left to our own devices. I mean, I know it's different because they stayed with host families and I had my mom, but she wasn't really around. If it hadn't been for my friends, I wouldn't have gotten into college. There were times when I wanted to give up because my mom kept insisting that I study a science like her. Sometime during high school, I started hiking when I just needed to get away." Alex let out a humorless chuckle. "It's so ironic—hiking alone to get away from feeling lonely."

I reached out and squeezed his hand. I was speechless as my feelings swirled inside. My heart was heavy, knowing that he went through that. I was honored that he trusted me to open up like that. But part of me felt guilty because I never imagined someone like Alex carrying so much heartache.

When Alex and I first met, part of me envied his confidence.

I'd attributed it to his looks and accomplishments. All fair assumptions, I'd say. On paper, it didn't make sense why he'd go for someone like me. We didn't share any common hobbies or ambitions. But maybe he knew something that I was beginning to realize: his lonely heart recognized a kindred spirit in mine.

"I'm sorry. That sucks." I shook my head, kicking myself. I wished there was something more I could offer, but I was coming up short. "Sorry. I don't know what else to say."

"You don't have to say anything," he said. "If anything, I'm supposed to be the one saying sorry to you."

Our waiter came and placed our food on the table. It didn't feel right to scarf down my food after what Alex just shared. Alex unfolded his napkin and picked up his breakfast burrito.

"Please eat. Your stomach has been growling forever. You should have taken that granola bar," he said, trying to lighten the mood.

I waited for him to take a bite before I picked up my fork and stabbed my scrambled eggs.

"Do you ever wonder what it would have been like if we had dated in college?" he asked in between bites. "Wouldn't it have been so much easier? We could have seen each other all the time."

"Yes and no. You don't know what I was like. I was all over the place. I mean, I still am, but it was much worse back then."

Alex smirked. "You say that like it was so long ago."

"Feels like a lifetime ago." I shook my head just thinking

about it. Alex looked expectantly at me, and since he had shared so much, I felt I should do the same. "I don't know when I would have seen you. I was always studying, and I came home every weekend. All my mom ever asked me about was whether or not I was dating someone, so I started treating dating like it was my job, and I didn't end up dating anybody during college. It kinda messed with my head. Got too much for me, you know?"

I tried to say more, but flashbacks from my dating history made me stall. How much of that did he need to know right now?

"I don't believe that." I knew he meant to say that in the best possible way, but he didn't understand the lengths I went to during my search for love.

"Well, you should be glad to know that you were the only one who saw potential in this," I said, gesturing toward my sweaty torso. "But even you would have made a run for it after—"

Why did I start a sentence I didn't want to finish? I should have quit while I was ahead.

"After what?" I had Alex's full attention now. "What did you do?" I refused to answer, not wanting to reveal my stalkerish ways, but because I stopped myself, Alex's imagination began to run wild. He started looking at me funny. If he was going to reconsider things, he might as well base it off the truth.

"I . . ." I couldn't look at him, so I shielded my face with my hands. "I may have looked up your phone number after you bought tickets and I may or may not have tried calling you." Alex didn't say anything, but my hands still covered my face, so

I didn't know how he reacted to this information. "But it went straight to an answering machine and I hung up without leaving a message, so it's not that bad! I—"

Alex's laugh caused our silverware to rattle on the table. "You called my house?" I failed to see what was so amusing about all of this. "Sorry, I used to leave my house number so I wouldn't get scam calls," he explained. "It's not that bad. You had me sweating over here, thinking like you were a serial killer or something."

"Please, no more sweating," I deadpanned.

Alex chuckled. "Well, I'm sorry I missed your call." He reached for my hand and waited until my eyes locked with his. "I'm sorry I didn't go up to the ticket office to ask about you so I could have looked you up. I'm sorry I work seventy hours a week. I'm sorry I see your texts five hours later. I'm very, *very* sorry about my mom and that I lied about you. I'm sorry I didn't think about how you'd feel. I'm sorry—"

I squeezed his hand. "You can stop there."

"There's one more thing."

There was? That seemed like grade A groveling to me. "I think you covered everything."

"I'm sorry that I was this close to being your boyfriend and I screwed it up."

I never knew I could feel my heartbeat through my eyes. "What are you talking about?"

"Last Sunday, before things went downhill, your dad kept

calling me your boyfriend. I know we didn't have a conversation about that yet, but I didn't want to correct him."

When I didn't respond, he let go of my hand and retreated. "Sorry. I misread the moment."

"Stop apologizing. It's not that." I swallowed. "Don't you think this is fast?"

"No, not for me. I care about you, Jas. I don't want to date anyone else. I thought you'd feel the same way."

I was floored. If any guy—literally any guy—had said that to me in college, I would have said yes so fast, I would have broken a world record. But Alex wasn't just any guy. I wasn't dating him to check off some imaginary dating to-do list written by my parents. He was open and kind and being near him made me hear swoony Taylor Swift songs in the background, almost loud enough to cancel all the noise—our parents, the donut shop, past dating regrets. Alex was different and I didn't want to jeopardize our chances by rushing into things. Not when there were still roadblocks to clear.

"I care about you too, but I want to take our time to get to know each other. We've seen each other what . . . three, four times? Half of those times, there were people around, sticking their nose in our business. I want to spend more time, just you and me."

"I want that too."

"Well . . . you need to give me some time. My parents still need to cool off. Until then, it's going to be very hard for us to get together. I had to lie to come today. I can't afford to keep lying to them."

"So, you're saying I have more groveling to do?" Alex's phone pinged. He meant to swipe the notification away, but its content caught his eye. "Hold on." He returned the sender's call, looking everywhere except at me as he waited. I knew right away it was his mom once he greeted her in their shared dialect that reminded me of Mandarin, but in watercolor. It sounded familiar but blurry at times. He spoke softly at first, dutifully agreeing to whatever it was she was possibly nagging him about, hoping to get her off the phone as soon as possible.

A part of me wished that he had taken the call outside so I didn't have to watch his demeanor change: hard at times and resigned at others. If that was the case, though, I wouldn't have seen the moment when his jaw hardened and his eyes lifted up to my face. His mom was asking about me. His response was short and not exactly the way I usually heard it, but I knew he just confirmed to his mom that he had not seen me since Sunday. In that instant, I felt my stock plummet. I couldn't help but think about all the times I said the same thing about Michael when my parents called. Damn, what a fucked-up feeling.

Alex finally got off the phone. "Sorry. My mom called to remind me about a few things she wanted me to bring for the trip."

"Why didn't you tell her I was with you right now?" I asked bluntly.

Alex stiffened. "I didn't want to get into it with her right now." When he noticed I was unmoved by his answer, he added,

"Trust me. You have to let me deal with my mom in my own way." If I hadn't heard myself say that before about my own parents, I would have been more upset than I let on.

He signaled the waiter for the check. "I'm sorry. I have to go pick up some stuff."

"Fine," I said tersely. I scarfed down the rest of my food so that I didn't have to box it up.

"Jas. Come on." He threw a few bills in the tray when the waiter came with the check. His phone pinged again. "Shit."

"What is it?"

"I forgot I have some work I have to wrap up before I leave," he said, irritated. "I was hoping to spend more time with you today."

"Oh yeah? What did you have in mind?" I ask halfheartedly.

"My original plan was to take you out to dinner, but now I might have to ask you to help me pack while I do some work."

"Sorry, but that's not worth sneaking out of the house for."

Alex lowered his voice. "You know, I don't always do work with my shirt on."

Flirty Alex was back. He was really reaching if he was trying to flirt his way into my good graces. It was a tempting thought, but our waiter happened to choose that exact moment to bring Alex's change with some judgmental side-eye free of charge. Alex face-palmed into our table while I snickered at him.

"I'm really killing it today," he groaned.

"So smooth." I snorted. We exited the diner. Before we split up to our own cars, I gave Alex a chaste kiss. "Have a good trip."

"I'm not going to see you for two weeks and that's all I get?" he complained. "I can't convince you to come over later?" He went in for a proper goodbye kiss.

I pressed a firm hand into his chest to stop him and stepped back toward my car. "You need to go. *I* need to go." I left Alex looking bummed, still standing in front of the diner. As annoyed as I was, something tugged at my chest. I didn't want us to part ways on bad terms, either, not when he was going to be gone for two weeks. Before I climbed in, I shouted, "I'll think about it."

## Chapter 16

*W*hen I arrived home, my dad was already asleep, sparing me from having to fake my displeasure at the long wait times at the DMV. I ran upstairs to take a quick shower and get dressed for work. While I rummaged through my closet, I called Linh, who was eagerly waiting for an update.

"Soooo . . . did you two kiss and make up yet?"

Seriously, this was how she answered the phone? "Linh," I scolded.

"Okay! Geez." She cleared her throat and said in a calmer tone, "How was your date?"

"We had a good time—"

"Yeah, you did," she said suggestively.

"—but let's just say we left things in a tentative place." I held out a few shirts and stuffed them back in. Too wrinkled.

"Why?"

"His mom called and he couldn't tell her he was with me and it . . . sucked."

"Oh no . . . I'm sorry. I was hoping you two would get back on track."

"I know." I groaned. "I really like him, Linh. Things started out so great too until . . . I shouldn't have let my parents get involved."

"I know it wasn't ideal for everyone to meet so soon, but Alex has already met your parents and it's not like they're going anywhere. They're always going to give you their two cents, but you have to tell them what you need."

That was easy for Linh to say. She spoke fluent Vietnamese and her parents were really supportive. We'd gone over this before.

"Give them a chance," Linh said, knowing what I was thinking. "You don't know because you haven't ever tried. But it's not just them, Jas," she continued. "Have you told Alex how much it bothers you?"

"Well, I didn't get a chance to say because we both had to leave." Linh didn't buy that excuse one bit. "And you know . . . I'm just *so great* with my feelings."

Linh quieted down, taking the conversation more seriously. "Jas, when was the last time you've seen your therapist?"

I cleared my throat. "A week before I moved home." Linh was silent. I knew my answer was not as recent as she hoped. My previous therapist was part of the school's counseling services. After I graduated, I didn't bother looking for another one, since working at the shop kept me busy.

"Alex is not like the guys you dated in college. He really likes you. Whenever I'm at the apartment, he asks about you. I just hope moving to New York will get me far enough so that he'll stop asking me questions. Let the man in, figuratively and then *literally*."

"Okay, this conversation is over."

"Wait! Before you go, I'm sending you my flight info for Sunday."

"I can't believe it's coming up so soon. I wish we could have hung out more before you left." I caught a glimpse of the time. I was already running behind, so I pulled the least wrinkled gray T-shirt over my head and put on yesterday's jeans.

"I know. I wanted to come up to see you this week, but I've been busy packing everything. I'm not even close to being done and it has to be shipped today. Hey, I'm going out to dinner with Owen tonight. I don't mind making it a double date."

"No, I don't want to impose." I ran downstairs and put on my shoes.

"Who's imposing? It's my farewell dinner and I'm inviting you. That way, you can see your man."

"Oh, don't say *farewell*. I'm still in denial." I opened the door and walked out to my car. "It's okay. I don't want to take away your time with Owen. I already saw Alex this morning. It's all good. I'll take you to breakfast before I drop you off at the airport."

"Fine, but if you don't come out, then Alex will be home all alone . . ."

"*Mm-hmm*," I said, knowing where she was going with this. The girl had a one-track mind. "Goodbye, Linh," I said in an extra sweet voice before I hung up and left for the shop.

UPON ARRIVAL, MY mom immediately made her grievances known. "Go help your brother with boxes. He's so slow. He has soft hands too!" She grabbed her purse and asked Pat for her car keys.

"Where are you going?" I asked as I split the stack of card stock with Pat.

"Auntie Helen take me to the wholesale warehouse to find cheaper price for matcha."

"Don't buy it just because it's cheap. Make sure it's good quality." I was afraid she'd buy anything that resembled a green powder.

"I know. I took a picture of the one we have. I'll look for the same kind. And we go to lunch and I go to the bank to make a deposit." She rattled off a list of chores to do as she walked out of the shop, as if I didn't do those things on a daily basis.

Pat and I started folding boxes side by side. He was prefolding the creases three at a time.

"You know that doesn't make it go faster," I commented in regard to his technique.

"Oh yeah? I'll race you."

We used to do this as kids when we had nothing better to do. Pat had yet to beat me, and he was sorely out of practice. I was game for an easy win.

"You're on." We double-checked our stacks to make sure we had the same number of boxes to fold. "Ready?" With his game face on, Pat nodded. "Set. Go!"

There was a flurry of arms as we tackled the boxes in our own ways. While Pat was busy prefolding, I put up the first completed box. He eventually caught up and we were neck and neck, building pink box towers around us. I was down to my last five boxes and victory was within reach.

"Jie, your phone is ringing," Pat said, his head down as he worked through his last few boxes.

I continued folding. "Stop distracting me. It's not going to work."

"I swear, jie." He stopped halfway through his last box so that I would stop. The brief silence was broken by my phone's faint ringing. As I ran back to dig my phone out of my purse, I heard Pat finish up his box.

"That doesn't count!" I shouted back when I pulled out my phone. On the screen, the caller ID flashed *Angel City Magazine.* Pat was making a case for his win while he stacked up the boxes.

"Shut up, Pat!" I picked up the call. "Hello?" I said, trying to calm my nerves.

"Hi. Jasmine? This is Ace. Rae sent me your résumé for our social media coordinator position. Is this a good time to talk?"

Ace Miller, founder and owner of *Angel City Magazine,* sounded so young. From the pictures I saw on the *Angel City Magazine* Instagram account, he couldn't have been a day over thirty.

I walked out the back door to the alley to get away from the loud humming and percolating sounds of the shop. "Yeah, I can talk now."

"Cool. So, I don't know if Rae told you, but we're a small team here at *ACM*. We all wear a lot of hats. No job is too small or too big to tackle. So, it's really important to me that we hire someone who fits in well with our team."

"Okay," I said, wondering where Ace was going with this. My heart was beating so fast. The anticipation for my first interview question was killing me.

"So, I need to know," Ace said, in all seriousness. "Two of the staff writers are Trojans. Is this going to be a problem? I don't want to deal with HR if a fight breaks out."

Confused, I said, "Um, no, it wouldn't be a problem." Ace seemed to have a sense of humor, so I took a chance and added, "But all bets are off during Rivalry Weekend."

Ace laughed. "Just take it off-site. Anyway, I know this is short notice, but would you be free to come in today? I can show you around the office. While you're here, HR can get your paperwork started. That way, we can get you set up and in here by . . . next week, maybe?" He didn't sound too confident. "Depends how fast the background check takes."

"Wait. I'm hired?" This was almost too good to be true.

"Yeah. Rae spoke very highly of you. She explained to me that she worked with you on a campaign to promote your parents' business. From what I saw, it looks really good. Most important, she told me you were adaptable and resourceful. Like I said, we wear a lot of hats and I could use someone who can jump in wherever it's needed. So, what do you say?"

I was speechless. Five minutes ago, I was elbow deep in pink boxes, and now all I could think about was a job where my co-workers weren't related to me and the possibility of never having to get coffee for anyone ever again.

"Jas? You still there?" Ace asked, stopping me from spinning.

"Yes." I was physically still there, standing in the alley, staring at the cinder-block wall. The rest of me was floating, fueled by the excitement over this new life that was feeling more and more tangible. I didn't know what the entire job entailed yet, but what I did know was that it would give me a front-row seat to an L.A. that I had primarily seen from afar. It compelled me to say, without reservation, "Yes, I'm here, and yes, I'm happy to accept!"

"Could you be here in the next hour or so?"

"Uh . . . yeah," I blurted, even though Pat would kill me for leaving him alone at the shop. Shit. How was I going to pull this off?

"Sweet. I'll email you the list of documents HR will need from you. Look forward to meeting you!"

I stood there, still holding the phone close to my ear long after Ace ended the call. What the hell was I thinking? I glanced down at my clothes. I was not at all ready to meet my new boss. How the hell was I going to get out of the shop? How was I going to tell my current boss?

Pat swung open the metal screen door into my shoulder. "Hey, what's going on?"

I hurried in without answering. Out of habit, I marched right up to the front counter, which Pat had cleared after finishing all the boxes. There was nobody in sight, inside the shop or out in the parking lot. It was a dead period of the day when the rest of the world was at work. Lunch wasn't for another hour and the summer camp at the elementary school wouldn't let out for a few hours after that. Now was as good of a time as any to make a run for it.

"Jie, why do you have that look on your face?" he asked cautiously.

"Pat. I got the job! Rae's old job," I clarified, still in disbelief. "I need to go right now to do some paperwork."

"Are you insane? I mean, congrats, but Mom and Dad are going to flip out!"

"I know, but I can't think about that right now. I already accepted it and I need to go. Can you please cover for me?"

The request alarmed Pat. "How am I supposed to do that?"

"It'll be fine," I argued. "It's so slow. At most, you'll get one or two customers at a time."

"It's not that, jie." He tilted his head back toward the security camera. "What if they find out you left? They're going to wonder where you are and where you drove off to in the middle of the day when you already supposedly went to the DMV, which was obviously a lie."

Damn it. The logistics never crossed my mind when I hastily agreed. I didn't want to flake out on my new boss, so I ran a few possible scenarios in my head. None of them sounded good or came without risk.

"Pat. We don't know if Mom will check the cameras, but if she does, tell her I'm in the back icing more donuts. She's going to be out for a while. I should make it back before then."

"What about your car?"

I wished I hadn't parked it so close to the front within the camera's view. If my mom found out I left Pat alone, I would set myself back before I could break the news that I accepted an "unstable" job. I swiped my phone. Uber was out of the question; the cost would eat up my first day's pay. I couldn't ask Alex or Linh. Both of them were busy and neither of them were in the area. I sent a desperate text into the group chat.

**JAS:** Guess what? I got Rae's old job! Thanks so much Rae!
**BILLY:** Congrats!
**RAE:** YAYYYYYY!
**KAYLEY:** CONGRATS!
**JAS:** Any chance someone's free to take me to sign some paperwork?

There were really only three viable options. Billy was back at Stanford and Josh was at work. I didn't care who it was as long as one of them could pull through.

**Rae:** That's fast! I would but I'm at my new job.

**Kayley:** Sorry. I'm not free

The group chat came to a halt.

"Well?" Pat asked as I frantically stared at my phone, willing Michael to respond. As minutes passed, I contemplated between shelling out the money for a ride and throwing caution into the wind and driving myself. What were the chances that my mom would check the camera anyway? Maybe I could make it if I drove fast enough. My phone pinged.

**Michael:** when?

**Jas:** right now . . . ? 😄🙏

I texted Michael outside of the group chat, explaining the situation. I let out a sigh of relief when he said he could come get me in ten minutes. I instructed him to park on the street near the alley behind the shop. I filled Pat in on the plan. I reassured him that I would get back as soon as I could, before my mom would get back. I offered plenty of excuses in case my mom checked the camera.

"Tell her I'm making a new batch of glaze. I'm washing all the trays. I'm doing inventory."

"Or I could tell her that you're taking a massive dump," he joked.

"Pat!" I scolded.

"Just get back before I have to tell her anything." He watched as I stepped out the back door. "You better know what you're doing," he warned, locking up behind me.

I waited in the alley behind the liquor store and ran up to Michael's car as he pulled up, just as I had instructed.

"Thank you so much," I said as I buckled myself in.

"Where to?"

I asked him to take me home so that I could change my clothes quickly and gather my documents.

"You're a lifesaver," I said as I plugged *ACM*'s address into my phone for directions. "I hope I didn't ruin your plans."

"I was about to run errands, but it's okay. I know you wouldn't have asked if it wasn't important." He gave me an encouraging smile as he turned onto my street and parked in front of my neighbor's house without skipping a beat. A feeling of déjà vu washed over me. I looked at Michael out of the corner of my eye and I could tell he felt it too. We were sitting in the same sky-blue car he drove in high school, parked at the same safe spot away from my house. It was way weird.

The door handle clicked as I opened the door. "I'll be right back."

I jogged off the awkward feelings as I quietly opened the door. I peeked inside to make sure my dad wasn't downstairs foraging for lunch. When I heard his quiet snore from upstairs, I tiptoed up to my room and picked out a black pair of jeans that was a passable substitution for slacks and switched my T-shirt out for a tank top, layering a pink button-up blouse over it. I stuffed my T-shirt and jeans into a bag to change back into later. I flipped through my desk for my Social Security card and slid it into my wallet with my driver's license. On my way out, I grabbed a pair of flats and sneaked back out of my house without incident.

I jumped back into Michael's car and told him to step on it. He sensed my nerves, probably because I was flip-flopping between keeping my hair up or letting it down. He kept our conversation topics light on the way there, catching me up on his family and some of the things he wanted to do before starting his job on Monday.

"I had these big plans like going on a road trip to Seattle, but I didn't think Misty would make it," he said, referring to his car. "I guess this will have to do."

I chuckled. "You still call her Misty?" I flicked the green pine tree air freshener that hung on his rearview mirror. I kept a lookout for the address and pointed it out when I spotted *ACM* on the marquee. We made it in decent time. I turned off the GPS and silenced my phone, not wanting it to interrupt my meeting with Ace. Michael took the first open parking spot down the block. He turned to me, surprised that I didn't jump out of the car the second he put it in park.

"Jas," he said, noticing my trembling hands on my lap. "Are you okay?"

I took deep yoga-style breaths. "Yeah," I huffed. I clamped my hands around my bouncing knees. "I can't believe I'm doing this. This is really happening."

"Hey." He gave my shoulder a gentle squeeze, startling me. "You already got the job. What's freaking you out?"

I vomited all the thoughts that were jammed in my mind. "What if I did all this and my parents kill me and I can't show up on my first day? Or what if this job sucks? Or my coworkers suck? Or I suck? And I end up posting something that wasn't 'on brand' and it's my fault because I don't even know what that means. Did I just accept a job without seeing anything in writing? What if—"

"What if," he interjected, "everything turns out fine? Jas. You'll figure things out. You always do." He squeezed my shoulder again before letting go.

I took a few more calming breaths before I nodded. Saying all my worries out loud helped, more than I expected it to. I reached over and placed my hand on his forearm. "Thanks. You always know what to say." And with that, I stepped out of the car and worked off the rest of my nerves as I headed toward *ACM*'s headquarters.

*ANGEL CITY MAGAZINE*'s open office space was on the third floor of a former toy factory building in Downtown L.A. Every surface in the space had been renovated like it was tailor-made for Instagram. There was a plant wall to my left with some hydroponic vases artfully placed on different levels. To my right, there was a huge mural of Los Angeles, capturing every enclave and landmark. Straight ahead was a white neon sign for *Angel City Magazine* in a modern cursive font. I felt so out of my element.

I greeted Amanda, the receptionist, who directed me to Ace's cubicle at the far corner of the floor.

"Hi, Jasmine!" Ace shook my hand. "Welcome to our humble abode." If I ever met Ace on the street, I would have never guessed that he was the owner/editor in chief of a digital magazine that was gaining clout among Angelenos. He had one of those deceivingly boyish faces, like Tom Holland.

"Hi, Ace." I looked curiously at his tiny workspace. Besides a few awards, nothing else graced his desk. His drab cubicle was a stark contrast to *ACM*'s colorful office.

"As you can see, we're tight for space." He pointed at an office on the opposite wall. "That used to be my office. We decided recently to do some podcasts, so we converted my old office into our set. My stuff is still in boxes." He pointed to the adjacent conference room. "That's our kitchen slash conference room slash storage space."

Ace walked ahead of me and introduced me to some of the staff.

"This is Riley Turner. She's our most senior writer. If you have any questions, she's a good person to ask."

I shook Riley's hand. "Nice to meet you," I said. I eyed Riley's bright coral athleisure outfit. It clung to her body in a way that made me think working out might be fun. The logical part of my brain knew it wasn't true, so I tried to hold on to that thought before I spent my entire first paycheck on what were basically expensive leggings.

Riley tightened her sandy blond ponytail and grabbed her water bottle. "Nice to meet you, Jasmine. I'm sorry to rush out, but I need to get to SoulCycle before I try this new tapas place for lunch. Looking forward to working with you!" Riley waved goodbye before stepping out of the office with such bounce that her ponytail swung like a pendulum.

"We aim to have good work/life balance around here. We don't work the typical nine to five, so as long as you get your work done, I'm pretty flexible with what you do with your time." Ace poked his head around a few empty cubicles. "A few people are out right now covering a cosplay event at the Convention Center and the protest in Boyle Heights over a new development. Some folks are off, since most events happen on the weekends."

I was so used to my schedule at the donut shop that it didn't occur to me that my new work schedule could be drastically different. I had assumed it was a Monday through Friday situation.

At the second to last cubicle, Ace introduced me to Mel, short for Melody, who previously covered the music scene before becoming *ACM*'s deputy editor. Mel had beautiful long braids and looked effortlessly chic in an orange-red jumpsuit. I had a sense Mel and I would get along right away. She had a warm personality, and it was apparent from all the concert and movie ticket stubs that were neatly pinned throughout her workstation that we had similar tastes.

He pointed at the empty cubicle closest to the entrance. It had an odd configuration, where the desk faced the wall, exposing the computer screen to the shared space behind it. "This will be your workspace. Sorry. Once Rae left, Marco, our graphic designer who used to sit here, jumped on her workstation real fast. Don't worry. Our office is more of a place to drop stuff off before heading to places and events we report on. We do have team meetings every Monday, so hopefully we can get your paperwork started so that you can meet everyone then."

Ace led me out of the newsroom and down the hallway to a nondescript office.

"Some of our administrative staff work from here. I didn't think I needed so much space when I started the magazine. Jeanette from HR will take care of the paperwork with you. I have to get going, but I'll email you more info about your first week with us. Mel will train you, so I have to check her schedule and let you know. If you have any questions in the meantime, you can email or text. You have my info, right?"

I nodded.

"One more thing. If you haven't noticed, we dress pretty casual here. We do dress up if the occasion calls for it, but nothing super formal. Cool?"

I gave Ace a thumbs-up like a dweeb. I had never done that before. I didn't know where it came from. I quickly curled my fingers around my thumb before it became a permanent fixture.

Alex left me with Jeanette, who pointed her pink bedazzled acrylic talon at every line that required my signature. I signed as quickly as I could, and before I knew it, I officially had a cramped hand and a real job, pending my background check clearance.

I TALKED MICHAEL'S ear off the entire drive home, giving him a play-by-play of my meeting with Ace. When traffic slowed, I showed him pictures of the office from their Instagram account. I was so elated that I didn't know where we were until he parked the car where he had picked me up just a couple hours before.

"Don't forget this," he said, hopping out and handing me my bag of clothes after I climbed out of the passenger seat.

"Yes, that's very important." I squealed as my feet tapped into their happy dance. "I can't believe I did that!" I threw my arms around Michael for a bear hug. "Thank you so much." I looked up at him with the wide smile that hadn't left my face since I walked out of *ACM*. "I wouldn't have been able to do this without—"

I didn't know what happened first. When Michael suddenly crashed his mouth onto mine, it disconnected the brain signals to my body. It didn't register when his hands came up and held my face or when my eyes closed. The kiss itself lasted a few seconds and ran on old muscle memory, like riding a bike. When my brain finally synced up and went back online, my eyes flew open and I stepped back.

I touched my swollen lips. "What was that? Why did you do that?"

Michael stared me, shocked at my bewilderment. "I thought . . ." He held his tongue and took a step back.

From the back door, the sound of trays clapping on the counter cut through our conversation. What was Pat doing?

"I have to go."

"Right," he said under his breath.

Though his voice was soft, his disappointment was loud and clear. "I'm sorry," I offered. "I didn't mean—"

Michael shook his head as he turned toward his car. "Yeah . . . whatever."

I winced when he slammed the door and drove off. How did this happen? My head was in the clouds, running over what I could have done differently as I headed toward the back door. I had one foot in the shop when I registered my mom's hurried voice, counting off donuts. My dad stood at the glazing station, dipping donuts into Froot Loops with swift precision as my mom flipped open an empty pink box.

"What took you so long?" my mom barked. "Your new boss made you work already?" *What the hell?* My eyes darted to Pat, who was standing behind my mom.

"Sorry," he mouthed.

Oh shit. He told them everything.

My mom stuffed donuts into the pink box with less of her usual finesse. "You leave your brother here by himself," she huffed. "You know he's slow."

"I didn't think—"

"No, you didn't think! He call me, tell me to come help. There were so many customers, like it was morning."

I was baffled. Afternoons were notoriously slow. Under different circumstances, this would have been a positive development. "Who . . . how?"

She ignored me. "Then we call you. You don't pick up your phone. You sneak out! With *that boy.* I knew something going on with that boy!"

I hated that she insinuated that there was something inherently wrong with Michael. As if his ethnicity had contributed to any of this shitstorm. "There's nothing—"

She shook her head in aggravation. "This is why you can't find boyfriend. You're no good. You lie to your family. You're *lazy.*"

I wasn't in any position to argue the no-good liar parts, but lazy? *Lazy?!* That stoked the fire in my stomach.

"How can you call me lazy? I work here every day with you guys. I've worked here all my life! You wonder why I don't have a life or a boyfriend? I don't have time for one because I'm always here! You know how many school events I've missed because of the shop? Don't you ever wonder why I don't have more friends? It's because of this stupid shop!"

"Don't talk back to your ma!" my dad scolded. My outburst tested his patience.

"This 'stupid' shop pays for the house you live in and the food you eat," my mom ranted. "Your college. Your clothes. Your—"

"I know!" I cried. She didn't need to list every single line item to get her point across. I struggled to find the right words to explain how I was feeling without coming across as ungrateful.

"If you think this shop so 'stupid,' move out then," my mom dared. "See how much food you can eat with your new job. Maybe you get skinny because you won't have money to buy food!"

"Ma!" It was becoming harder and harder to feel remorseful when my mom dealt in petty arguments. They weren't anything I hadn't heard before, but they were easier to brush off when they came in small doses, not when she was piling them all at the same time.

"You'll see. Then you wish you study to be a lawyer like Linh or engineer like Pat."

Part of me knew I was meant to take her comment at face value, but it compounded this deeply rooted idea that my life would be so much better if I was smarter, thinner, stronger, more poised, less sarcastic, or less disruptive. More or less, not me. Anybody else but me. This part broke me, bringing resentment into this volatile mix of insecurity and guilt.

"You think Pat is so fucking perfect?!" I yelled in a blind rage. "He fucked up his internship! Why do you think he's fucking home?"

"What the fuck, jie!?" Pat shouted from the entryway.

"What? Is that true, Pat?" my dad asked Pat. He got his answer when Pat wouldn't meet his eyes. "You!" He wagged his finger at me. "This is your fault."

"How?" I threw up my arms. "He's the one who didn't check his fucking email!"

"Fucking hell, jie." Pat retreated to the safety of the front counter.

"Everyone stop saying *fuck*!" my dad shouted.

"Because you always lie. My daughter, the liar," my mom declared.

I had enough. There was plenty for me to feel bad for, but I wasn't going to take Pat's shit too. I pulled my car keys from my purse.

"Where are you going?" she called after me.

My instinct was to reply back with "Moving out!" but I kept it to myself. As I crossed the entryway, Pat appeared, arms crossed, blocking my way. He wouldn't budge, so I bumped past him. He could deal with his own mess this time.

## Chapter 17

*W*hen I arrived home, I ran up to my room and lay in bed. All the huff and puff from my earlier rage had deflated. I finally checked my phone to see the slew of Pat's messages that I had missed.

PAT: shit jie. That one guy came back for his free coffee
   and brought back a bunch of friends.

PAT: some Yelp group?

PAT: when are you coming back?

PAT: they're taking all kinds of pictures of the shop

PAT: they want to know if there's some secret ingredient
   in the sesame donut

PAT: should I make some shit up?

PAT: a lady from the school wants to do a special order
   for the camp kids

PAT: 6 dozen!

PAT: you need to come back ASAP to ice the donuts

**Pat:** where r u?
**Pat:** sorry. I had to call mom.
**Pat:** hurry back

Fuck. I imagined Pat flailing as Yelpers bombarded our shop. I checked Yelp, but the reviews hadn't posted yet. What if that was our opportunity for the shop to get more positive reviews and I blew it?

I closed Pat's texts and checked if I missed any others. There was one from Michael, but I skipped it. I couldn't deal with him right now. The only other text came from Alex.

**Alex:** Are you sure you can resist these?

Below was a picture of his bare calves, flexed in a Captain Morgan stance. I deeply regretted telling him that I thought they were sexy, but a smile tugged on my lips, wondering how he could have possibly taken this photo.

**Jas:** you're getting desperate and it shows

My phone rang.

"Is it working?" The humor in his voice melted away some of the stress from the day. "Do you want to come over? I just finished with work. I think I can still make reservations for the place I wanted to take you."

That sounded so good, considering the alternatives. Being at home felt like a slow death, biding my time until round two with my family. In the background, I heard Owen's muffled voice, reminding me of Linh's farewell dinner.

"I don't know. I'm not in the mood to go out tonight."

"Did I say go out? I meant stay in. You can help me pack." When I didn't reply with a snappy comeback and the pause in our conversation had gone on a touch too long, he asked, "Is everything okay?"

I didn't know where to begin with that question, so I changed the subject. "Where's Owen taking Linh tonight?"

"Owen's driving to Garden Grove to help Linh ship her stuff. Seriously, is something wrong? You don't have to help me pack. We can just hang out. Or I can come to you if—"

"No!" If I was trying not to raise suspicion, I failed miserably. "No," I repeated, calmer this time. "I . . . I got into an argument with my parents," I offered as a temporary explanation. As for the rest of it, I was still making sense of it myself.

"About what?"

This simple question, a mere two words, filled me with dread. It was the gateway to a million more questions that I realized would be better answered in person. That way, I could better convey context and rationale. That's what I hoped, at least.

I swallowed my anxiety. "I'll come over. Text me your address."

"HEY." ALEX TOOK my purse as I entered his apartment and placed it on the side table before greeting me with a hug. It had the warm coziness of being wrapped in a comforter, making it the perfect antidote after a rough day. I let myself melt into it, savoring it while it lasted.

"Nice place," I said after I cracked an eye open.

His loft was modern and neat, but very much a bachelor's pad. The white walls were unadorned. Past the small island, the kitchen looked like it had never been used with still shiny appliances and an empty bright white countertop. If it weren't for the mismatched furniture, his place could have stood in for a model apartment.

Alex assessed my tired eyes and weak smile before he bent down for a reassuring kiss. "Do you want something to drink?"

I declined as he laced his fingers with mine, leading me down the T-shaped hallway for a brief tour. In an effort to keep the conversation light, he injected random, unnecessary observations.

"Here's the bathroom," he said at the first door on the right. "And that bougie soap that Linh likes." Pointing at the closed door across the way, he added, "Closet, just in case you want to see our collection of . . ." he pretended to count—"three towels?" Alex made a quick left when we reached the end, letting go of my hand at the doorway. "And here's my room."

Alex rolled his luggage to the side to clear the way for me.

"I thought I wasn't here to help you pack," I said as I walked in, eyeing the pile of clothes on top of his bed.

"You're not." He swiveled the chair out from behind his desk and plopped me down. "You can sit here and look pretty," he said, winking as he threw my words back at me.

That wink at point-blank range was set on stun, and if it had been under different circumstances, I would have closed the few inches that divided us—because come on, his bed was right there. Instead, I let him back away and watched him fold his clothes.

"My laptop is on if you want to watch something. Are you hungry? We can order takeout."

I shrugged, not sure if I could eat.

Alex paused. "If you don't want to tell me what's wrong, that's fine, but what can I do to help you feel better?"

Did he have a time machine so I could restart this day?

"What time will you arrive in Hangzhou?"

Alex's eyebrows knitted together while he stacked his shirts. "With the layover, I won't be there until Monday morning. That reminds me . . ." He tossed aside a pair of shorts and picked up his phone. "I just sent you an invite for WeChat, so we can still text."

"Oh, okay," I said, my voice distant. I swung around and aimlessly browsed his desk to keep busy. Alex didn't seem to mind as he observed from the opposite side of the room.

"Out on the hunt, the stalker creeps upon her prey: the defenseless desk drawer," Alex narrated like a National Geographic documentary while he tucked a pair of socks into a zippered compartment.

It was so unexpected that I laughed, which made him chuckle. His shoulders visibly relaxed with the change in my mood. I had no idea I affected him that way. With a bashful sidelong glance, I began to slide the drawer back into its rightful place.

"I didn't mean to stop you," he said with his normal voice. "Not that it would be interesting. Just some receipts and other stuff that I don't know where else to keep."

As he said this, I noticed a folded insert from the *Daily Bruin*, our college newspaper, under a heap of receipts. At the top, there was a gray-scale photo of Alex, surrounded by suited-up fraternity brothers and sisters in some hotel conference room.

"That guy at the end of the second row, that's Terrence. He's the guy I'm meeting up with in Shanghai," Alex said.

"We clearly ran in different circles." I skimmed the article, which read like their fraternity's year in review—their fundraising, their alumni mentoring program, and professional conferences they attended together. "How did you have time to do all of this?"

Alex shrugged. "Some people might hit the gym after a breakup, but I threw myself into school, I guess."

His voice was more pensive than the previous times his ex came up, but I couldn't bring myself to ask him to elaborate. He didn't give me much of a choice either way.

"You should look on the next page. There's another picture of me with my mentor, who helped me get my job."

I unfolded the newspaper, and below the article, my eyes landed on a face I tried hard to forget. The pages crinkled with my tightening grip. "I'm glad we didn't date during college. I don't think you would have liked me then."

From the corner of my eye, I caught Alex's confused reaction at my cryptic comment. He dropped whatever he was folding and sat at the edge of his bed across from me. "Where did that come from?"

I placed the newspaper facedown on his desk. "At the diner, you asked me if it would have been better if we dated in college, but we wouldn't have been good together." Alex's face was marred with the look of concern. I chewed on my lip as I considered what to say next. When I came here, recalling one of the worst moments of my life wasn't on the docket, but here we were. I didn't want to talk about my past as much as he did, but today, it all caught up to me and I had nowhere else to turn.

"My GPA was shit after taking my science classes. I was studying around the clock, repeating classes, and I couldn't catch up. By senior year, I was burnt out because after all the time I put into studying, hunting for boyfriends, and working at the donut shop, I was supposed to have figured out my future. So I kinda . . ."—I swallowed hard—"went on a bender. Partied a lot."

My mouth glued shut at that understatement. It started with the occasional party. It quickly escalated to partying on Thursdays, Fridays, and Saturdays. Weekend after weekend, I drank free booze and danced my way through strangers' apartments with Linh. I remember that euphoric high the first time I tried molly, thinking there was no better way to make up for lost time. Linh was happy that I was finally having fun instead of being a hermit. So much so that she didn't mind babysitting me as I let loose. I didn't make Linh's job easy. Soon it had extended into Sundays and Hangover Mondays, or what I thought were Mondays. I didn't always know what day it was.

Alex gave me a look like he wasn't quite following. "So, you went to a few parties. Everybody parties senior year."

"I was . . . I don't want to say 'dating someone,' because that's kind of a stretch, but I went out with someone. We were at a concert and I got wasted and passed out. Ended up at the hospital and my parents found out. They didn't take it very well, so I guess you can say I've been groveling in my own way." I cleared my throat, punctuating this abridged version of events.

At one party, I recognized Nate Sutton, who wrote for the *Daily Bruin.* His picture was printed every week next to his pop culture columns. I remember telling him how cool it was that he wrote articles about movies and concerts, even though I disagreed with his reviews half the time. I can't say for certain how coherent my arguments were, but I thought he was cute, so we danced to an awful remix of John Legend's "All of Me."

When a couple of drunk girls spilled their drinks on me, I didn't mind Nate following me into the bathroom as I cleaned myself up. He was the first person who showed even a remote interest in me in three years, so I took all the attention he was willing to give me. Even though it was consensual, having a one-night stand in some rando's bathroom during a party was a new low for me. There's nothing less romantic than having sex in a moldy frat-house bathroom while people knocked on the door the entire time to see if the bathroom was really occupied.

Linh found me doing the Walk of Shame that night. She tried to make me feel better about it, but we both knew it was out of character for me. It was too reckless. I was lucky that I didn't get an STD. When Nate texted me the following week about going to the Odesza concert, I was hopeful. Maybe I didn't have to write him off as my college one-night stand. Maybe it would turn into something promising. Linh insisted that she come with me, and I'll always be forever indebted to her because of it.

That night started out pretty normal. We pre-partied at Nate's apartment. At the concert, I had more drinks and molly before the floor became too crowded. At first it was amazing. I felt so free and happy, dancing against bodies that I knew belonged to strangers, yet I loved them for no apparent reason. Nothing was on my mind except for the music. It was the most fun I'd ever had.

Until it wasn't.

Within the hour, the music started to feel heavy. My clothes were drenched. Was everyone dancing around me sweaty or was it just me? The colorful, glowing lights from the stage turned pitch-black in an instant and my body met the floor. The last thing I saw before I passed out was Nate's glowing white V-neck shirt backing up when Linh approached the scene. Luckily, Linh took me to the hospital right away and called my parents. If Linh hadn't been there, I don't know what would have happened to me, since Nate was nowhere to be found.

The first thing I saw when I woke up in a hospital bed was the disappointment written across my parents' faces. I knew right away that I had hit rock bottom. All the years I spent carrying extra responsibilities, handling everything myself, thinking I was protecting them, came crashing down. I lost their trust and I would have done anything to earn it back. My parents didn't want to let me out of their sight, but with graduation so close, they enlisted Linh to be their eyes as I completed my last quarter. I checked in with them every night and went home every weekend. After graduation, I moved home and worked at the shop ever since, hoping to show them that I was fine. But now it had been over a year of this redemption tour and I didn't feel fine.

How did I get this so wrong? I hadn't done anything differently, still using work-arounds, yet I expected new results.

"I screwed that up, though," I muttered. "Things got pretty ugly between us today."

"Why?"

"I got the job . . . at *Angel City Magazine.*"

"Oh." Alex blinked at the news. "Isn't that a good thing?"

I tried to recall the explanation I rehearsed on the drive there. No matter how many different angles I took, I knew he was not going to like the Michael-shaped parts of the story. Alex's warm hands wrapped around my fingers, which had been rapping on my knees. They stayed there as I rambled about the swarm of customers, missed texts, and how I accidentally threw Pat under the bus as my mom and I got into it. But there was no amount of practice that could have prepared me for the chill that replaced Alex's hands when he let go upon hearing about Michael's involvement.

Alex didn't say anything for a while. When he first withdrew, his eyes bored into mine, searching for confirmation that he'd heard correctly.

"Why didn't you call me?" The question came out slow and measured, but I heard the edge in his voice.

"You were busy—"

"I would have come, especially if *your ex* was your only other option." I opened my mouth to reply when he elaborated further. "Don't say he's just a friend. Exes don't drop what they're doing to help their ex-girlfriend out of the goodness of their hearts."

My face grew hot as Alex stared, like he was waiting for me to defend Michael. To say that nothing happened.

"You're right." My heart raced as I committed to full transparency, knowing that it wasn't going to go over well. "I should have known, and I should have asked you." His eyes widened and before he could jump to conclusions, I added, "He kissed me after he dropped me off, but it didn't mean anything."

"Wait a minute." Alex held out one hand to stop me while the other braced his chest. "How . . . Why would he kiss you if . . . Did he not know about me?"

I blanched at the question. It never crossed my mind to tell Michael about Alex because I avoided talking to Michael as much as possible.

Alex clenched his jaw as his eyes darted down to my twisted mouth. "I think you should go." His voice was soft, but his words stung. He shot to his feet and resumed packing, throwing clothes into his luggage.

"Why? I didn't do anything wrong." Alex shot an indignant look toward me that took a second for me to process. "It's not like *I* kissed *him*. I didn't—"

"You lied to me," he said with undeniable conviction. "You said your ex wasn't in the picture, but there he is, conveniently at your shop or picking you up or who knows what else."

I winced at his accusation, but I couldn't feel the cut of his words over my anger. How dare he call me a liar when he had been doing the same? Putting up smoke and mirrors to present the arguably best version of him and me to his mom? Saying his ex was in his past, but letting jealousy cloud the truth? These conversations were long overdue, but after an emotionally draining day, I had no energy left for them.

"If you want me to leave, then I'll go, but nothing else happened, okay? I'm not going to sit here and let you project whatever insecurity you have on me." I stood up, squaring my shoulders. "You can say all you want that your ex is irrelevant, but she's not. Otherwise, you wouldn't be spewing all this bullshit about me seeing Michael behind your back. Honestly, if you think I'm so terrible, why are we even dating?"

Alex's eyes darted to mine. "That's not what I—"

"Isn't that why you lied to your mom about me . . . again?" I scoffed as I stalked out of his room.

"Jas, you know it's not like that," Alex said, following me down the hallway. "You of all people should understand."

I didn't bother turning around as I reached the front door. "What's that supposed to mean?"

"You lied to your parents just this morning."

"That's not the same thing." I shook my head and threw my purse over my shoulder. "I do it to have a life . . . to . . . to be more of who I am. Not to pretend that I'm something I'm not. So, you can take your apology and shove it."

It wasn't the most articulate thing to say, but it felt warranted. With his hands on his hips, Alex met my glare with a resigned gaze. There was that lingering pull toward each other, but neither of us wanted to cross the invisible line drawn between us.

Eventually, Alex broke first. "You're right. I shouldn't have said that, but it's just . . . how do you think I feel? My ex cheated on me, telling me she had to stay late at the lab, conveniently leaving out that she was staying late with her lab partner."

I wanted to tell him that it sounded like a personal problem, but the vulnerability in his voice and the pained expression on his face caused my frustration to dissipate. Even so, it didn't resolve anything.

"Well," I said, trying to keep my voice even, "I don't know if you've noticed, but I'm not her."

"Jas."

I turned around to leave, but he reached for the doorknob just as I had, stopping me in my tracks. The shock of his warm touch put every inch of my body on high alert, sensing him standing close behind. I closed my eyes as his arm relaxed onto mine and his chin descended on my shoulder. It ached, wanting to lean into him, but I was tired. Tired of past mistakes. Tired of putting myself out there only to get hurt.

Twisting the knob, I opened the door and left.

## Chapter 18

*W*hen I returned home, everyone went into their respective corners. My mom went to the kitchen to warm up leftovers. My dad, having had his normal sleep interrupted, went straight to bed to rest up for tomorrow morning's bake. Pat went to his room, threw on his headphones, and shut the door. I went to the kitchen to gauge how my mom was feeling. She pretended that I wasn't there and walked around me. The silent treatment was in full effect.

She did let me eat, despite what she had said to me earlier. I wasn't sure how I was supposed to act. We had eaten in silence plenty of times after long days at the shop, but not due to a fight. Was I supposed to show shame and beg for forgiveness, even though there was a part of me that had no regrets about getting a new job? How could I explain that I wanted the shop to thrive, but I didn't want any part in it anymore? Would any of that matter if they didn't trust me? I ate quickly without looking up from the table. As I stood up to take my plate to the sink, my mom said the only thing she would say to me for the rest of the night.

"Don't come to work tomorrow," she said sternly.

At first I wasn't sure if it was a test. Was I to show up anyway to prove my loyalty or was I supposed to do as she asked? I studied her for a moment. Her face was long, tired from an unpredictable day. She could barely tolerate sitting across the table from me for a short meal. She wouldn't be able to keep her cool with me being so close behind the front counter, with customers as our audience. I nodded, intent on meeting her request.

"WHY AM I always driving to the airport?" I grumbled. I was sitting in traffic with Linh and her parents, who decided to help Linh settle into her new place. They were bickering over being late. It was giving me a headache, adding to the shortness of breath I was starting to feel as we inched closer to Linh's departure. I wasn't sure what her parents were so worried about. We were almost there, and even with the delay, I estimated that they had at least two hours before they needed to arrive at their gate.

"Because you love me, Jas. You wanted to spend every last minute with me before I leave. I know you're going to run past security and try to catch me before I board the plane, only to see my airplane take off. Just like in the movies."

I snorted at Linh's rom-com vision. "Have you seen me run? Seriously, next time take an Uber."

"You do realize I'm about to pay law school tuition, right? I need to save every dollar I have." Linh narrowed her eyes as she studied my profile. "Are you okay? You don't look like you've had much sleep."

"That's because I haven't," I said dryly. "I haven't heard from Alex and my family's still giving me the silent treatment." If I had needed a sign about how anyone was feeling, my dad left me a Post-it Note on my bedroom door with an angry face drawn on top, flared nostrils and all.

"You and Alex can work things out." Linh held my hand. "And your family will come around. You'll see."

"What makes you so sure?" I whined.

"Because . . . at the end of the day, they'll always want what's best for you. They don't know what that entails yet, but that's where you come in. You have to tell them what you need."

"I tried," I said, recalling our shouting match at the shop. "I even thought about typing all the things I wanted to say into Google Translate, but it didn't sound right."

"It's not always about the right words, Jas. You have to let them in here." She reached over and pressed her hand on my left boob.

"This will be our last memory together. You, fondling my boob."

Linh shrugged before she placed her hand back on her lap. "What? You have nice boobs."

"What am I supposed to do without you, Linh?"

"Stop being dramatic. I'm just moving to the East Coast. Even when I'm drowning in torts, you can always call me."

"Thanks," I said with a weak smile as I pulled into the drop-off zone at John Wayne Airport.

I helped Linh and her parents unload their luggage. Linh's mom wrapped her hands around mine as she thanked me for driving. I humbly nodded, wishing them safe travels. I stood in front of Linh and we both tried to play it cool, but we failed miserably. We embraced in a big bear hug. As we separated, I blinked away the tears that welled in my eyes.

"I'm going to miss yo face, Jas." Linh sniffled as she pressed her hands on my cheeks, making my lips pucker.

"There's always FaceTime," I muttered out of my squished face. "You're going to do great, Linh." Linh's mom offered to take a picture of us two before they departed. Linh insisted that we wear our sunglasses because our eyes were already red and puffy. After squinting at my phone and holding it out at an un-flatteringly low angle, Linh's mom snapped a couple of photos. Linh and I hugged one last time before I watched her disappear into the airport.

I returned to my car and opened my camera roll to see the photos. I laughed and cried at the same time. Instead of taking a normal smiling photo, both Linh and I had exaggerated ugly crying expressions on our faces. In this sad moment, we still spoke the same language.

I posted the picture on Instagram. I typed the first caption that came to mind before someone honked at me for parking at the drop-off zone too long.

"My BFF. Ride or Die. Roomie. California Gurl. NYU won't know what hit 'em!"

I CALLED MY mom when I was almost home. She had broken her silent treatment, though we spoke only when necessary. I was planning to help her close the shop, but traffic pushed me behind schedule. She told me not to bother since Pat was with her. It was for the best, since I cried most of the way home. A tearstained, swollen face would surely scare away customers.

By the time I walked into my house, I still hadn't shaken off my somber mood. I went upstairs to my room and sat at my desk, hoping to gain some inspiration on how to explain things to my parents.

The blinking cursor on my laptop taunted me, counting every second that I left the page blank. I began to feel restless. Unable to sit still, I paced around my room. Being at home made me feel itchy and I needed to get out. I opened my window to get some air. Looking out, all I could see were the mountains. Between the golden light and the smog, the mountains looked two-dimensional. The dark slate silhouette of the uneven mountaintops looked like the void of a sheet of paper hastily torn in half.

In a momentary lapse of sanity, I ran downstairs and grabbed my sneakers. I didn't bother to change my clothes. I had to go before I talked myself out of it.

I took a deep breath as I approached the hiking trail. I didn't plan to hike the entire trail since there was only an hour left before closing time. Because I came here impulsively, I didn't have any supplies with me except for the bottle of water I had in my car.

The sun was starting to set and the sky had a cool orange sherbet hue. I embarked on the trail at a slow and steady pace. I said hello whenever I crossed paths with other hikers, but I mainly focused on the hike itself, making sure one foot made it in front of the other. I concentrated on the crunchy sound of the gravel underneath my feet instead of the noise in my mind. I stopped when I came across a field of tall yellow wildflowers, admiring their almost neon highlighter tone that called my attention away from the dry gray brush.

"Miss!" An older hiker walking in the opposite direction called toward me. He lifted his walking pole and pointed it downhill toward the entrance. "The trail is closing soon. Might want to turn back around."

"Thanks!" I said. He saluted me as he continued walking back down.

I cradled a flower in my hand, grazing my thumb across its petals. Its unassuming beauty left an inexplicable imprint on me. As the wind brought the petals to a flutter, it also gave way to a sense of calm and clarity that I sorely needed after the past few days.

In that moment, I thought of Alex. I understood why this was such an important part of him.

With my phone, I snapped a picture of the entire hillside. The sunset cast shadows from its uneven dips and curves. The clouds overhead gave the photo a sense of movement to an otherwise unyielding mass.

I made my way back down to my car and posted the picture on my Instagram. I watched my photo load with the following caption: "First solo hike."

MY MOM WAS clearing the table when I walked into the house. She frowned in confusion at my arrival. "You took that long going to the airport?" she asked, skeptical.

I pointed down at my running shoes. "I went to exercise," I said, knowing she wouldn't understand the concept of hiking as a voluntary activity.

Her eyebrows shot up, silently questioning me before she disappeared into the kitchen without further comment. I waited around to see if she'd ask me if I had eaten yet, but I gave up on it once I heard the water running as she washed dishes.

I climbed upstairs. Pat's door was ajar. Peeking through the one-inch sliver, I found him sorting his clothes, his back facing me.

I knocked on the door as I popped my head in. "Hey, can I come in?" He shrugged without turning back. "Doing laundry already?"

"I hadn't planned to stay so long," he mumbled, throwing a shirt into his pile of whites. "What do you want, jie?"

"I'm sorry, Pat," I said. My apology garnered zero reaction. I sat down on his bed, sitting perpendicular to him. "I didn't mean to throw you under the bus. You were just . . . collateral damage."

"Thank you for saying that. It makes me feel *so* much better," he said sarcastically.

"I'm sorry," I repeated. "I shouldn't have gotten you involved in the first place. You could have been back in Santa Cruz and none of us would have known any better."

"If I really wanted that, I wouldn't have come down at all." The bed dipped as he sat beside me.

"Why'd you come down then?"

"I had a rough quarter and . . . I don't know." He perched his feet on the bed frame and hugged his knees. "Why not? Do I need a reason to see you guys and eat Mom's food?"

"I guess not." I picked up his video game controller, pressing random buttons to give my hands something to do. It hadn't crossed my mind that Pat might miss us. "But you didn't have to stay or help me."

"How could I not?" he said incredulously.

I cringed. "I'm sorry. I know I shouldn't guilt you. It's bad enough when Mom and Dad do it."

"No, not that." He twisted his body to face me, his hands gripping the side of the bed for balance. "You know, it was the first time you ever asked me to help you."

"Well, I never needed your help before," I said, unsure where he was going with all of this.

"I know. Didn't you think I'd want to help you? After what

happened last year?" He found confirmation on my face that I hadn't thought that of him. "Jie, when Mom and Dad told me that you were in the hospital, I was still at school. I felt so useless. When I came home last summer, everyone just acted like everything was fine. You were going to live at home and work, and nobody ever brought it up again. It was weird, ignoring this big thing that happened to you. Every time I asked you if you were okay, you'd just say you were fine when nothing felt fine. So, when you asked me—blackmailed me—to help you with this plan, I thought it was the least I could do, you know . . ."

He hoped he didn't have to complete the sentence, but I glanced at him, encouraging him to go on. He let out a reluctant sigh. "It was the least I could do after all that you've done for me."

I shrunk at his admission. He had never acknowledged any of the things I did for him before. Just as neither of us had explicitly shown gratitude to our parents for all they did. It was an unspoken rule that we showed our gratitude with our actions and not our words. Even as I sat there, letting Pat's words settle, it felt different. Almost like trying on a shirt that looked good on the mannequin, but looking in the mirror, you weren't sure if it was quite your style.

"Thanks, Pat. For everything." He replied with a single-shoulder forget-about-it shrug. How could he be so nonchalant about it? "How did Mom and Dad react after I left? About your internship, I mean?"

Pat avoided my eyes. "You know how they are . . . They were

mad that I lied but . . . they got over it once I told them I would still get to intern in the fall."

"Oh . . . that's . . . cool," I managed to say. Good for him, I guess. My hands strangled Pat's controller.

"Don't break it." Pat swiped the controller out of my hands and placed it back on his desk. "Jie, it's me. You can tell me that it sucks. I know I got off way easy."

"In all fairness, you didn't sneak out, take a job they don't approve of, and drive off with a secret ex all in one afternoon."

"True, but it still sucks that they gave you so much shit. I honestly didn't remember how much work goes into the shop, and you did it for so long."

"You don't remember because I saved you from going when we were kids."

"Yeah, you're a real Katniss," he said dryly, which earned him a shove. He laughed it off. "There is something that might make you feel better, though."

"What's that?" I sulked.

"I didn't exactly get off scot-free. Now that they know I'm free for the rest of the summer, they asked me to fill in for you."

"What?" I couldn't believe it.

"Well, what were they going to do? You accepted the job already. You didn't leave them much of a choice. They've already started having conversations about possibly hiring someone after I go back to school. Mom's still working out the numbers, though, but I overheard her tell Dad that sales look promising."

I blinked at Pat. "Are you telling me . . . that my plan worked?"

"Your methodology sucked, but yes, it worked."

"We did it?" I whisper-screamed. "We did it!" I fell back into Pat's bed and kicked my feet in the air.

Pat let me relish the moment before popping my balloon. "Did you forget that our parents are pissed at you, you psycho?"

I sat back up and smoothed down my shirt. "Right." I cleared my throat. "About that . . . I have a plan. Can you help me?"

## Chapter 19

There was a short window in the evening when both my parents were up at the same time. My dad typically gave himself about thirty minutes to get dressed, briefly discuss business with my mom, and maybe eat if he woke up hungry before returning to the shop. During this time, my mom tried to wind down for the evening, either playing slots on her phone or watching the latest C-drama.

The mission I sent Pat on was to wrangle my dad early to sit down for a meal. Unfortunately, my mom made dinner *Chopped* style, using random items from the fridge and pantry. Pat said it tasted okay, but it wasn't going to whet my dad's appetite. I let him figure something out while I thought about what I wanted to say. I opened up my laptop and went to work.

I kept my bedroom door open to listen out for my dad. At 9:45 P.M., I heard my dad step out of his room and shut the door behind him. Ten, maybe fifteen, seconds later, I caught a whiff of frozen pepperoni pizza bites getting zapped in the microwave and the sound of my mom scolding Pat for warming up junk food so late. It was time. I quickly saved my file, folded my laptop, and carried it under my arm.

My dad happily stuffed his face while sitting in his usual seat, ignoring my mom's nagging about the pizza bites being unhealthy. I set up my laptop in front of my dad's plate and opened my presentation.

"What's this?" he said with his mouth full. My mom stood next to my dad, one arm resting on the back of his chair. They gave real king and queen vibes, if kings ate tiny pizzas and queens wore pajama sets from Costco. Pat sat at the table beside me for moral support.

There wasn't much time before my dad had to leave, so I jumped right into it. "Ma, Ba, I'm sorry for lying. I never wanted to lie to you, but sometimes you guys make it so hard to tell you stuff. You guys tell me every day what you want me to do, so if I want to do something different, I know you won't like it. You either get mad at me or ask me why I don't know how to do something, as if I'm supposed to know everything."

"So what? You still tell us even if we don't like it," my dad said, like it was clear as day.

"And what? Just take your lectures and feel bad about myself?" I scoffed.

"Yeah. I'm your dad. I'm supposed to tell you when you're being stupid," he argued. "Right now you're being stupid."

"No, Ba. *This* is why I don't tell you guys stuff!" I rubbed my eyes. This conversation escalated way too fast in the wrong direction. I couldn't have him derail my presentation before I lost my nerve. "Please, Ba. Can you wait until I'm done before you say anything else?"

My dad chafed at my request, unaccustomed to getting directions from his own daughter. Asking him to listen was purely for logistical reasons, not the act of disrespect he interpreted it to be. I quickly pressed enter to transition into the next slide before my dad went on a tirade about respecting elders.

A photo of me sitting at my dorm room desk appeared on the screen. I was in my oversize white UCLA hoodie and flannel pajama pants, staring into my general biology textbook.

"Linh took this picture to show me that I was studying too much. She was trying to get me to take a break." I pointed at the screen. "See that? I hadn't washed my hair all week." I zoomed into my face. "Look how red my eyes were. I was trying really hard to get good grades. I studied all the time." I moved on to the next slide, which had an image of the human body labeled with the endocrine system. I had entered all the terminology into Google Translate for my parents to read. "This is one of the things I had to study. Do you understand any of this?"

My dad leaned closer to the screen, mouthing the words as he read the simplified characters. "I don't know what that means."

"I don't, either!" I flipped to the next slide that contained pictures of my old chemistry homework problems. "I don't know how to do this, either." I steeled myself, imagining sad Post-its in my future as I moved on to a screenshot of my transcripts, which they had never seen before. "Ma. Ba. I'm showing you all of this to tell you that I tried really hard, even though my grades don't show it. I was . . . I was so tired and then you guys always asked me to come home on the weekends to work and I'd do it because I knew you guys needed a break more than me. But then I'd come home and all I'd hear you guys say is how great Maggie or Pat or whichever cousin is doing," I said bitterly. "You guys would ask me if school was good and it wasn't. Or if I had a boyfriend yet and I didn't. Then that was it. Like the rest of me didn't matter."

The last sentence slipped out with the rest, unplanned, but it spoke to a truth that I'd never once said aloud to anyone, not even Linh. It was a surface level statement that was greater than the sum of its parts. I hoped its simplicity could reach across this gap between us. My heart was pounding during this excruciating silence, but as I looked closer, I saw their feelings etched across their stoic faces. The concern on my mom's slackened face once the shock wore off. The slight frown from my dad as he lowered his eyes.

They felt the distance between us too.

To think, for all the times they turned away, seemingly impassive, perhaps they struggled to find the right words for me. It filled me with regret knowing that if I had realized that sooner, then maybe I wouldn't have given up on them so long ago.

Finally, my mom tapped her hand against the back of my dad's chair. "Almost time to go," she said in a low, steady voice.

She walked off for her room, knocking the back of my chair as she passed me. "You go to sleep. Work tomorrow."

My dad read the confusion on my face. "Give her some time."

"Why is she still mad at me?"

"What? You think because we know why you lie that the lying was okay?"

"No," I said defensively. "That's why I said I'm sorry."

"You know she doesn't like surprises."

I hoped my dad would elaborate, but he didn't. He left his vague answer up for interpretation. But I recalled all the times she texted and stayed up to make sure I came home. The stakeouts and her neurotic bookkeeping. Her need for structure and control was her coping mechanism.

"Con, wǒmen dōu ài nǐ," he said matter-of-factly. My eyes darted to Pat's, who looked equally stunned. My parents had rarely told us that they love us verbally. It wasn't like we didn't know. They showed us love in many ways, but hearing the actual words was a new feeling I had to break into.

"If we didn't care, we would ask you nothing," he explained, stuffing one last pizza bite into his mouth as he stood up. "But we care." He held the sides of my head and bent down. "Wait. Did you wash your hair?" he asked slyly.

I rolled my eyes and nodded.

My dad held my head in place as he affectionately inhaled the top of my head. "Sweet like jasmines." He tilted my head until we had direct eye contact. "Next time, tell us when something bother you."

"Even if it's stupid?" I mumbled.

"It's better that we think you're stupid than you're lying," he said, letting go of my face.

"I didn't want you to worry about me," I explained. "I thought I could handle things myself."

"Con, we will always worry about you. That's what parents do. You'll see one day."

"Ba," I grumbled. "Really? Can you not say that?"

"I say one day! Not tomorrow!" He pointed a stern finger in between my eyes. "I go now, but we talk about your boyfriends later."

"They're not my boyfriends," I grumbled.

My dad grabbed the meal my mom packed for him and took off for the shop.

Pat stood up as I closed my laptop. "How are you feeling?" he asked.

"Fine," I said automatically.

Pat tilted his head, waiting expectantly for more.

Right. "Fine" was no longer sufficient. "I feel okay. Redemption Tour 2.0 is off to a slow start."

"It's only day one." Pat started to walk away, but I blocked his path, wrapping my arms around him.

Pat stilled. "What are you doing?" he asked, his voice a monotone.

"What does it look like I'm doing? I'm giving you a hug." He had never shown me so much support before. "I'm trying to say thanks."

Pat tried to shake me off. "We don't hug! Everyone's so touchy-feely today."

I squeezed harder. "We can be like normal families who hug. Just accept it."

Finally, Pat gave me two quick taps on my shoulders. "There. You're welcome. Now let me go before I have to hear about the made-up bands for your redemption tour."

I released him. "I don't have made-up bands yet, but obviously I'm headlining. You're the surprise guest."

"You're so weird, jie." He picked up my laptop and we headed up the stairs together. "Jasmine thee Stupid," he threw out.

"Lil Pat X."

"Dumb." He chuckled. "The Disappointments."

"No Direction," I shot back as we clomped our way up.

"Panic at the Disco."

"Too soon," I groaned. "That's a real band, by the way."

"Sorry." Pat handed me back my laptop before we went our own ways. "This was good, though. I think they got it."

I hoped he was right.

I WALKED INTO the shop the next morning, anxious about the reception my parents would give me. There was no one at the front counter, but listening closely, I heard my parents conversing in the back. I poked my head in to see what they were up to only to be distracted by the rolling rack stacked with trays full of matcha and Oreo donuts.

"What's going on?" I asked as I counted the trays in my head.

"Special order," my mom said simply. In Khmer, she told my dad that they'd talk more later. Walking past me, she told me to make a pot of decaf. That was my answer. It was going to be business as usual for my mom today.

I walked behind my dad to drop off my purse while he wiped down the icing station. "Hey."

It was an attention grab rather than a morning greeting. He stuck out his index finger, signaling me to wait, building the suspense. He pretended to look over his shoulder for my mom, but it was all for show. There was nothing in the shop that my mother didn't know about. He bent down to the racks where we stored all of our icing, wiggling his fingers before he pulled out the second tray from the top. It was full of milky green icing.

"Wow," I said in hushed amazement. He had finally made a dedicated tray of matcha icing, promoting it up to the regular rotation. He slid the tray back, this time with less showmanship.

He slapped my back before he left for the day. "No more icing for you," he said, relieving me of my short-lived baking apprenticeship.

I was pleased to hear it, but I kept my feelings in check, since I still didn't have a strong read on my mom. I returned to my station and started a pot of decaf while my mom greeted Sam before she toasted a ham and cheese croissant for the next customer in line. I recognized that lady's face but could never remember her name.

I flipped over a Styrofoam cup and poured Sam his usual cup

of coffee. "Can I get you anything else, Sam?" I placed it on the front counter between us.

He looked back and forth between my mom and me. He tossed a dollar bill on the counter. "No thanks. I know better than to stick around when Mom is mad."

I scowled at him when he turned around. I didn't have time to dwell on it. I jumped back behind the display case, moving around my mom as we packaged donuts for our waiting customers.

I tried to get on my mom's good side. I was proactive about cleaning up and restocking things as needed. As things slowed down through the afternoon, I made sure to get up before she did to assist our customers. A hint of a smile appeared on my mom's face when a customer complimented her youthful looks. Customers refused to believe that my mom was pushing fifty.

We continued this dance around each other all day. Sometimes I would catch her looking at me, but she'd turn away if I tried to meet her eyes. At closing time, I was about to help my mom reconcile our cash register when a customer walked in. We simultaneously looked up at the sound of the door chime. My mom stiffened.

"What are you doing here?" she said icily to Michael. My mom, who can be nice to even the worst customer, made no attempt to be polite to him.

Michael's eyes widened at my mom's unwelcome tone. "Um . . . can I speak to you, Jas?"

I wiped my hands on a towel and stepped away from my mom. She grabbed my wrist without taking her eyes off Michael. I gently removed her hand.

"It's okay, Ma. I'll be right back."

I led Michael outside to the curb. He paused and reluctantly sat down on the dusty concrete in his brand-new black slacks. I inspected the area for gum before I sat down, leaving a healthy distance between us.

"How was your first day at work?" I asked, hugging my knees. Normally, I hated small talk, but I needed to break the ice. It was uncomfortable talking to Michael knowing that my mom was watching us from inside the shop.

"It was fine. Sorry to show up out of the blue. You didn't return any of my texts." Michael stared straight ahead at the empty parking lot. He stretched his arms forward, uncomfortable in his fitted oxford shirt. His arms returned to his sides, his hands gripping the edge of the curb. "I'm sorry about Friday. I misread things."

"I can't even make sense of all of this. Yeah, we agreed to be friends, but what the fuck, dude? Kissing me? What happened to your girlfriend?"

Michael rubbed the back of his neck. "Vanessa and I broke up when I left San Diego. It wasn't that long till I saw you working here. I thought it was a sign." He turned and scanned my face. When he didn't find what he was looking for, he sighed. "I should have expected this," he said, defeated.

"Expected what?"

"That you wouldn't want to get back together. Deep down, I always knew I liked you more than you liked me."

"That's not true." I hated that Michael thought about our relationship that way.

"Yes, it is. If you really liked me, you would have told your parents about me."

I let out an exasperated breath. This was the same argument we had in high school.

"Me not telling my parents had nothing to do with you. If they knew about you, I would never have been able to go out with you after school. They would have kept me at the donut shop to make sure we would never see each other and lectured me every day about not dating you. I thought it was the best thing to do, even though . . ." I remembered how it felt when Alex asked me to lie to his mom. "I know you got the shit end of the deal."

"It wasn't all bad." Michael's lips curled up into a sad smile.

Letting go of my knees, I stretched my legs. "I'm sorry I didn't text you back. I was . . . I was seeing someone," I admitted. "And . . . he wasn't too thrilled that I called you for help."

Michael's head swung toward me. "You were dating someone? How come you didn't tell me?"

"You could have asked," I pointed out.

He threw his hands up. "Well, I don't know! You've been MIA. You don't respond to texts. You don't update your social media. How would I have known?"

"Again, you could have asked."

Michael shook his head in disbelief. He kept his eyes down when he asked, "You really didn't feel anything when we ran into each other? Was it just me?"

I wanted to be honest with Michael. When I first saw him a few weeks ago, I did feel the rush of my first love, the novelty of the ups and downs of being a couple. Looking at Michael's kind face, I knew there was nothing in the world that would take that feeling away when it came to him. Nothing could erase our history together, but those feelings didn't extend to the present or the future.

I faced him so he'd know what I said next came from my heart. "I think what we had was very special, and even though we're not together anymore, it doesn't make it less special."

With his head still down, Michael nodded slowly. He understood. "I hope things work out for you guys."

"I don't know," I muttered, not wanting to get into this conversation with him.

Michael thought for a moment before he said, "Well, if you want him back, you should tell him. What's the worst thing that could happen?"

I gestured at the both of us. "This! This is the worst thing that could happen," I said incredulously. Michael was the last person I expected to give me relationship advice.

Michael rolled his eyes. "I'm just saying, if he's worth it, you should try," he said, giving me a knowing look.

"I will keep that in mind," I said before looking back into the shop. "I better go back inside. We close soon."

Michael and I stood up. We did the awkward should-we-hug-or-not dance. I decided for us and wrapped my arms around him. After he got over the initial shock, Michael relaxed and hugged me back.

"Goodbye, Michael," I whispered into his shoulder.

With a wistful smile, he replied, "Don't be a stranger."

When he stepped into his car, I turned on my heels and walked back into the shop. My mom quickly redirected her attention to the cash register as if I didn't know she was spying on us the entire time. She finished counting all the five-dollar bills as I sidled up to her. Before she moved on to the one-dollar bills, she rested her wrists at the corners of the cash drawer.

Looking straight ahead, my mom said quietly, "Tell me everything about him."

I closed my eyes and took a deep breath. "What do you want to know?"

I aimed to answer her questions as truthfully as I could. I gave her the gist of my relationship with Michael—how we met, the school events he took me to, how things ended between us. It wasn't the conversation I expected to have with her today. But, as I told her more, I realized it was the one we needed to have.

"So, whenever you said you had a project, you were spending time with that boy?" my mom asked, trying to recall every lie I told.

"I really did have to work on projects some of those times," I asserted.

I could tell that she wanted to ask me if Michael and I had had sex, but she couldn't muster the courage to ask me. I wasn't about to volunteer that information.

"Was he a good boyfriend?"

"Yes," I said definitively. "I think you would have liked him. He's really nice."

"Do you still like him?" she asked, cautious.

"No. Not like that."

Relieved, she asked, "But he still likes you?"

It annoyed me that she was relieved. If she had given him a chance, then we wouldn't be in this situation. There wasn't anything I could do about that now, so I simply replied, "No, not anymore."

"*Mmm.*" My mom nodded before she sighed. "All this time, I thought nobody liked you. I was so worried that you'd never get married. I kept praying for you." She tapped the stack of dollar bills on the counter to straighten them out and tightly snapped a rubber band around it.

I rolled my eyes. "Is that really such a big deal? It's not the end of the world. I could take care of myself."

My mom raised her eyebrows. "You sure about that?"

"Ma, a boyfriend or a husband isn't going to make my life better." In fact, boyfriends were the reason why my life was so full of drama right now.

My mom waved my comment away. She didn't want to argue with me anymore.

"Let's go, Jas," she said. She shooed me out the front door and locked up behind us. My mom sighed wistfully. "If only you took Chinese class in college," she mumbled under her breath.

"I did!" I shouted in exasperation, surprising my mom. We both stepped into my car.

"Then why is your Chinese still bad? And how come you couldn't get a boyfriend? Do I need to teach you how to talk to boys?"

"*Arrrrgggh.*" I knocked my forehead against the steering wheel. "Let's go home, Ma."

$\mathcal{M}$y mom and dad peppered me with questions about my new job. I was tempted to do another presentation with all the pictures and facts to address their frequently asked questions. Then maybe they could just email it to whichever relative inquired about my life. It was nice that my parents were warming up to it, even though they didn't know exactly why my job existed in the first place.

"Can't anybody just post stuff on their phone?" they'd ask.

Apparently so, because they hired me.

Since this was the last week I would be working at the shop, Pat and I insisted that we watch the shop so that my parents could enjoy some time off. This time, they put up less of a fight. My mom had already rounded up a few aunts to go to the casino together on Friday.

Pat tapped on the book I was reading as he walked past me. I flipped it around so that he could see the cover.

"What the fuck are you reading?" Pat asked.

"Exactly," I replied. The book Alex gave me was not a page-turner. Fortunately, it wasn't very long. It was written by some so-called millennial/Gen Z expert, but despite the blunt, flashy title, it didn't have any original information.

"You don't need the book anymore, Miss I Have a Job Now."

I knew that, but it was Reading Wednesday, and I was a creature of habit. I thumbed through the remaining pages. "It's not like I have anything better to do," I said, referring to the empty eat-in area.

"You can help me fold boxes. First one to finish their stack gets a dollar," Pat said with a fake enthusiasm that made me laugh.

"No thanks." I sat on the stool and stuck my nose back in the book.

"Come on. You have to fold some, for old times' sake. You're never going to fold boxes ever again! You're going to miss it, just watch."

"Okay." I shut the book and crossed my arms. "I'll watch."

Pat was not amused and proceeded to fold boxes at a snail's pace. It was painful to see, so I went back to reading. It was the lesser of two evils. I finished reading before Pat folded seventy-five boxes. I admit I skimmed past the job search chapters since I already had a job, but I did get the main points. If I had to write a book report on it, I think I would get at least a B.

After Pat moved the boxes from my view to their rightful corner, the natural lighting caught my attention. I propped up the book with a sugar dispenser and placed a sprinkled donut

305

and a cup of coffee around it. I took a picture and posted it on Instagram and captioned it, "In case you donut know what to do with your life . . ." It was my last week at Sunshine Donuts, so I gave myself a pass on donut puns.

After it posted, my feed refreshed. I scrolled down. Linh posted a picture of her new apartment. Rae posted a picture of herself geeking out over the two computer screens at her new desk. In the mix, a post from Alex appeared.

I obsessed over the picture. It was of a walkway full of tourists at West Lake. Along both sides of the path were tall, elegant weeping willow trees. The wispy bright green branches were suspended in the air, working their magic. The caption was just one word: "Hi."

*Hi? Hi who? Hi me?!*

Those two letters infuriated me more than those damn winking emojis. I hadn't heard from Alex since Saturday and out pops this vague-ass message from the other side of the world. I began to type a real salty text when I realized, *He's not going to get this*. I scoured through all the apps on my phone and tapped on WeChat for the first time. After I set up my account, I had to sit back down because there were more than two letters waiting for me.

*Monday*

 **ALEX:** I made it
 **ALEX:** Thought you'd want to know

*Tuesday*

**ALEX:** I'm sorry

There was a voice message below his apology. The storefront was empty, but I excused myself to the restroom, afraid that I wouldn't be able to hear the message above the sounds from the shop and over my own heartbeat. Leaning against the sink, I pressed play. I held my breath as Alex's gravelly voice rang in my ears.

*Hi Jas. I didn't want to write a long text and the Wi-Fi at my grandma's house sucks and uh . . . I'm still a little jet-lagged, so if this doesn't make any sense, that's why. Um . . . I thought about what you said and you're right. I shouldn't have said what I said, especially when you've been honest with me. Your honesty catches me off guard sometimes. So does your humor . . . and the face you make when you don't think I can see you looking at me . . . I'm sorry. I know I keep saying that to you and you must be tired of hearing it but . . . can you call me when you hear this? I miss you.*

I replayed the message to make sure I'd heard every word. Though the soft sincerity of his deep voice weakened my resolve, it was the assured conclusion of his message that convinced me to hear him out.

"Hello?" Alex answered with a low, groggy grumble.

"Hi," I replied. In my eagerness, I'd forgotten about the time difference. "I'm sorry. Did I call at a bad time?"

There was a shuffling sound in the background. Alex cleared his voice. "It's okay. It's only . . . four in the morning." He groaned. "It's fine. Really," he added quickly.

"I saw your Instagram post," I said just as he said, "I miss you."

Why did I always get those fluttery feelings whenever he said that? Especially when I added the image of him talking dreamily while lying in bed. It was very annoying because it made it difficult to stay mad at him.

"They reminded me of you," he said.

"Can you stop saying that?" I said at the same time.

I pursed my lips, attempting to resist the smile growing on my face. "We have to stop doing this," I said. The whole talking over each other was getting tiresome.

"Wait. What?" His voice grew wary. "Are you breaking up with me?"

"Oh no." I slapped my palm on my forehead. "No, when you said you missed me, I wished you'd stop having to miss me. You know?"

"Jas. I'm still getting over my jet lag and I think I slept maybe two hours before you called, so you have to spell it out for me here."

"I meant . . . I wish you were here."

And I did mean it. Despite everything, I missed him too.

"Oh," he said with a relieved chuckle. "Yeah. Same."

"I heard your message." I pinched the bridge of my nose, trying to synthesize all my thoughts. Who knew if Alex would remember having this conversation later? "And um . . . I know you don't like talking about your ex, but I'm not your ex, okay? And I've always been up front with you. That's why I told you about Michael, even though I knew you wouldn't like hearing it. And I know we both have stuff going on with our parents, but I'm working on it. I hope getting this job and not being with them all the time will help set some boundaries. And I'm not about to tell you how you should handle things with your mom—that's not my place to say—but if you want us to move past this, then I don't want you to lie about me anymore."

"Jas . . ."

"I know that was a lot." So much for keeping it concise. "We can talk about this later if you want, but that's where I'm at."

"No, this is good. I needed to hear that. I needed to hear that from *you*," he amended. "I've never told you this because I know it's going to sound narcissistic, but I knew I liked you because I thought we were so similar. Like, I could tell you would understand some of the things that I don't usually share with other people. But I made wrong assumptions and I shouldn't have said all those things to you."

I nodded even though he couldn't see me. There was a restorative effect from his acknowledgment. Even though this was likely the first of many conversations, it made me hopeful that Alex was willing to reflect and come back to the table.

"I did try talking to my mom, by the way. It was brief, but . . . I don't want to say what she said after, but I did try."

"Thanks?" It was nice that he tried, but it did nothing for my self-esteem that Alex felt the need to filter their conversations. "I don't want to make things worse between you two."

"No. Please don't think that. It has always been like this between me and my mom. But . . . I did tell my grandma about you."

I couldn't help smiling when his voice suddenly became shy. "Oh yeah?"

"When I arrived, she asked me why I was in a bad mood. She made me go to West Lake—I didn't want to go. I took that picture of the willow trees because they reminded me of you, but my VPN wasn't working, so I didn't know it went through."

"See? I told you they're magical." I smiled way too big for someone staring at a dirty mop in the corner.

"I showed her your picture too. The one from Dodger Stadium. She thinks you look sweet," he said with a hint of mirth, knowing how I'd react to that description.

I snorted in the most unladylike way. "And what did you say to that?"

"I said, 'It's because she's around donuts all day.' And then I had to explain to her what donuts were," he replied, his voice trailing off into a yawn.

As much as I wanted to keep talking to this adorable, dreamy Alex, I wasn't sure how much longer he'd last.

Someone banged on the door, startling me on my feet.

"Are you done pooping or what?" Pat shouted. "I need your help! And wash your hands!"

The motherfucker.

"Hey, I have to go," I said with an extra sunny disposition, hoping Alex hadn't imagined me sitting on a toilet yet. "You should rest. We can talk later."

Judging by Alex's laugh, it was too late. The damage was done. I was going to kill Pat in a deeply personal way that only a big sister could.

"Okay. Talk soon."

Alex called me when he woke up, close to noon (his time). His circadian rhythm was way off. We talked while he ate lunch and I settled down for the night. At one point, his grandma asked if we could video call, which I declined as politely as possible in my panicked, pajama-ed state. We made a rain check for another day. During their brief interaction, I couldn't help but notice the stark difference between the way Alex conversed with his grandma compared to how he spoke to his mom.

"I'm her only grandson. Of course she spoils me," he noted.

"I don't want to take too much time away from her," I said. "You have so few chances to visit. I'll still be here when you get back."

"Is that a promise?"

"Yup. Pinkie swear."

We made a verbal binding agreement, but it didn't stop Alex from staying on the phone until it was my turn to fall asleep.

THE NEXT DAY, three girls from the Hacienda High School volleyball team came into the shop giggling. They whispered among themselves, egging one another on. One of them glanced at my dopey, clueless brother, who was helping my mom roll pennies.

I kicked his foot. "Your fan club is here," I whispered. "Obviously, they're blind."

Pat disregarded my insult and offered a warm smile as he assisted them. One by one, they pointed at the glass, picking out their donuts. I rang them up as Pat passed along their orders.

"Five-fifty," I said, looking up at the first girl. She was very tall. Made sense when I saw C embroidered on her jersey.

She handed me a twenty-dollar bill. "I'm paying for everyone."

"That's nice of you," I said, smiling as the other girls got excited for their free food. I looked into the other individual parchment bags that Pat lined up at the front counter, totaling up the orders.

One of the girls grabbed her bag and peeked inside. "It looks just like the picture," she squealed.

"Picture?" I handed over the change. "What picture?"

She showed us an article on her phone that had image after image of Sunshine Donuts. The exterior shot was taken at an angle with sunspots. The interior included pictures of our entire display case, the tray of croissants, and our vinyl tables. There was a stunning photo of a dozen matcha donuts, neatly lined up in our pink box. There were two candid shots—one of Pat and my mom with her big smile behind the cash register and one of Alex and me from a few weeks back, smirking at each other behind the front counter. The photo of us gave me a prickly feeling. On the one hand, it was a little creepy that someone took this picture of us without our knowing, but on the flip side, it was such a cute picture of us.

"What is this?" I flicked my finger to scroll to the top of the article. "The Glaze Report?"

"It's a donut blog. They really liked your donuts." She flipped her phone once she heard a text notification. "Then we looked you guys up on Yelp and came over."

When she looked up, she smiled at Pat before her friends swept her away, giggling their way out the door.

"What was that about?" I pulled out my phone to find the article for myself.

"I gave the team captain my number," Pat said, going from charm to smarm.

"Ew, gross. That wasn't what I meant." I scrolled through the pictures. "Ma, look."

She paused from counting change and squinted at my phone. "Where you get my picture?"

"The customers from that day wrote about the shop." I read her an excerpt:

> Sunshine Donuts offers a variety of tried-and-true standards that are exceptionally made, all evenly golden brown and made fresh every morning. They remind you that when done well, classics are classics

for a reason. They recently added new flavors to their menu, including their Instagram-worthy matcha and black sesame donuts. They are a must-try! Come for the donuts and stay for the friendly service.

"Oh my god. It's so nice," I said as I continued reading. I took a few screenshots to post on the Sunshine Donuts Instagram account.

"Jie, look at our Yelp reviews," Pat said with awe. We'd jumped to a total of sixteen overwhelmingly positive reviews. "Check this one out. 'The donuts and coffee are fresh. The older lady and daughter (?) usually run the shop, but did they hire new people? The last time I went, there were some hotties behind the counter. I will be coming back!'"

I peered over Pat's shoulder, which proved to be difficult with his inflated ego. "You read it wrong." I pointed at his phone. "It says *a* hottie. Singular."

"What makes you think this person wasn't referring to me? You know those girls came in to see me."

I tossed him a skeptical look. "Yeah, *high school* girls. Please make sure that girl is of age," I warned.

"Come on! I'm not that old. I'm still nineteen," he asserted.

"Why you guys fight?" My mom stuck her head in between us, looking at our phones to see what we were arguing over.

There was an easy way to resolve this.

"Ma, if someone saw Pat and then saw Alex, which one would they say is better looking?"

I wondered if my mom heard the little tremor in my voice when I mentioned Alex's name. It was the first time any of us had brought him up since the Dinner. With things barely getting back on track, I was waiting to feel out the best moment to tell her that Alex and I were still dating.

One thing I did know about my mom was that she would never let personal feelings get in the way of judging superficial things. She pushed up her glasses and analyzed Pat's face for a generous three seconds. "Sorry, Pat."

"Doesn't feel so great, does it?" I teased a humbled Pat.

She patted his back. "Okay okay okay. Enough phones. Pat, go mop outside."

I hunched over my phone, posting the screenshots of the article and of Pat's favorite Yelp review. I captioned it: "Come for the donuts. Stay for the friendly (good-looking) service."

I felt a strong hand on my back.

"Okay, Ma." I straightened my posture.

"How many times do I have to tell you . . ."

Here we go again . . .

My mom flipped my hair over my shoulder to the front. "Go get a haircut."

"What? Right now?"

She walked to the back, picked up my purse, and shoved it into my arms. "Yeah. For your new job."

A secret smile stretched across my face. Did my mom just approve of my job by way of nagging? Damn, she was a true master.

"Why you look like that, shǎ nǚ?" She gave me a football pat on the butt. "Go now!"

Before I left, I gave my mom a hug, which she quickly dismissed. "Thanks, Ma."

ON FRIDAY, MY mom opened the shop as usual, even though I told her to sleep in and enjoy her girls' trip with my aunts. She said she was too used to her schedule to sleep in anyway. She went over the numbers with my dad as he finished his last tray of donuts. I started making fresh pots of coffee while Pat grumbled his way toward his napping spot.

When the morning rush began to trickle in, my mom came out front and stood next to me. In tandem, we slid donuts into bags and stacked them inside boxes as we fulfilled the orders.

My mom rang up Ivan/Combo #1, sliding his small black coffee and sprinkled donut toward him. "You know, it's my daughter's last day."

I knocked my head in the glass display, dropping my tongs, which scattered down the tray. "What?"

"Oh yeah?" Ivan asked, hovering over the front counter to look at me.

"She got new job," my mom said proudly. "She's going to be a . . . how you say?" She rolled her wrist, hoping the word would come to her. "Jurr . . . you know . . . write for newspaper."

"Congratulations!" Ivan grabbed his donut and coffee. "We'll miss you!"

This announcement garnered more congrats and some *aww*s from the other regulars waiting in line.

I rubbed the crown of my head, smiling and thanking the customers as they gave me well-wishes. I leaned close to my mom. "Why did you say that?" I whispered. "I'm not going to be a journalist."

"Close enough."

"But it's not my last day." I was set to work through the weekend, mainly to continue training Pat.

"You don't think customers will ask why you're not here next week?" she said as she walked behind me, smiling as she greeted the next customer.

I scanned down the line, paying closer attention to our regulars' faces, looking past their usual orders. These were our Monday through Friday customers. For years, they've stopped by our shop every morning to fuel up before they started their day. To our elderly customers, our shop was their spot for an early bird social club. For the others, this was their pit stop before heading to work at construction sites, corporate jobs in Downtown, or early shifts at the hospital. I never considered from their perspective that my leaving would disrupt the few minutes of their morning routine. Just as I'd marveled at some of their kids growing up, I never stopped to consider that they felt the same about me.

I jumped back into the groove of service, letting my mom brag about me even if it was not a hundred percent true. At least it was based on the truth.

## Chapter 21

*I*t was a good thing I didn't eat breakfast. Between my nerves and the bumpy, hour-long bus ride to Downtown, I wouldn't have been able to keep anything in my stomach. Not to mention, the person who sat next to me was in dire need of deodorant and dandruff shampoo. I scooted as far away from him as my seat would allow.

On top of that, I nearly missed my stop. I assumed the bus pulled over at every stop. No one told me that I had to press a button to alert the driver. Fortunately, the bus stopped anyway at the traffic light. I elbowed my way between standing commuters, almost getting stuck when my lunch bag got caught on an elderly lady's walker. I would have died if I was late to my first day of work.

I jogged half a block to the *ACM* office. When I walked out of the elevator with haggard breath and slightly disheveled hair, I gasped when I saw my workstation completely covered with streamers and a *Welcome* banner.

"Oh no! We're not done yet!" Amanda tried to shield my eyes.

"Oh my gosh! You guys didn't have to," I said.

"No. This is an *ACM* tradition. Close your eyes!" Amanda linked arms with me. "Follow me. Keep 'em closed!"

Amanda guided me to the kitchen area so that I could put away my lunch. She warned me that enticing-looking food was prone to get stolen and that I should label my containers. She also pointed to the locker wall, specifically at the bottom right corner.

"Sorry. You got stuck with Rae's old locker. I'll give you the instructions on how to reset your combination." Amanda looked out into the office space. "Okay. We're ready for you now." She made me close my eyes again and walked me to my workstation.

When I opened my eyes, a group of familiar and unfamiliar faces shouted, "Welcome, Jasmine!" I was blown away by the warm welcome. Ace introduced me to the other writers, Yadi and Will, and Marco, whose desk I was inheriting.

"Jasmine, just letting you know, we will vote on your nick name by the end of the week," Ace said.

"You can call me Jas. That's what everyone calls me," I said, embarrassed by all the attention.

Ace shook his head. "No, you have to have an *ACM* nickname. For instance, Marco's nickname is Bieber 'cause of the hair. Yadi's is Yadda Yadi, and Will's is Bert."

"Why Bert?" I asked.

"Doesn't he just look like a Bert?" Ace asked. Will rolled his eyes. That's when I noticed Will's thick eyebrows. I couldn't unsee them.

"Anyway, we already have a poll for yours." Ace pointed at the poll taped to my overhead cabinet.

The current options were Jazzmatazz, Jazmanian Devil, and the very unoriginal Jazz Hands. I secretly hoped that someone would come up with a better option by the end of the week.

"Someone suggested New Rae," Yadi said, looking directly at Will, "but we figured that was a little racist."

*Just a little?*

"Thanks?" I said. My new colleagues were an interesting mix of personalities but got along like family. They were going to keep me on my toes.

"Everything you need is on your desk: ID, which also gives you access to the front door, computer log-in, purchase card, log-in info for all of our social media accounts, and a list of all of our phone numbers. Rae also created a manual for you to help you get started," Mel explained. She must have noticed how overwhelmed I was because she added, "We can also go over all this stuff after the meeting."

Everyone returned to their desks to gather their things for the meeting. I sat at my desk and dusted off the round paper confetti. I looked around for a notepad and pen to take to the meeting. I peeked out of my cubicle and saw everyone taking their laptops into the conference room. I quickly logged in to my laptop and unplugged it in time to join everyone.

Ace had everyone provide quick updates on the stories they

were working on for the week. The main agenda item was the pop-up food and craft beer festival that *ACM* was co-hosting in two weeks. *ACM* created a name for itself for reporting lifestyle and news from underrepresented enclaves. Accordingly, the pop-up event reflected up-and-coming local chefs and brewers that didn't have brick-and-mortar establishments yet.

I learned that as the sole communications person, I was in charge of managing *ACM*'s social media presence. Staff writers were responsible for creating posts related to their work, but I had to make sure they were posted strategically to drive more traffic to the website and our partners. I also had to help coordinate the pop-up event. I was in over my head. Rae didn't explain all of this in great detail before she referred me. I was anxious to study the manual she left me.

"Jas, you okay? You look like you've seen a ghost," Ace said.

"Don't worry, Jas," Mel reassured me. "This is the third time we're hosting this event. We're here to help as you get the hang of things." I was so grateful that she would be training me.

After the meeting, Mel brought me up to speed on the day-to-day tasks I was responsible for. She left me to study the manual and familiarize myself with where Rae left off for the rest of the day.

When noon rolled around, I was prepared to eat my lunch at my desk. Most of the writers left the office to cover their stories. When Marco and Yadi invited me to join them for tacos at Grand Central Market, I threw my sad ham sandwich back in the fridge.

While eating our tacos with a view of Angels Flight, I learned that Marco and Yadi were the two USC alums in the office. After we exchanged our obligatory disdain for each other's alma mater, we agreed on a peace treaty under which the winner of the rivalry game may gloat only during the Monday after. Besides that day, we called a truce. Both Marco and Yadi were from East L.A. and had a general idea of where Hacienda Heights was, which was cool. Some L.A. natives weren't familiar with anything east of Downtown unless they were coming to the San Gabriel Valley for good Chinese food.

By four o'clock, I wasn't sure what to do. Everyone except Amanda had left. Ace said *ACM* wasn't a typical nine-to-five place, but I was hesitant to leave early on my first day. I spent all afternoon studying and absorbing as much information as I could. My brain couldn't compute any more data. Just as I thought about texting Ace, he texted me.

ACE: Are you still in the office?

JAS: Yup

ACE: It's cool if you want to leave early

ACE: You should start getting notifications soon

ACE: Next round of articles get posted at 4

ACE: Don't respond to trolls

ACE: Keep it light and fun

ACE: If you're not sure, don't respond

ACE: But engage as much as you can

Not long after, my phone blew up with notifications. Twitter. Instagram. Facebook. I spent most of my commute home glued to my phone. I wasn't sure what to make of this part of my job. Posting about *ACM* seemed easy enough, but responding to comments—the good, the bad, and the ugly—was not fun. The number one rule of the internet is to never read the comments, but now it was my job to read and respond to them. After a while, I was getting cross-eyed. I almost responded a few times with my personal handles.

I finally arrived home an hour and a half later. I was so drained that I went straight to my room and took a nap. My mom had to wake me up for dinner. She asked me all sorts of questions about my first day.

"Jas. Jas! Do you hear me?" my mom said, frustrated that I was paying attention only to my phone. My mom attempted to grab my phone, but I dodged her as I finished my response to a complaint about a broken link. "Jas! Stop looking at your phone!"

"It's for work, Ma."

My mom leaned over and squinted at my phone. "That's Facebook. How is that work?"

"It just is." I didn't have the energy to explain to her what I was doing. Not that I knew what I was doing. I finished my post just as Alex texted a good morning message through WeChat.

"Who that? Alec?" She never could quite get the *x* in his name. "You still talk to him?" she asked behind a mask of indifference, but I knew better.

"Yeah." I cleared my throat. "We're still dating. He apologized for his mom and the dinner and . . . I really like him, Ma."

"Humph."

I sulked in my seat as I tried to decipher her neutral tone while she shoveled rice into her mouth with her chopsticks, chewing for a long time. Without looking at me, she picked up an over-easy fried egg splashed with Maggi, which she made to lure me out of my room.

"I was waiting for you would tell me," she said before taking a bite.

I gawped at her. "What are you talking about? How did you know? Did Pat tell you?" I wouldn't put it past Pat and his loose lips.

Her eyes cast a sidelong glance over her glasses. "What? You don't think I notice you smiling at your phone like a crazy girl? Or laughing in your room late at night? I know you're not talking to Linh. She don't make you laugh like that."

She tapped my shoulder, so I automatically pushed her hand away, not wanting to fix my posture. I didn't bother asking her to elaborate what she meant by a "laugh like that." Any answer would have been mortifying.

She sighed. "If you think he's a nice boy and he treats you good, then okay. Just don't bring up his māmā anymore."

Her mouth pressed into a line with some residual disdain from the Dinner, but her knowing eyes gleamed with encouragement. This was big, like we reached some unspoken milestone in our relationship. Damn, I underestimated her. This whole time, I didn't think she was paying attention to me, but she had been. I just didn't know it.

"Okay, con?" She rubbed a small circle on my back this time to reassure me. The foreign feeling made me sit up straight anyway, which was some real Jedi mind trick shit. She seemed dismayed by my startled reaction.

That's when I realized that she was trying to connect with me. Her grand gesture.

So I stopped resisting and rested my soft, mochi-like cheek on her sturdy shoulder. Shoulders that had carried sacks of flour and our family through ups and downs. We didn't exchange any more words as my mom patiently sat there with great fortitude.

When I felt ready, I sat up. I smoothed my hair and nodded again at my mom. With that acknowledgment, my mom picked up her chopsticks and tapped my bowl. The gentle clink signaled that it was time to eat, time to move on.

AFTER DINNER, I retouched my makeup to insert some life into my face for the video call with Alex and his grandma. It felt like a much bigger deal meeting his grandma than his mom, so I wanted to look my best. This time, Alex prepped me the night before with a list of possible topics his grandma might ask and gave me some quick facts about her, like how she was a single mother herself, but that she had a tight-knit group of friends from the neighborhood who helped her raise her only daughter. They also had a weekly get-together to play cards, which Alex claimed he hated because of their raucous competition and gossip sessions. Still, I heard the adoration in his voice as he reminisced about his childhood with his grandma, so I hoped she would like me.

During the call, Alex stayed by her side while we conversed, only stepping in when I stumbled with my Mandarin. She asked me the basics—where my family's from, if I had any siblings, how Alex and I met, and where I worked (I was happy to have a decent answer to this question now). His grandma didn't sneer at my horrible accent as I thought she might. She actually complimented the fact that I knew any Mandarin at all for an ABC (American-born Chinese).

What could I say? I reveled in surpassing low expectations.

Loaded with an adorable picture of Alex in his school uniform at seven years old, his grandma joked that she didn't mean to dote on Alex so much as a child, but he cried so easily. She recounted a story that Alex refused to translate for me. It didn't matter so much because seeing Alex squirm, exasperated with this presumably oft-repeated story, was priceless.

When I told her that I liked the silver streak in her hair and that she looked great for her age, she said she'd send some products along with Alex, who arched an eyebrow. I brushed it off. I was shameless in collecting cheap brownie points.

"You don't have to bring any of that stuff back," I told Alex after his grandma excused herself from the call. It was getting late, so I tied my hair into a ponytail, wiped off my makeup, and slipped on my glasses.

"Are you sure? I was thinking that it might make for a nice gift for your mom."

"Don't worry about it," I said, although knowing my mom, it wouldn't hurt. "You don't need to overdo it with gifts."

Alex bit his lip as he smiled, making me count the days until I could kiss that mouth of his. "What if I already bought you a gift? Would you be mad?"

"No, but there's only one thing I want."

"Name it."

My mouth set on a sheepish smile. It was a little ridiculous, my suddenly feeling shy. The battle scars from my ill-fated quests for love prevented me from making hasty declarations, but I summoned the courage to open my heart for the person who made me feel like we were at the center of our own universe.

"Just you," I said like it was our own secret language.

Alex blushed at my succinct answer. "I think I can manage that through customs."

I hoped so. He was set to arrive at LAX Sunday morning from Pudong International Airport. I offered to pick him up, but he said he'd already arranged for a ride. Until then, we planned to keep up the routine we had over the past week—starting and ending our days together, respectively, on opposite sides of the world.

## Chapter 22

*T*he next day, a small bouquet of yellow and orange wildflowers was delivered to my desk.

> *Jas,*
> *Congratulations on your new job!*
> *Alex*

When I was met with questions about Alex, I didn't know how to answer, which caused some light teasing about my "secret admirer." It didn't help when a box of cupcakes arrived on Thursday. At first everyone in the office circled around me, hoping I would share. But then they discovered the cupcakes were covered with fondant and shaped like pimples that, when popped, squirted a custard filling. I found them wonderfully delightful. My colleagues, not so much.

Alex's gifts were a fun diversion because work ramped up as the week progressed. During the day, I jumped into planning the pop-up event. Amanda had been handling the registration, so I suggested that she collect all the vendors' social media handles when they signed up to save me the trouble of looking everyone up later on. On Wednesday, I was on the phone for hours with someone at the Department of Recreation and Parks who claimed that we didn't have a permit to hold the event. I was put on hold and transferred to four different people before someone confirmed that the permit was indeed approved and on file.

I don't know how I managed to drag myself to work on Friday. I stayed up late every night this past week, managing all of our social media accounts. Did I even talk to Alex yesterday? The only thing I remembered typing before going to bed was some snarky response to some jerkface commenter. Hopefully, nobody noticed or it was at least on brand.

This job was going to kill me.

Ace knocked on my cubicle before he came in and sat on my desk. "Happy Friday! How are you holding up, Jas?" His annoying chipper attitude turned into pity when he saw my dazed eyes. "Are you okay?"

I rubbed my eyes under my glasses, which I had to wear all the time now with the increased screen time this job thrusted upon me. "I'm sorry. I haven't been sleeping. My phone has been going nonstop," I grumbled.

Ace's eyebrows knitted together. "You know you don't have to respond to everything, right? Rae used to turn off her phone around ten."

I gave Ace a deathly stare. "Now you tell me."

Ace held his hands up and backed up a little like he saw a rabid animal. "I told you. Work/life balance." It was easy for him to throw around work/life balance as a solution, but it was harder to practice when a huge part of my job was a relentless, ever-evolving 24/7 online beast. When I stopped scowling, Ace added, "I do appreciate how you've engaged with our readers. I noticed a few of them had a bit of . . ." Ace's voice trailed off as his hands morphed into claws.

"I'm sorry. I was a little tired when I wrote those."

"No! Don't be sorry. I thought they were funny. It shows more personality and readers kept commenting afterward. So, that's good!"

"Thanks." I gave Ace a thumbs-up. What was wrong with me? I was so out of it.

"Hey. Let's get you a coffee to celebrate your first week. My treat."

That was the best thing he could have said. As the owner/founder of *ACM,* Ace was constantly on the go. It was a rare opportunity to get one-on-one time when he was pulled in so many directions. Because of that, I learned quickly that this coffee chat was not a social event.

We talked about work the second we started walking toward the small Starbucks not far from Pershing Square. Ace kept the conversation light as we walked since the sound of cars and buses passing by made it difficult to hear. Once we made it inside Starbucks, Ace asked me how the pop-up event was going.

When we sat down with our drinks, we discussed strategies to maximize exposure of the event through traditional advertising and posting giveaways on our social media accounts. Ace was rattling off so many ideas, I had to take notes on my phone before I forgot.

"I'm going to pick up coffee for the whole office. You mind carrying some back?" Ace asked as he texted everyone in the group text for their coffee orders.

"No, that's fine." What was I going to say? No?

Ace lined up to place the order. I stood off to the side where drinks were picked up. I yawned as he began to order.

Ace chuckled. "Do you need another one?"

I smiled and shook my head. Ace walked around to the left of me to lean against the wall to check on his email. I spotted our barista, Eli, adding a final touch of almond milk into Marco's Flat White. He was cute, but not worth texting Linh about.

I hunched over my phone as I checked *ACM*'s social media accounts, shuffling to the side when more customers filed in. Before I checked the *ACM* Twitter account, a text from Alex popped on my screen.

> **ALEX:** good morning. How were the cupcakes?
>
> **JAS:** delicious and oddly satisfying
>
> **ALEX:** because you sent me that one pimple video, I keep getting suggestions for podiatry videos.
>
> **ALEX:** Want to watch some fungal toenail clipping with your breakfast?

Just reading that made me gag.

**JAS:** I draw the line at toenail clippings
**ALEX:** now you tell me. I had one more surprise planned
**JAS:** what is it? A pedicure?

That didn't sound half bad. I wouldn't turn down some pampering after this week.

**ALEX:** It was supposed to deliver at lunchtime, but I
    arrived early.

What? His typo gave me false hope.

Eli packed our eight drinks on two trays, double-checking the order with Ace. Everyone except for Marco ordered an iced drink on this hot day.

Once Ace confirmed everyone's orders, he picked up a tray and said, "Thanks, man. You got it, Jas?"

I tucked my phone away and picked up the other tray, tossing in a few extra napkins and sugar packets while I was at it. "Yeah, I got it."

"Jas."

My ears perked up. The lack of sleep was getting to me. I must have been delirious because the baritone voice sounded so much like Alex. I shook the thought out of my head when the man next to me turned around.

My mind ran down my Alex checklist at lightning speed.

Perfectly parted hair, slight five-o'clock shadow, strong jaw, and a hot face that lit up when he saw me. When I realized that Alex was not a figment of my imagination, my tray wobbled. My conflicted arms wanted to chuck the coffee and toss themselves around Alex's broad shoulders. As a reflex, Alex reached out to catch my tray, his fingers bracing mine. With a secret smile, he held my gaze until my hands were steady, unhurriedly grazing my fingers as he let go. The moment felt so intimate, I almost forgot we were standing in the middle of Starbucks.

"Surprise." His eyes twinkled at me while his voice remained neutral. "What are you doing here?" The question made me aware that people were watching us. Normally, I would have cared about that sort of thing, but I was so shocked by his appearance, which was too damn good for someone who just flew back. He had a crisp white dress shirt on with his sleeves rolled up to his elbows and navy-blue slacks. He was way too dressed up for a Friday.

I eyed the spot of coffee that landed on one of the blue flowers dotting my yellow sundress. "I should be asking you that. I thought you weren't coming back until Sunday."

"My friend Terrence bailed on me, so I caught an early flight back," he said. "And I decided to come in for a meeting." He gestured to his terribly pretty colleague. "This is Quinn. Quinn, this is Jas." Quinn waved, since my hands were full. I returned a polite smile, even though on the inside, I irrationally hated everything about her because Alex was going to spend his morning with her instead of me.

I was met with curious faces, waiting to be introduced. I tilted my head toward Ace. "This is my boss, Ace. Ace, this is Alex . . . and Quinn." I supposed I couldn't leave her out.

"Hey, man," Ace said to Alex. Wanting to make a quick exit, Ace added, "We better get going before the coffee gets cold. Nice meeting you guys."

"Same," Alex said to Ace. "Call you later," he mouthed to me.

I dragged my eyes away from Alex and quickly followed Ace out. I felt Alex's eyes watching me as I left the coffee shop.

I was still reeling over the fact that Alex was back when Ace asked, "So . . . was that your boyfriend or something?"

"Or something," I replied, stifling my smile. I willed myself not to skip the rest of the way.

"Ah, the secret admirer," he said as we crossed the street. "Heads up. The office decided on your nickname."

"Oh yeah?" *Please don't be Jazz Hands.*

"You'll find out when we get back."

When we returned, I found my cubicle covered with wallpaper made up of Arnold Schwarzenegger memes. Taped to my laptop was a screenshot of the "Hasta la vista, baby" response I left last night to an extremely rude Instagram commenter who threatened to unsubscribe to the magazine.

"Welcome back, Jasinator," Will said, in his best/worst Arnold impression. Everyone else in the office stood up from their cubicles and gave me a thumbs-up.

I laughed. "I like it. Thanks, guys," I said, genuinely touched.

This past week, my coworkers welcomed me in with open arms and appreciated my work. I still felt like I was flying by the seat of my pants, but they planted a seed of confidence in me. Embracing my new nickname, I was ready to kick some ass.

Marco and I finalized the artwork and signage for the pop-up event. We received the shipment of merchandise with the event logo, all of which was created by local artists. I bundled an organic T-shirt, glass water bottle, and mini beer mug as one of our prize packs. Marco took photos of the prizes by our plant wall so that I could post our first giveaway.

Marco finished his coffee, which left a touch of foam on his beard. "Is it me or is it hot in here?"

"It's probably your coffee," I said.

It turned out that it wasn't just Marco. An hour later, it took both Yadi and Will to crack open a window to free the stale air in the office.

"The A/C must be broken again," Yadi said. Her typically bouncy, curly hair succumbed to the heat. "Amanda, can you call facilities to fix it?"

"I already did. They said they have to look for a part. They always say that. They're too cheap to replace the whole thing," Amanda said.

"I texted Ace. He said if it becomes unbearable, we can work from home," Mel said as she packed her backpack. "I have to get to the Westside anyway, so I'm out. See ya!"

Everyone started to follow her lead. I stopped Marco before he stepped out.

"Hey, can we finalize the program? It's the last thing I need before I go," I said.

"Jas, it can wait. Escape traffic while you can," he said.

I pressed my hands together. "Please? I promise it won't take long."

"Ugh. Fine, but if you keep me here past noon, you owe me lunch."

It was a real possibility that I might owe him lunch because I quickly learned that Marco, while he had amazing artistic skills, was the world's worst speller. He managed to misspell 90 percent of the chefs and brewers attending the pop-up event. I made sure he corrected each and every one. It almost went to print when I caught a typo in our own web address. I should have made him buy me lunch for having to double-check his work.

I beamed at Marco when I pointed out it was 11:51 A.M. He was not amused by my enthusiasm, but he was relieved to finally go home. I didn't know he was so affected by the heat until he threw his messenger bag over his shoulder, revealing his huge pit stains.

As I gathered my things, I heard the door open. After years at the donut shop, I almost greeted the person with "Welcome to Sunshine Donuts!"

"Does anybody work here?"

I turned around to find Alex peering over Amanda's abandoned reception desk with a smug smile on his face. "I called you, but you didn't pick up. My meeting wrapped up. Wanna go to lunch?"

I narrowed my eyes at him. Who did he think he was, strolling into my office unannounced, looking that good?

"What are you doing here?" I asked as I brushed past him.

Alex caught my hand before I got too far, zapping me with that buzzy feeling I'd gone too long without. "You know this wasn't the warm welcome I was expecting," he said, following me into the elevator.

"And what were you expecting? That I'd throw myself at you at my place of work?"

His arms folded around my waist, facing me toward him as the doors closed.

"Never stopped you before." With his free hand, he cradled my face toward his, pressing a soft, teasing kiss that made my body arch into his, wanting to feel as much of his body as I could on mine. Unfortunately, we were rudely interrupted by the short elevator ride down to the first floor.

"You're going home already?" he asked when we stepped outside, finally noticing my purse and the tote carrying my laptop and lunch bag.

"Yeah, I'm off for the day." I think that's what I said. Who knows? I was too busy drinking him in. After all, we'd spent two weeks making eyes across a screen, so it was hard to resist looking at them up close and personal, while his hand at the small of my back kept me close, generating the hum between us.

"Me too." He tucked my hair behind my ear, gingerly running his fingers through it until the ends fell at my collarbone. "Did you want to hang out at my place? I left your real gift there." Alex deserved an Oscar for how cool and calm he said this, but I knew what was going to happen. He knew that I knew. We couldn't call an Uber fast enough.

Once we were in his apartment, Alex's hands clasped my face for the kiss I'd been waiting for since I first laid eyes on him this morning. Alex gave me a beseeching kiss, no holds barred. Like he was trying to prove himself. Like he was pleading. Combined with his apparent desire, it was a heady mix. I could hardly keep up, so I let him sway me until we stumbled into his bed.

"I missed you," he said on my lips while his hands crept up my thighs, lifting my dress along the way.

"I missed you too," I panted, losing my self-control as I unbuttoned his shirt. It's true what they say. Absence made my heart grow fonder. And damn it! I wanted to see his abs in real life.

"Ahem. My eyes are up here," he said, amused, when I ran my hands gratuitously over his toned core. "And all this time, I thought you wanted me for my calves."

A laugh bubbled out of me, but the interruption gave my greedy hands pause. It'd been so long since the last time I had sex, and it wasn't with anyone I liked as much as Alex. But this time it would be different. The warm caress of his hands made me feel safe, and the way Alex looked at me showed me this would mean something for him too.

"It's okay if you don't want to," Alex said, interpreting the shift in my mood as cold feet.

"Oh, I want to," I corrected him, wishing he'd taken off his pants already. "It's been a while. That's all."

He groaned when I parted my legs wider, bringing our bodies closer. His nose trailed the curve of mine, planting a soft kiss on my lips before he made his way lower.

"Then I better make it good for you."

Over and over, he fulfilled his promise.

## Chapter 23

*W*hich ones do you like so far?" Alex asked as I sampled the chips selection that he'd brought back for me at his kitchen counter. There were plenty more snacks stuffed in his carry-on that surely made a TSA agent pause.

Out of the four open bags, I pointed at the braised-pork-flavored potato chips.

Alex raised his eyebrows. "You would." He opened his mouth wide for the chip that was on its way to my mouth. Begrudgingly, I obliged.

"It just tastes salty," he said, crinkling his nose while he munched on the chip.

"Don't eat them, then." I slapped his hand away when he reached for another chip. I was starving. Our afternoon activity precluded our eating lunch. "So, what was your big plan if you hadn't run into me this morning?"

"I was going to text you after my meeting to take you out

to lunch. If I overslept, I considered showing up at your house or the donut shop, but I wasn't sure if it would have upset your parents."

"Please. You're part of the reason why the shop is doing so well," I teased.

I was about to show him the Yelp review when I saw all the notifications from the *ACM* giveaway. My phone had been on silent because the contest was already creating a ton of buzz. Alex watched as I lost myself to work.

"I can't believe that's your job. You don't like posting on your own social media accounts."

"This is only a part of my job. I do other things too," I stated as I toggled between all the Instagram accounts I handled.

Alex wrapped his arms around my waist and looked over my shoulder as my personal account reloaded, pointing at my recent updates.

"I can't believe you went hiking by yourself. Does that mean you'll go hiking with me tomorrow?" he asked hopefully. "I could recommend some new shoes."

I shuddered at the thought of wearing real hiking boots. They were not my style. "I can't. I have to work. There's a bone marrow registry event happening in Monterey Park that I'm covering in the morning. They wanted me to get the event more exposure since there aren't enough Asians on the registry." Speaking of which, I opened up my work calendar to double-check the address.

A confused look crossed Alex's face. "I didn't know you wrote for the magazine too. I thought you just did the social media stuff."

"Well, I'm the only Asian person on the team, so they asked me to cover it. Ace just wanted a basic write-up, so it's a good one for me to start with."

"What are you doing after that?" Alex asked.

"Mel invited me to go with her to see some local band at the El Rey. She claims ska is making a comeback."

"What a hard job you have," Alex joked. "Damn. How do I get on your calendar? Can you pencil in lunch with your boyfriend somewhere?" Alex started tapping on my phone, about to add an event into my calendar.

A smile crept on my face as I swatted his hand away. "Oh yeah?" I said dryly. "Is that what you are? Since when?"

"Since today? Or would you prefer two weeks ago, when you kissed me on the hill?"

"You kissed me. Get it right."

"Either way, I'm not picky." Alex hung his head on my shoulder, inhaling deeply. "*Mmm.* You still smell like vanilla."

"That's impossible," I said, trying not to let Alex distract me. "I haven't been at the shop all week."

"I swear!" he insisted, burrowing his head again to take another whiff, tickling me.

My shoulders shot up to my ears, ejecting Alex from the crook of my neck. "Stop changing the subject. I have conditions."

Alex straightened up from my accusation. His eyes, full of mirth, narrowed at me. "Like what?"

"Like . . . my boyfriend might also have to come with me to some of my work events. Night markets. Sustainability fairs. Art exhibits, for example."

"So hard," he mocked, placing his hand on his chest. "But I think I'm up for the challenge. What else?"

"One more thing."

"Let me guess," he said next to my ear as his hands made their way under my dress. I promptly slapped them away.

"This is very important." Alex lifted his head, his hands still on my knees. "You need to grovel to my parents."

Alex hung his head as he backed up and crossed his arms. Nothing like bringing up parents to ruin the mood.

"They're cool with us dating, but I think it would be a really nice gesture if you apologized in person."

Alex shifted his stance. "Yeah, I knew I'd have to at some point." He pointed his chin toward his room. "Okay. How about right now?"

Geez, someone was in a rush. Not that I minded. "I don't know," I said as I stretched. "Can't we eat lunch first, at least?"

Alex busted up laughing. "No, not that. I also brought some things back for your parents." He walked back into his room and came out with two large gift-wrapped boxes.

"How come theirs are wrapped so nice?" I pouted, gently touching the gold wrapping paper. My snacks were loosely stored in his luggage, mixing around with his clothes.

"They came this way," he explained. "Can't say I saw any potato chip gift boxes."

We left soon after, making sure to grab lunch first. Alex would need the energy for the groveling, I argued. I gave my mom a heads-up that I was bringing Alex to the shop. I tried to stop her from calling my dad, since he needed to rest, but she insisted that he be there too. When we pulled up to the front of Sunshine Donuts, both of my parents were at the front counter, waiting. Pat was in the corner, glued to his phone.

My mom eyed the two boxes in Alex's hands as she gave him a lukewarm reception before walking into the back of the shop. The rest of us followed her lead, leaving Pat to watch the front. He gave Alex and me an encouraging nod as we passed by.

My parents stood on one side of the icing station while Alex and I stood on the other. It felt like we were about to go on trial instead of a mediation. They didn't say anything, giving Alex the floor.

"Uh . . ." Alex rubbed the back of his neck as he struggled with his words. I gently rubbed his back for encouragement. He glanced at me with a small, warm smile before turning his attention back to my parents. In Mandarin, he apologized for himself and on behalf of his mom. He presented them with the two gifts, which my mom tentatively opened. The first box contained a gift set of different teas, each in its own beautiful tin. My dad slid it toward himself, knowing it was for him. My mom lifted the lid on the second box, her eyes widening in awe at its contents.

"My mom helped me pick that out," Alex said of the premium box of ginseng.

"Your mom?" It was my turn to be stunned.

"Yeah," Alex said, facing me. "I told her I was going to see you when I came back, and if she didn't like it, then, oh well. I think when she realized how serious I was, she offered to help me pick the gifts."

Warmth rushed to my face so quickly, it rendered me speechless.

Inside the box was a handwritten note from Alex's mom. I don't know what it said, but as my parents read it, whatever reservations they had left seemed to melt away. My mom tossed a look to my dad, to which he replied with a single nod, passing the ball back on my mom's court. It was going to be her call.

"Alec," she said, slipping the note back into the box. "I have one condition."

"What is it with you Tran women? Always drive a hard bargain," Alex said under his breath, just loud enough for me to hear. I pressed my lips together, trying not to snicker right before my mom delivered the verdict. "Yes, Āyí?"

"Go up front and help Pat for a little bit." Pointing at me, she said, "Con, go take some pictures for online so people think he works here."

I couldn't help but laugh at Alex's horror. "Look at you. You've become the face of our shop," I said, pinching his cheeks.

Alex eventually obliged for about fifteen minutes, during which many photos were taken and zero customers were helped.

After his "shift" was over, he offered to take our photo, since everyone in my family was present. The four of us shuffled into place behind the front counter, Pat and I bookending our parents in the middle. Alex backed up to the glass panes, triggering the door chime, which my dad must have fixed, because it rang like a perky doorbell.

When Alex handed my phone back to me, I studied the photo before looking up at him, my eyes hovering over my glasses.

"Why are you looking at me like that? Do you need me to retake it?"

I rolled my eyes. The picture was disgustingly perfect. A profile picture contender. The late afternoon light reflected on our stainless-steel counter, illuminating all of our smiling faces, centered between our display case to the left and our tower of pink boxes to the right.

I TRUDGED ALONG the uphill path, feeling the burn in my calves. I had hoped after all the hikes I had been on with Alex over the last two months that this would get easier. I stepped off to the side, using my hand to shield my eyes from the low sun as I looked behind me.

"Come on, Pat! You're so slow," I called out. Pat took his time lumbering his way to the palm tree I was standing under. All the time he spent playing video games must have caused his muscles to atrophy.

"You're walking fast for someone who doesn't even want to be here," he said. "Where's Alex?"

"He's at the gate up ahead. Come on," I said, trekking up toward the entrance where Alex was waiting for us.

"You couldn't get parking covered with your press pass?" Pat complained.

"You're lucky I invited you at all," I replied.

It wasn't like I wanted my brother to be the third wheel, but I took pity on him. He spent all summer at the shop with my parents. I chipped in one weekend so that my parents could take a weekend trip together—their first vacation ever—to give my parents and Pat a break from each other. My uncle Tin came in to help us bake donuts so that we didn't have to close. I helped him make our specialty donuts and had a chance to observe how far Pat had come along. Pat made great strides at the shop, but he was ready to go back to Santa Cruz. It was hard not to empathize. When Mel offered me the chance to cover this concert, I managed to get an extra ticket for Pat to reward him for his service.

As we approached the entrance to Dodger Stadium, I found Alex checking the time on his phone, waiting restlessly. He wasn't sure if he was going to be able to get out of work on time, so we'd decided to meet here. Since he was distracted, I took the opportunity to sneak up on him. I blended in with a herd of screaming teenage girls. When the group parted around Alex, I made my way behind him and slid my arms around his waist, startling him.

"Oh my god!" I said in a mock squeal. "Are you the eighth member of BTS?"

Alex chuckled in relief, giving me a quick kiss. "Where's Pat?"

"Over here. Hey, man," he greeted Alex with a head nod. "I almost lost you in that group of girls," Pat muttered to me.

"Boohoo. Worse things have happened," I said as I pulled the lanyards with our passes out of my purse. They weren't back-stage passes, but it gave us access to stand in a reserved section where the soundboard was set up. Linh would have snatched away Pat's ticket if she had been around. Anything for the chance to fawn over her favorite BTS member in person, who I now knew was J-Hope because I did my research for strictly professional reasons. Linh would have loved this. Law school deprived her of enjoying the fruits of her labor.

"How's it going?" Alex chatted up Pat.

"Good. Glad to get out of the shop," Pat said, adjusting the lanyard around his neck.

"What are your parents going to do when you go back to school?"

"They're looking into hiring Jas's former fiancé," Pat joked.

That asshole was referring to Hansen. My parents threw the idea out to Auntie Helen and Hansen, but it was a temporary so-lution at best unless they could figure out another way he could stay. They were currently shopping him around to other single cousins.

"I'm sorry. Did you say fiancé?" Alex asked.

"Don't pay attention to him." I punched a cackling Pat in the arm. "I'll explain later."

"Can't wait for that," Alex said dryly, leaning down for a chaste kiss. "Are you ready?"

Alex unfurled his fingers, revealing his open palm as the crowd inside began to clamor. He was no magician, but the simple gesture conjured the feeling of anticipation. So I accepted his proffered hand because where others saw nothing but warm autumn air, I saw the promise of possibilities.

# Acknowledgments

The idea of writing a novel was something I kept to myself for a very long time, but never thought to put into action. For this book to come to fruition, it took the help of several people, from small kindnesses to big gestures. I really want to thank just about everyone I've ever met, but I will try my best to restrain myself.

To my agent, Laura Bradford, thank you for seeing the potential in my book and helping me shape it into what it is today. You are one of the hardest-working people I know, selling this book during a pandemic no less, and I'm convinced you are superhuman. Thank you to Hannah Andrade and Jen Chen Tran for reading early drafts and providing valuable feedback.

To my editor, May Chen, for taking this book to the finish line and for all your encouragement. Your comments give me life! I feel incredibly lucky that you understood this book and I've learned so much from your insights. To Elle Keck and the amazing team at Avon/Morrow/HarperCollins, thank you for supporting my book and helping it shine in ways I'm ill-equipped to do.

I'm eternally grateful to my beta readers, whose loud cheerleading drowned out all my impostor syndrome as I wrote and rewrote this book. To my BFF Laura, I'm sorry you had to hear me drone on and on during my commutes home about my neurotic book thoughts (on top of my usual nonsense). To Joyce, for being a fast reader and for reading multiple(!) drafts. You are a lifesaver and I'm so thankful to call you my friend. To Jenn a.k.a. Dr. JLo, thank you for being my first secret writer friend when I thought this book would only exist on my hard drive.

Many thanks to the #WritingCommunity on Twitter who shared advice to a literal virtual stranger and newbie like me. I learned so much just by observing from afar. I specifically have to thank Beth Phelan for creating #DVpit and making space for marginalized authors. To Brian Kennedy, for helping me refine my #DVpit pitch and for reading my query. To Suzanne Park, for your encouragement and taking the time to answer my random questions. To Kathleen Nguyen, for your enthusiasm and kindness.

To my critique partners, Linh Pham and Joanne Machin, thank you for reading my chapters, for your honest feedback, and for being all-around wonderful humans.

To my fellow 2021 debuts (you all know who you are), thank you for being a sounding board and celebrating with me during this wild publishing journey.

To my teachers who saw something in my writing that I didn't always see in myself, thank you for your kind words.

Ba, thank you for your love of writing and for being a word nerd. I'm sorry that I didn't pay enough attention during our Mandarin lessons. If there are any mistakes, it's on me. Ma, thank you for your pragmatism, entrepreneurial spirit, and for leaving me alone (for the most part) when I wrote at the house. To Phuong and Sue, for reminiscing about our donut shop days with me since both of you certainly clocked in more time than me. Thank you for reading and helping me with a long list of random things. I'll always be riding the coattails of your talents. Thank you, Jared and Mitch, for your dumb jokes. Superfriends, I love you for life.

To David, thank you for simply saying "Oh okay" when I decided out of the blue to start writing this book. You put together my writing desk and took care of our girls (and took them to Grandma's—thank you, A-Ma!) whenever I needed time to write. This was not in the plans, but you adapted to my author life so lovingly.

To Alice and Sophie, thank you for not touching Mommy's computer.

Finally, to the readers. While this book is a work of fiction, I wanted to depict a slice of my diaspora life—the day-to-day joys, frustrations, and most of all, love. Thank you for choosing my book and spending time with these characters who are near and dear to my heart. I hope you enjoyed reading about them as much as I enjoyed writing them.

# About the Author

**JULIE TIEU** is a Chinese American writer, born and raised in Southern California. When she is not writing or working as a college counselor, she is reading, on the hunt for delicious eats, or dreaming about her next travel adventure. She lives in the Los Angeles area with her high school crush husband and two energetic daughters.